Never Let Go

By Allison B. Hanson

Never Let Go

Nick of Time

When Least Expected

Never Let Go

A Blue Ridge Romance

Allison B. Hanson

Allison B. Hanson

LYRICAL SHINE
Kensington Publishing Corp.
www.kensingtonbooks.com

LYRICAL SHINE BOOKS are published by

Kensington Publishing Corp.
119 West 40th Street
New York, NY 10018

All Kensington titles, imprints, and distributed lines are available at special quantity discounts for bulk purchases for sales promotion, premiums, fund-raising, educational, or institutional use.

Special book excerpts or customized printings can also be created to fit specific needs. For details, write or phone the office of the Kensington Sales Manager: Kensington Publishing Corp., 119 West 40th Street, New York, NY 10018. Attn: Sales Department. Phone: 1-800-221-2647.

Lyrical Shine and Lyrical Shine logo Reg. U.S. Pat. & TM Off.

First Electronic Edition: May 2016
eISBN-13: 978-1-61650-964-4
eISBN-10: 1-61650-964-3

First Print Edition: May 2016
ISBN-13: 978-1-61650-965-1
ISBN-10: 1-61650-965-1

Printed in the United States of America

For my husband, Pete. Thank you for always being there for me, even when I insist I can do everything on my own.

Chapter 1

There was nothing worse than being awakened from a very intense sex dream right at the best part. Riley squeezed her eyes shut and tried to go back to sleep, but there was no use. Her son was crying. With a sigh, she sat on the edge of her bed, taking a second to let reality return before she went across the hall to her two year old.

"Momma," he whimpered as she entered his room.

"What is it big guy?" He didn't waste any time climbing into her arms and winding his chubby arms around her neck.

He pointed, his face wet with tears. "Bad," he said.

Red and blue flashing lights reflected in the window throwing eerie shadows across the ceiling.

"That's from a police car," she said as she carried him to the window and pulled the curtain back so he could see. "Police are good guys. They protect us from bad things." Like the abusive boyfriend the woman across the street kept letting back into her life.

Riley hadn't had it easy, her ex had cheated on her and then left when Luca was only a few months old, but at least he'd never been abusive. But she was an optimist. Always able to find the good in any situation. The good in her failed marriage was in her arms at that moment with his sleepy head resting on her shoulder.

"Are you okay now?" she whispered and Luca nodded. "Let's get you back in bed." She tucked him back into his twin-size, big-boy bed and kissed his forehead.

"Momma," he said in that voice that melted her heart.

"You want me to stay with you for a little bit?" She knew exactly what he wanted.

He nodded and scooted over to make room for her in the bed. He had her wrapped around his little finger.

Fortunately, she wasn't a big person. Barely five feet tall, she could still wear clothes from the girls' section at the department store. She shifted to get comfortable as Luca nestled up against her, his thumb instantly going into his mouth as the fingers on his other hand found her hair. It was a routine they had perfected over the years.

"Love you, buddy," she said as he fell asleep.

She had only planned to stay until Luca drifted off, which was why she hadn't worried about an alarm. A mistake she wouldn't make again. The next morning Riley jerked out of bed and rushed to get them both ready to leave.

No time for a shower, she put her hair up in a twist and dabbed on some makeup while Luca ate dry cereal out of his *Toy Story* bowl.

She had planned to wear a nice spring dress to welcome May, but looking outside at the chilly drizzle reminded her how unpredictable May could be. Riley threw on a pair of khaki dress pants and a sweater before tossing Luca's clothes in his bag and leaving the house.

Guilt kept her speed under control as she crossed busy streets to get to her mother-in-law's. Technically, Anita Fisher was her *ex*-mother-in-law, but she had told Riley many times that her son was wrong and that she still saw Riley and Luca as family. That was why she was willing to watch her grandson for free every day while Riley worked at Valley Jewelers. And occasionally when Riley worked her second job at the Mountain Gate Hotel.

Riley's lawyer/brother-in-law Cooper had forced a garnishment against her ex to pay child support, making his payments more predictable. But it still didn't cover daycare along with her other expenses.

"Running late?" Anita asked as she came out on the porch to greet them.

"Yeah. I fell asleep in his bed and didn't hear the alarm in my room."

Anita just smiled and kissed Luca's head as Riley passed him over. "How's my boy today? Are we going to try the big-boy potty?"

"No," Luca said.

"Oh, come on," Riley said. "The potty is great. Much better than yucky diapers."

"No," Luca said, just as uninterested as ever.

With a frown she ruffled her son's white-blond hair and kissed his chubby cheek. "I'll see you later. Love you."

"Love you, Momma," he said in return. He waved as she backed out of her mother-in-law's driveway. It felt as if she was leaving half of herself behind with him.

"You're graduating?" Sam said as he sat at his sister's table for dinner.

"Yes," his niece said with a huffy air he didn't appreciate. "You knew that. Remember back in September when you said, 'You're in twelfth grade?'" She used a low voice he guessed was supposed to sound like him as she rolled her eyes.

He did remember that part. But apparently it hadn't registered that her being in twelfth grade last September meant she would be graduating this June. Sure he *knew*. He wasn't an idiot. It was just that he still saw her as the eleven-year-old she'd been when he got out of the service and came to Roanoke to live with his sister.

Helping to take care of McKenna had kept him sane when he came back to the States after three tours in Afghanistan. It was easier to forget about explosions and the friends he'd lost while watching *SpongeBob*, playing Candy Land, and teaching a kid how to divide fractions. It put things into perspective.

It didn't, however, stop the bad dreams, or the way he still over-reacted to loud noises, but he felt like he was doing pretty well considering. After all, he was alive.

"So what do you want for a graduation present?" he asked.

"A car?" McKenna's eyes lit up with excitement.

"Hello, I'm Sam Brooks, your uncle who believes you should get off your ass and get your own car. Nice to meet you."

She laughed and rolled her eyes again before she took the dishes to the kitchen.

"I'm worried her eyes might actually fall out of her head from all the rolling," he whispered to his sister when McKenna was out of range.

"It's a possibility," Georgie said with a laugh.

"So what kind of car do you think she wants?" he asked. He had money put aside. He had a pretty good job and a low cost of living since he traveled a lot. His apartment was small and cheap.

"No car," Georgie said firmly.

"Come on. She's going to need one for college."

"You know how I feel about it, Sam," she snapped.

He did. Georgie's husband had been killed in a car accident eight years ago, turning her into a single mother. It was one of the reasons Sam moved in when he first got back. So he could help. It turned out they had all helped each other.

"Georgie, she's going to drive someday. You can't protect her from everything."

She nodded and rubbed her temples.

"I know. But I still think it's important for her to buy things for herself. She'll appreciate and respect it more if she pays for it with her own money."

That was an excuse he could get behind, but he was sure it was just that. An excuse.

"How about if she comes up with half, and then I front her the other half?" he compromised. "I don't want her driving around in something unsafe." He had learned how to manipulate people from the best. Namely Georgie.

Georgie was technically his half-sister, and was ten years older than him. Her father left their mother when she was six. When their mother started dating Julio Alvarez a few years later, Georgie latched on, happy to have a father again.

They were married and a year later Samuel Alvarez was born. Georgie always said those were the "good years" when her mother was happy and her Dominican father made *mangu* on Sunday mornings.

Julio died in a work accident when Sam was four. He had only two distinct memories of his father. One was riding on his shoulders during the fireworks display, and the other was of him singing in Spanish while dancing with Sam's mother.

When Sam was seven, his mother married again. This time it was more for security than love. Even Sam could tell. But Wayne Brooks adopted Georgie and Sam, giving them all the same last name and uniting them as an official family. Wayne wasn't a bad guy, he encouraged Sam to go into the service and he walked Georgie down the aisle at her wedding. But after their mother died, he drifted away, leaving only his name behind.

"I don't want her driving something unsafe either," Georgie said, giving in. "What mother would want that?"

McKenna left to meet a friend after the dishes were done.

"What should I get her for graduation until I can help with the car?" he asked Georgie as he got ready to leave.

"I'm sure if you tell her the plan she'll be happy with that."

"But I have to get her a gift on the actual day."

"Another memento?" She laughed. "She has a whole box full of stuff you've sent her over the years."

"Really? She kept all that?"

Georgie went down the hall and came back with a blue plastic box. She pulled up the lid, exposing all the treasures he'd sent his niece over the years.

"She always asked me to send her something when I left." He remembered as he picked up a rock, knowing exactly where it had come from.

"I know." She plucked out a piece of china he'd picked up from the wreckage of a house in Iraq. He dropped the stone and pulled out a small bottle full of sand from Qatar. "I think you'd be hard pressed to get her anything that means more to her than this junk."

"Hmm. Do you think she'd notice if this box was missing for a few days?" He had an idea.

"Probably not. Why?"

"No reason." He took the box and with a kiss on the top of her head and a 'thanks for dinner' he left to go home to his lonely apartment.

He had just gotten back from a long job in Mississippi, and would be spending a few weeks at home. He didn't mind traveling. It kept him busy—and kept him from noticing how pathetic his life was. It wasn't that he didn't want more. He'd often thought it would be nice to have someone to come home to. But he'd tried that when he first got out of the military, and it hadn't worked out so well.

He spent the rest of the evening working on plans for an addition for his friends Ian and Lexi Montgomery. They'd just adopted three kids and with the one they already had, they had outgrown their cabin in the mountains.

He pulled into the Montgomery driveway the next morning, proud of the results of his labor the night before.

The sounds of laughter and noise escaped when Lexi opened the door looking a little ragged, but smiling. "Hi Sam, come in. Do you want some coffee?" she offered as two little kids went running past him.

"Uh, sure." He followed her into the kitchen taking in the mess. There was cereal all over the table, mixed in with crayons and an abandoned sock.

"Excuse the mess. We went from having one handful to four. It's only been a week and a half, and we haven't worked out our schedules yet. But we'll get there." She was still smiling as if this was the best thing in the world.

A shout in another language from the other room made Sam jump.

"Sasha! English please!" Lexi called.

"Jamie bit me."

"Jamie! Don't bite your new brother!" She was still smiling as if she didn't notice she was caught up in the middle of a hurricane. "Are those the plans?" She pushed some things aside on the cluttered island. After she wiped up some jelly, he rolled them out.

Ian came into the kitchen with a giggling little girl hanging over his shoulder.

"It looks like you got a little something on your shirt," Sam joked.

"Really? I don't see anything?" Ian spun around quickly making the little girl laugh even more. He righted her and as soon as her feet hit the floor she ran off in the direction of the living room where all the noise was coming from. "What do we have?"

The Montgomerys looked over the plans, oohing and ahhing appropriately. Even though they had been impressed with his work in their master bathroom, Sam was surprised when they'd asked him to do the work instead of his boss Dalton.

He made note of the changes they requested and then rolled up the drawing. The necklace hanging around Lexi's neck caught his eye, and he thought of his idea for McKenna.

"Do you know where I might be able to get a chain and some kind of charm thing I could put sand in to make a necklace?" he asked while pointing at her jewelry.

"You should go see my friend Riley at Valley Jewelers. She'll help you, and if you tell her you know me, she'll even be nice to you."

"She's not normally nice?"

"It depends—" Lexi was interrupted by the sound of crying from the other room. Looked like Sam would have to figure this one out himself.

"That no good, low-life *asshole*," Riley muttered as she slammed her car door and walked up to her mother-in-law's house to retrieve her son. She didn't feel a moment of guilt trashing her ex-husband on his mother's very doorstep. *Bastard.*

Evan had visited her at work, asking once again if she could have the garnishment stopped for child support. The reason Cooper had to set the automatic payment up in the first place was because Evan wasn't paying. *Anything.* Today he'd promised not to let it happen again.

As if she could believe his promises. She remembered about five years ago when he promised to love her for the rest of his life, forsaking all others. Turned out he didn't *forsake* very well.

Evan had promised that once he got out of college, he would support Riley so she could finish school. That also never happened.

The more she thought about it, everything he'd ever promised had gone unfulfilled. Even that one night after their first anniversary dinner when he promised he was going to make her feel so good her head would explode. As she recalled, nothing exploded at all.

"That mother—"

"Momma!" Luca ran up to her, interrupting her expletive about his father.

"Hey baby! How was your day? Did you go in the potty?" She hoped.

"No." He laughed as if her expectations were entertaining.

"You know you can't stay in diapers forever, Luc. One day you're going to want a girlfriend, and she's not going to be interested in a guy who goes in his pants." Luca laughed again as his grandmother came out. "What is his problem?"

"They do it when they want to. Kind of like everything else." Anita chuckled. "Evan was three and a half before he started."

Riley twitched at the sound of Evan's name. She was still full of rage.

"Uh-oh." Anita winced. "Did something happen?"

"Go clean up the toys," she said to Luca who ran off obediently. Since Anita asked, she decided to share. "Evan asked me to stop the wage garnishments. He said he would pay it on his own. He just doesn't like it coming out of his paycheck."

"It would be coming out of his paycheck anyway," Anita mentioned.

"Do you think I'm being unreasonable?" She watched her son picking up blocks in the other room. "Please tell me if I am. He left me with a baby after I put him through college. Now I don't have a degree to get a higher-paying job. I can't support Luca on my own. Shouldn't he have to help? Isn't he responsible?" Riley hated crying more than almost anything, besides feeling sorry for herself. The fact she was doing both in front of her mother-in-law pissed her off even more.

"You're not being unreasonable, sweetie. He has a responsibility to you and Luca. It's his own fault he also made a responsibility to Celia and their daughter. He doesn't get to pick which of his children he supports. He needs to take care of both of them." She stepped away and came back with a handful of coupons. "Here, I clipped these for you. There are two good ones for diapers."

Mrs. Fisher was retired and living off the pension her husband had from the Department of Transportation. She helped where she could, but money was tight for her too.

"Thank you, these will come in handy." Riley put the coupons in her bag and gave the woman a hug. As she gathered Luca's things to go home, the anger and frustration she'd felt all afternoon faded away. She might not be rich, but as she drove home listening to Luca tell her about the kitty next door, she felt lucky. Whatever struggles she was faced with, she had the love of the little boy in the backseat. She would make it through anything for him.

Sam stepped into the small jewelry shop late the next morning. There were two women behind the counter. A cute blonde was smiling at him in greeting, while the other woman was older with a sour expression.

He silently hoped for the blonde.

"I'll go check the back stock. You have things out here?" the older woman asked. The short girl nodded and turned back to Sam. It was going to be a good day.

Sam's father had blessed him with dimples which he found came in handy when charming the ladies. He'd been told his caramel skin and muddy green eyes made him look *exotic*. Using all his assets had been drilled into him during basic training, so he flashed the blonde a smile, hoping for the best.

"Can I help you?" the girl asked, sounding friendly enough. He wasn't sure what to expect after Lexi's vague comment.

"I'm looking for Riley." He was surprised to see her shoulders fall as she closed her eyes and let her head fall forward.

With a sigh, she tilted her head to look up at him. "Are you serving me papers or something?" She eyed the box in his hand nervously.

"No. I actually need a special piece of jewelry made. My friend's wife said maybe you could help."

"Oh! I'm so sorry. Okay." The smile was back. "What is it you were looking for? Something for your wife?" Her gaze brushed up and down his body and he grinned as he did the same thing to her. Although his trip was somewhat shorter since she was probably only five feet tall.

"No. My niece. She's graduating from high school and I want to give her something special. At least until her mother will let me help her with a car."

"Rich uncle. Why couldn't I have one of those?" she joked.

"Not rich." It was best not to make things sound too appealing.

"So what's in the box?" She rubbed her palms together excitedly.

"Mementos." He opened the lid and watched her frown. "Okay, maybe it's more like trash. They're things I picked up for her when I was overseas."

"Military?"

"Yes. Marines."

"And what were you thinking you wanted to do with it?" She tilted her head and a single blonde curl fell against her cheek.

He fought the urge to push it back as an excuse to touch her cheek. Her skin looked soft. Why was he thinking about her skin? He never even considered the softness of a girl's skin before. Other than the size of their rack, and how well they filled out their jeans, he didn't normally care about the rest.

She had plenty of other nice features besides soft skin. Her chest was nicely proportioned and from what he'd seen of her ass, it was cute. *Soft skin?* What was wrong with him? Maybe it was the estrogen from all the jewelry.

"Uh. I'm not quite sure. Maybe you could find something in here that would make a nice necklace?" He shrugged as he held up the piece of broken china. "Or maybe not."

"Can I borrow the whole box?" she asked, still studying the contents.

"Sure."

"You don't seem to have any expectations, so is it safe to say you'd be happy with whatever I came up with?"

"It would be safe to say that, yes." He nodded with a smile.

She gave him a form to fill out his information. "Give me a few days and I'll give you a call when I'm done."

"All right. Thanks." He stepped back. "I have complete faith in you."

She laughed as she picked up a stick from the box. "It's not like I could make this stuff look worse." She smiled and he couldn't help but notice she had a dimple on her left cheek. He'd never seen what women saw in his dimples before, but now he had a clue.

Riley didn't know why she wanted to do a great job for Sam. He was cute, yes. But he wasn't the kind of guy who went for the short girl with a two-year-old.

Regardless, there was something sweet about a big tough guy wanting to do something special for his niece for her graduation.

She'd taken the box home to work on in the evenings after Luca went to sleep. As she worked she wondered where the things in the box came from, what he must have felt being in a strange place, carrying a gun, and hoping he would make it home someday. Had he been scared when he picked up this rock? Had it been sunset when he scooped up this sand? Looking through the scattered collection of his life in the military gave her an intimate connection with the stranger with the cute smile.

It only took two days to finish. When the project was done she called and left a message to tell him it was ready.

Sam came in the next day. He smiled his dimpled smile and rubbed his palms together. "I'm kind of excited to see which one you picked," he said as he came closer to the counter.

"Actually," she said as she opened a box and pushed it over to him. "I used a lot of them."

He picked up the charm bracelet and studied it with a smile. "Wow. This is perfect."

She was pretty proud of it herself. She'd filled glass beads with the different specimens of sand. The broken piece of china was polished and hanging from a link. She wound gold wire around a stone to hold it in place, turning it into a charm. She'd even added a few colored beads to give it some splash.

"Do you think she'll wear it?" Riley asked, hoping he was pleased.

"Hell, yes. She's going to love it. Thank you so much." He didn't even ask how much it cost, he simply held out his credit card.

"The total is forty-eight sixty-four," she said and he pulled the card back before she had a chance to take it. Was it too much?

"That can't be right. It has to be more." He pointed at the bracelet. "This is amazing."

She smiled, happy he didn't think he was being ripped off. "No, that's it. Just some wire, a link bracelet, and a few beads."

"What about your time?"

"It didn't take much time." She didn't want to admit she'd taken it home. It seemed too personal.

His shoulders relaxed and with a frown he held the card out again. "Are you sure? I would pay more."

"It's fine. Maybe you'll stop in again for a gift for your wife."

"I don't have a wife." He looked around the store nervously.

"Really?" She smiled at him, not even trying to hide the fact she had done that intentionally. Why was she fishing? She couldn't act on it. She had responsibilities.

"If you won't let me pay you for your time, would you consider letting me take you out to dinner on Saturday night?" He cocked his head to the side and flashed those dimples.

How could she say no to that face? It didn't matter that she couldn't come up with an answer, because she didn't want to say no. Luca was spending the weekend with his dad. She had the weekend off from the hotel and was going out with the girls on Friday night. But Saturday was wide open. She'd planned to take a relaxing bath, but maybe Sam would be up for something more relaxing. She shivered at the uninvited thoughts that inspired. What had gotten into her?

"I would like that," she said before she had a chance to chicken out.

"Great." He was holding out his phone so she could enter her number and address when a garbage truck lost its grip on the Dumpster across the street. It fell to the pavement with a loud clang.

Before she knew what was happening she was on the floor behind the counter with Sam's weight crushing her. His caramel skin was almost pasty white as he used his own body to protect her from . . . a loud sound.

Okay, it might have been more heroic if there was actual danger involved, but she was still impressed. She had visions of Evan cowering behind her.

"Customers aren't allowed back here," she managed to squeak out with the last of her breath.

"I'm sorry. I guess old habits run deep." He jumped up and held out his hand to assist her to her feet.

"Reacting to loud noises, or jumping women when they least expect it?"

"You'll have to wait to see," he said as he brushed her off. "Sorry."

She noticed how bad his hand was shaking when he held out his phone again. It was pretty obvious the noise had startled him, and now he seemed embarrassed by his reaction.

"I wish I had a dollar for every time I've had a guy lying on top of me behind the counter. Pauline frowns on it." She waved her hand as if it was no big deal.

To be perfectly honest, it was the most action she'd seen in a very long time. Dating had been problematic with a baby not to mention her unrelenting hatred of all males. It had taken a while to get over Evan's betrayal.

Sam's body was hard and warm. She kind of wished there had been danger so he would have stayed on top of her a little longer. Again a shiver ran up her spine at the visual. She'd thought these urges had died a horrific death years ago, but here they were, taunting her in front of the sexy soldier guy.

"I can gift wrap it for you," she offered as a way to get him to stay a bit longer.

He shook his head. "No, thanks."

"It's really no trouble, and it comes with the purchase."

"Thanks, but I want to look at it some more before I give it to her."

"Maybe I should have made one for you too."

"Maybe." He winked at her.

She gave back his phone and handed him the box of leftover items.

"So Saturday. I'll pick you up at seven," he confirmed with a nod.

"Seven. I'll be ready." She almost said she was ready right then, but kept it contained. She needed to rein it in before she scared him away.

After packing every toy Luca owned and giving Evan strict orders, she watched her ex-husband load her child in his sports car and drive off with him. Every time Evan had visitation, Riley spent the first half hour crying and worrying that her baby might not ever come back. She'd heard horror stories where the father took the kid to another country, and the mother had no way to get the child back.

Of course to pull something off like that Evan would need intelligence and motivation. Two things he lacked immensely.

She took a breath and went to get ready for her night out with the girls. It had been months since she'd gone out alone with adults.

"I have a date tomorrow night," Riley said as soon as she sat down. It was possible her friends Lexi and Nichole or her sister Roz had more exciting news, but Riley didn't give any of them the chance to share.

"That's awesome. Congratulations," Roz said. "Is he nice? He'd better be nice."

"You thought Evan was nice," Riley pointed out.

"Okay, but he'd better be nice for real."

"It's too soon to tell. He was a marine. He did do a fine job of protecting me with his body from a loud noise yesterday."

"Ooh. Romantic," Nichole said with a laugh. They were all happily married and thought Riley should be too.

A few minutes later they were talking about kids, morning sickness, and laundry, but Riley had a happy heart and a date with a sexy soldier.

Chapter 2

Sam had no idea why he was nervous as he drove across town to pick up Riley. It was a date. He'd gone on thousands of dates. Okay, maybe not thousands, but hundreds at least. He'd never felt nervous before, and didn't like the feeling now.

He wiped his hand over his short hair and took a deep breath before ringing the doorbell.

Riley opened the door with a smile and stepped out of the house, pulling the door closed behind her. He didn't so much as get a glance inside first.

Was she neat? Messy? Serial killer? Were there bodies piled up? He didn't smell anything except her soft vanilla scent so he assumed her home was corpse-free. Besides he was pretty sure he could handle her. Petite girls weren't normally his thing. He generally liked a pair of legs that were long enough to wrap around his waist twice, so he was surprised he found Riley so appealing.

She was wearing a red dress, and her blonde hair hung down her back in waves. He held out his arm and led her to his truck with all the manners his mother had beaten into him.

His truck wasn't raised, but it was high enough that it wasn't going to be easy for her to get inside. Especially not in the dress and the heels.

"Up you go," he said as he put his hands on her waist and hefted her up into the truck like a bag of concrete mix.

"Thank you." Her cheeks flushed red. "Height challenged," she explained.

"I'm a full-service kind of guy." He hadn't meant it to be a line, but it turned out to be a good one.

"Hmm." She smiled, and he knew she was interested.

He had become a one-night-stand kind of guy out of necessity more than choice. Usually the date portion of the evening was only to ensure the sex portion. But as he drove them to the restaurant, he found he liked joking with her. Especially as she laughed about the pitfalls of being short.

"So then I leaned out to pull the door closed and realized I couldn't reach it. So I had to get back out of the car, pull it closed, then squeeze myself inside the small opening so I could sit down and shut the door."

"Wow. I've never been happier to have long monkey arms than I am right now." He laughed. "Although being big is not all it's cracked up to be either."

"Oh really?" She raised her brow.

"Yeah. Do you know how hard it is to get through the grocery store without some short woman stopping me to get something down from the top shelf?"

"Oh, no! I have to do that all the time. I hope I've never bothered you."

"I think I would have remembered you," he said without thinking. It was true. Her warm brown eyes made him want to look deeper, to see if he could find the bottom.

Her cheeks—the ones he still thought looked soft—flushed at his compliment. He'd thought he was in. Now he worried he was in over his head.

He took her to a nice Italian restaurant she'd been to only once before. Unfortunately it was where Evan had taken her to celebrate a new job—the first of many new jobs he would come to have—after they were married. They had shared an order of calamari, and she thought her life was going to be perfect.

It didn't turn out that way, but the calamari was pretty good.

Evan told her he'd found someone else when Luca was three months old. Not only had he found someone else, but the new girlfriend was pregnant. He apologized and even cried while she tried to work up to some emotion. Any emotion. But at that time, nothing came. She couldn't be angry, hurt or sad. All she could think of was her son, and how his life would never be the way she'd planned it for him. He would never be able to climb into bed with his parents on Sunday mornings to snuggle. He would never have a brother or sister that looked like him, instead he would have half-siblings and step-siblings.

He would be passed back and forth, forced to eat two meals on holidays, and he would wonder what he did to make his dad leave, just like she had wondered when she was a child.

"You okay? It looks like you're pissed off," Sam said with his brows pressed together.

"I'm great." And she was.

Sure, she eventually got around to the anger and hurt, and there was a time when she hated Evan with every fiber of her being. But over the last two and a half years she'd moved on.

Her son was happy and loved, and he crawled in bed with her on Sunday mornings to snuggle. She didn't need anything else.

Except maybe a night of fun with the man sitting across from her.

"So are you Italian?" she asked the very inappropriate question. He was obviously some perfect mix of nationalities. His skin was a magnificent bronze color, and his eyes were hazel. His dark hair was thick, and might have been curly if it wasn't cut so short.

"No." He paused and for a moment she thought she was going to have to ask. "My father was Dominican, but I don't really remember him."

"I never knew my father." Why had she said that? As if they could make a club or something.

"So we're going straight for the hard stuff, huh?" he said with a laugh as the waiter came over to take their drink order. He ordered a beer and she got a glass of wine. She didn't get the chance to go on many dates, she was going all out.

"I'll briefly discuss my failed marriage and then that should be it for the hard stuff on my end."

"How long were you married?"

"Three years." She deliberately didn't mention they had a son together before he took off. On the few dates she had gone on, she'd found that the men backed off immediately when she mentioned having a child. She didn't want to risk having Sam back off. At least not tonight.

And what would it matter? She was an adult. She wasn't seeing anyone. It was perfectly acceptable for her to take him back to her apartment and have a great time with him. Then she would send him on his way in the morning. People did this. She could do this. There was no harm in keeping some parts of her life a secret. As long as they didn't get attached, no one would get hurt.

It was official. He liked her.

Not just because Sam was pretty sure he was going to get an invite back to her place, but because she ordered a glass of wine without giggling and pretending she shouldn't. And she ordered real food; not just a salad. She wasn't going out of her way to try to impress him which meant one of two things. She was secure enough not to care what he thought, which he found incredibly sexy. Or she was only looking for a short-term fling. Also sexy.

"So you said you travel a lot for work. What do you do?" she asked, and damn if she didn't seem genuinely interested.

He went on to tell her about his responsibilities with Roanoke Restoration and Repair. "I take pieces of old houses that are being demolished and either put them in a newer home right away, or have them shipped back here to our warehouse. People are starting to miss the classic details that have been lost in modern construction. They want something with character."

"That's really neat," she said. "So part of a house from Boston could be getting repurposed into a home in say Denver?"

"Yes. But it's mostly the fancy parts that get repurposed. While people like the looks of older architecture, they also like the convenience and efficiency of having new windows."

"But it makes the house original, instead of just being a box that looks like all of the other boxes out there."

"Yes. My boss is really good at drawing up plans for a house that can encompass both aspects. Culture meets functionality."

"And you help build the houses."

"Actually, I hire the crew on location, and check in on their progress. That kind of thing. I'm usually running a couple of jobs at one time. I've also been trying my hand at drawing up plans. Nothing quite as big as a house yet." Though he had played around with some different ideas.

"Do you ever forget what state you're in when you wake up?" she asked.

"All the time. Fortunately the hotel people usually have a list of state laws on the back of the door. I find it helpful for remembering where I am."

"Yes. I know about that. I work at a hotel some weekends."

"Really?" He would have thought the jewelry gig was enough to support a single woman with an apartment and a compact SUV. Maybe she had a shopping issue.

He tilted his head to the side. She didn't look like she had a shopping issue. Her dress was pretty, and her bag was nice though it didn't have a brand name printed all over it. The only jewelry she wore was a pair of simple gold earrings.

"I have a friend who runs a hotel, and she lets me take a few shifts when I need extra money. I check in guests and make sure their room is okay. It's not rocket science."

"Is the jewelry store?"

"No. But sometimes I do get the occasional job that lets my artistic juices flow." Oh how he liked the idea of having any of her juices flow, artistic or otherwise. "I liked working on the charm bracelet for your niece. I could tell how much those things meant to you. I wondered why the sand from Kandahar was coarser than Qatar. And where that dark brown stone came from. It was like I was being entrusted with someone's most valued treasures."

She meant what she was saying. They weren't just words to make some attempt at a connection. He looked into those brown eyes again, and while he still couldn't see the bottom, he thought he'd gotten a glimpse into her soul.

She'd shared something with him, and he wanted to share part of himself with her.

"The sand from Qatar came from a beach. That is why it was finer than the sand from Kandahar." He never talked about his time in the service. He blinked and looked away.

"Oh." She glanced down at her plate. "I didn't mean to bring up something that's uncomfortable for you." Whether she brought it up or not, it was always with him. Every second of the day. When he'd first come home he met with a therapist who told him that would be his life. Memories and ghosts, and the inability to get close to someone without causing them pain.

He thought for a therapist the guy hadn't offered him much hope. But maybe that was because there wasn't any.

"I generally don't talk about it, because it seems to make other people uncomfortable."

She reached out and placed her hand over his.

"You can tell me. I'm not uncomfortable." She squared her shoulders as if prepared to make him tell her. He thought maybe she could.

To Riley's surprise, he told her more than she expected. She could see he was holding back some details, whether because they were too intense or were classified, she couldn't be certain. But he shared enough that she got a picture of what his life was like for the years he was overseas.

Basically he broke into homes looking for people. Sometimes he was faced with frightened locals, and sometimes it was hostile insurgents. When he broke through a door, he didn't know for sure which it would be. She couldn't imagine that level of fear lurking behind a closed door.

As the evening progressed, Riley did a good job of steering their conversations away from children or what she did with her free time—something she had very little of.

By the time he paid the bill, she felt comfortable enough to invite him back to her place. She'd cleaned her apartment, and put Luca's toys in his room. Maybe Sam wouldn't notice the refrigerator art and the kid's movies.

She was trying to remember if she had picked up the Transformers towel from the bathroom floor as Sam walked her to his truck. She turned toward him, waiting for him to assist her into the vehicle like the last time, but instead he drew her closer, bending his head so he could kiss her.

It wasn't that she didn't expect him to kiss her. That was what happened at the end of the date, regardless of whether it was truly the end of the date. But his closeness surprised her, causing a startled gasp.

"Are you okay?" he asked, frozen inches from her lips. She could feel his warm breath on her face.

"Mmmhmm," she mumbled, not sure if she should pull him in the rest of the way. She wanted him to kiss her. Her reaction was just nerves about what would come next. This wasn't her thing. She was out of her element.

Not that it was a bad thing. Her element of late consisted mostly of Bubble Guppies and diapers. She wanted something hot and wild, despite the fact she was not normally hot or wild.

Letting out a breath, she confessed. "I'm nervous. I haven't done this in a while."

"Haven't done what exactly?" Sam hadn't backed off so when he smiled at that range she worried his perfect white teeth might cause blindness.

"Any of it. Dates, kissing, and..." She gestured the rest with a wave of her hand. "You know." Great. Now she sounded like a twelve-year-old.

He laughed, low and sexy. "Is it okay if I kiss you, now? You've already survived the date, and we can discuss the *you know* part on the way back to your place. No pressure."

"I would like you to kiss me," she said, feeling her face heat with embarrassment.

He moved slowly for those last few torturous inches. As if giving her the chance to stop him. She definitely didn't want to stop him.

When his lips finally touched hers the tension left her body in a rush. She'd never felt so comfortable during a first kiss. Maybe because it didn't even feel like a first kiss. There was plenty of excitement, but the nervousness had gone, leaving a tingly feeling she'd never experienced before. It could have been that she was desperate, but she guessed it was more a testament to his skill in the art of moving his lips against hers.

Their conversation over dinner had become quite personal, and she felt the comfort and familiarity in his touch. A *zing*, as she'd heard it described by women in movies and romance novels. An honest-to-God tingle moved up and down her body, heating her skin in a matter of seconds. And unlike the last time, it wasn't due to embarrassment.

When he moved away, she clung to him, pulling him closer like a starving person despite having just finished off a plate of fettucine alfredo.

She made a lusty sound, deep in her throat and she didn't even care enough to be ashamed. So what if he knew she wanted him. Big deal. She was planning on making it extremely obvious very soon anyway. She decided to look at it as a head start instead of a problem.

When he answered her with an equally primal sound, she was certain the night was moving in the right direction.

The kiss progressed, turning into groping and petting. He moved his lips down her neck, catching her skin lightly between his teeth.

Then he pulled away and looked around as if he'd forgotten they were still in the parking lot of the restaurant. She understood the sensation. She too was a little stunned.

"I think we'd better go, before we get carried away," he suggested, his voice rough.

Carried away? Too late. She was already carried away. She was thinking about buttons and zippers while he picked her up and set her in the seat.

She took a deep breath, wanting to get herself together so she could play the cool seductress. But as soon as he got in the driver's side, she slid across the seat and had her tongue in his mouth. Surely that could be considered seductive, if not exactly cool.

She knew they still needed to get to her apartment, but she wasn't sure how she could possibly wait that long. Especially when Sam's hand was moving up under her dress, touching the moist fabric of her panties.

"We really need to go," he said, his breathing ragged.

He pulled away from her to put the key in the ignition. After he shifted himself and cursed softly he drove out of the parking lot.

She focused on looking out the window instead of thinking about the man sitting next to her or what they were about to do.

Her sister surely wouldn't approve of this situation. Roslyn thought she should be trying to find a father for Luca. She was convinced Riley could still have a happily-ever-after if she only found the right man. That was easy for her to say. She was married to a lawyer and their daughter Maddy, was an angel on Earth.

Well, Riley didn't have a lot of free time to search for that man. Sam was here now. He was hot and from the way he was clenching the steering wheel as he drove, they obviously had some sexual tension going on. She was going to enjoy the evening, and when Evan brought Luca home tomorrow night, she would go back to reality with a smile on her face.

Sam parked at her house and was out of the truck a second later. She didn't wait for him to get around to her side to help her out. She just jumped, hoping she wouldn't twist an ankle in her heels.

He placed his hands on her face, covering her cheeks and neck as he claimed her with his lips and walked backward toward the house. He didn't release her as he backed up the steps. He must have had some kind of radar navigation ability.

She didn't have the same ability. She needed to pull away so she could look in her purse for her keys.

"So we need to talk about *you know*," he said, his dimples popping out when he smiled.

"I'm in," she said quickly, making him smile wider.

"You're sure?"

She unlocked the door and stepped inside. "I am." She was. Whether she'd still feel sure in the morning, she didn't know. But for tonight she was sure.

As she raised her hand to flip on the light, he scooped her up and carried her down the hall.

"Where's your bedroom?" he asked, his lips so close to her ear.

"First door on the left."

He went inside and placed her on the bed, covering her with his body. Somehow he was still able to reach the light on the nightstand and flip it on.

He stopped long enough to pull back and meet her gaze. "Riley, are you sure you're okay with this? Just say no if you don't want this. No pressure."

"I do. I want this." So much. She'd never gone this far with a virtual stranger so quickly. But Sam didn't feel like a stranger.

"I need to see you," he told her as he moved both hands under her dress.

She would have agreed to anything he wanted by that point. It had been so long since she'd had sex, she was about to explode. And Sam seemed capable of making it happen.

He had her dress rolled up to her chest before she got in the game and reached for his jeans. With shaky hands she fumbled with his button until he rolled to the side giving her better access.

For the sake of efficiency, she gave up on his jeans and focused on getting her own clothes off so he could work on his. She didn't need the seduction, she just needed him. Quickly.

Before he threw his pants he took out his wallet and tossed it on the nightstand. Then he moved to his shirt, unbuttoning the navy blue fabric and shrugging it off to reveal a multitude of muscles, sexy tattoos, and a few jagged scars.

She wanted to ask him about them, but not now.

He hooked his thumbs through the strings on the side of her panties and pulled them off in one swift movement. She heard him mutter a curse, but it sounded like the good kind so she reached for him, wanting to pull him in.

He resisted for a little while longer, teasing her with kisses on her neck and breasts. Then she heard a noise. The best sound in the world.

It was the quick tearing sound of a condom wrapper being opened.

Thank God! Sam wasn't the kind of guy that wanted to tease her forever. He simply rolled it on and pushed inside her as if they'd been doing this together for years.

The small room echoed her moan back to her as he rocked out and in at a perfect pace. She wasn't able to think about anything but the feeling of him filling her over and over as the tension built.

For a second she thought it was way too soon. He would think her a wanton nympho if she went that quick, but as the feeling intensified, she didn't care what he'd think of her. She gave in completely.

There were more mumbled curses by her ear as his tempo quickened and then she felt it. The tightening of her muscles she had missed for so long. Her short legs were up for the task of pinning him in place for the few moments it took to take her over. And over. And over.

This is real, Sam thought as he felt her muscles contract around him. This was no fake orgasm. She hardly made a sound as she held him in position, tensing, and then she moved—just a tiny shift really—and her breath left her in a rush along with a loud groan of pleasure. He had satisfied her. And fast.

Of course she'd said she hadn't done this in a while, so maybe it wasn't him.

He wasn't a rat bastard who never cared whether a girl got off with him, but there had been occasions when it took more work than he was willing to invest. This time, with Riley, he actually wanted to make her feel good. He'd held back his own release to make sure of it.

And now it was so much better to thrust into her two more times and finish, knowing she'd had her pleasure first.

Her heart was pounding as he slid off of her and rested his head on her chest. She was so small he didn't feel comfortable with his full weight on her. She wrapped her arms around him and he felt her kiss his hair. He'd never felt so peaceful.

He wanted to stay.

His body shuddered as this thought flitted through his mind. It was as much a surprise as when he'd thought her cheek looked soft. What was going on with him?

He never stayed. It wasn't safe. He knew that from experience. He also knew he couldn't have a girlfriend. He was much too messed up for that. It wasn't fair to her—no one would knowingly sign up to deal with him. What if he hurt her?

Sam had come home from the service with more than just a few tattoos and a box of trash. He had some heavy shit in his head that came out at the worst times.

Rather than panicking, as he expected, he snuggled in closer to her soft skin and cool sheets. He let out a sigh and closed his eyes for a few moments.

"Sam?" she said with a nudge. She must have wanted him to go. He should go.

"Right." He shook the beginnings of sleep from his head and got out of bed. There was a trashcan in the corner where he tossed the condom before he turned to search for his pants.

Instead of seeing his pants, he was distracted by the sight of Riley. The sheet had wound around her, exposing one leg and her flat stomach. Her right breast was bare while the left was covered in blonde waves of her silky hair. She was a goddess.

"Heading out?" she asked, as if she was completely fine with it.

"Actually," he paused for a moment as his brain and his body got into a short argument over what was the safe thing and what was the fun thing. "If it's okay, I'd like to stay. I have another condom with me."

The smile that took over her face told him she was definitely on board with this plan.

"Maybe we can use it in the morning," he added.

"I think . . ." She tilted her head to the side before she leaned over and opened the drawer of her nightstand. She held up a strip of condoms with a grin. "They're not expired!"

He chuckled at her excitement before he crawled back in bed with her.

Taking his time to appreciate her body, he tossed the second condom in the trash a while later. He cuddled next to her and pulled her against his chest. Her small stature was a perfect fit to his body, and he refused to think about how comfortable he was or how right it felt.

There would be regrets and disappointments soon enough. Right now, he wanted this. He wanted her for more than her body, he craved her comfort. Maybe she would be the light he needed to keep the bad dreams away. He would try not to drift too deeply, where the demons lay.

The next morning might lead to another round of fun, but after a shower he would leave and probably keep his distance. Just to be safe.

"Goodnight, Sam," she murmured against his neck before her body grew heavy with sleep. He didn't say it back, but it had been a very good night.

Sam woke to the smell of bacon and the sound of voices, surprised that he'd slept straight through the night.

Riley was gone.

He frowned at the empty bed and got up. So much for his chance at morning sex before he left. Although he couldn't be too disappointed. They'd had sex again in the middle of the night, and from the scents coming from the kitchen he guessed she was making him breakfast. It was a pleasant compromise.

He pulled on his boxers and his jeans, not bothering with his shirt or shoes.

"What did I say?" Riley said as he walked out into the living room. There was a wide cutout in the wall so he could see her standing at the stove looking down. "I said, put it away."

He didn't know what he was supposed to be putting away, and he didn't need to wonder for very long. She wasn't talking to him.

A little blond boy darted around the wall and stopped still. His chubby feet made sticky, slapping sounds on the hardwood floor.

"What the—?" Sam started.

"Shh," the boy said. "S-S-Sam is sleeping."

Despite the fact that Sam was frozen in place, staring at a child who was the spitting image of the woman in the kitchen, he managed to look up to see her face.

She was frowning.

It was such a huge difference from the way she'd looked the night before, he hardly recognized her.

"Come have breakfast," Riley ordered. Sam wasn't sure who she was speaking to, but he followed the little boy into the kitchen and took his seat. It could have been the lure of the bacon, but he was pretty sure it was blatant curiosity.

Maybe he'd woken up in an alternate universe or something.

He'd spent hours talking to Riley the night before, and she'd never once mentioned having a kid, and yet here one sat. Holding his pancake like a cookie and staring at Sam.

Chapter 3

"**D**rink your juice," Riley told her son to distract him from staring rudely at their guest.

She was so angry she thought her head might explode all over their breakfast. But she worked very hard not to let it show. It wasn't Luca's fault and it wasn't Sam's. She had never intended for the two to meet, and now her worst worry was playing out over bacon and chocolate chip pancakes.

"So, who are you?" Sam asked, looking only at Luca.

"Luca Fisher." He ran his name together making it sound like one word.

"And this is your mommy?" Sam pointed at her and Luca nodded. "Funny, I don't seem to remember you mentioning him last night." Sam's voice was flat but not accusatory.

"Luca was supposed to be at his dad's until this evening."

"I cried," Luca said.

She reached down to brush his fine hair with her fingers. "I just wanted to go out and have a nice time. Thank you."

"So I'm free to finish my breakfast and leave with no strings attached?"

She almost laughed at his expression. She pictured him being chained to her bed as her prisoner. "Of course." She picked up a piece of bacon and took a bite, chewing harder than necessary. *Freakin' Evan.*

While she loved to see her son and have his little arms around her neck in a choke hold, she would have been just as happy to have that later in the evening—as planned. But according to Evan, he had an appointment. At least that was what he'd told Riley when he dropped off a sleeping Luca at six in the morning.

Who had appointments that early on a Sunday morning?

"S-S-Sam," Luca said. "Snake."

Sam looked down at his bare chest, which was covered in tattoos, none of which was a snake.

"This is a dragon. Not a snake," Sam told Luca.

"That's not what he's talking about." Riley shook her head.

Without a word Luca hopped down from his chair and ran out of the kitchen. He came back a few seconds later with a book and Hops, the stuffed white bunny he'd gotten from his grandmother at Easter. Riley had hoped many times Hops would be abandoned. It was nearly impossible to keep a white rabbit clean when it was owned by a toddler.

Luca put both items on the floor by Sam's feet and flipped through the book to find the appropriate page. It might have been easier if he knew the alphabet so he could have flipped right to it, but eventually he found the page he wanted and held the book up awkwardly.

Sam helped.

"S-S-Sam the snake," Luca repeated while pointing.

"Huh." Sam nodded. "Look Riley, I'm a snake." He flipped the book back around and pointed. "Who is this?"

"T-T-Tommy the turtle."

"Ulysses the unicorn?" Sam said and gave Riley a look of disbelief. "Unicorns aren't real. You know that, right?"

Luca nodded and held up the bunny. "Hops," he introduced Sam to his stuffed friend.

"Hmm. Very manly."

"Luca, I think Hops is sleepy, why don't you go tuck him in your bed so he can take a nap?" Riley suggested.

"Okay." She waited until she heard Luca in his room and turned her attention to Sam. "I'm sorry if you feel like I lied to you."

"You did lie to me."

"Yes. I guess I did. I'm sorry about that. But can you honestly say you would have followed through on the date if you'd known I had a kid?"

He gave a noncommittal shrug.

"I haven't been out with a guy in a while. I haven't had sex in a very long time. So yes, I used you to have some fun. Sue me. It's not like this was going to turn into anything anyway. You were going to come out here this morning, eat your breakfast, and come up with some stupid plan to get out of having to deal with me ever again. I've actually made it easy for you. You can just finish your bacon and leave knowing I'm not going to call you names when I never hear from you again."

"How long has it been since you had sex? Like years?" he asked.

"Really? That's all you heard?"

"No. I heard the rest. I get it." His brow furrowed. "If you're okay with how this ends, then I'm okay too."

"I am perfectly fine with how this is going to end." With him walking out the door and never coming back. "I don't want to expose Luca to a bunch of men who come and go in his life. I grew up with that and it was difficult. Every time I thought someone was going to stick around and be my dad, they left while I was at school and my mother never spoke about him ever again. I don't want that for him."

"I can respect that."

"Thank you." She relaxed and ate another piece of bacon. Anger made her hungry. "Yes, it's been years."

"Maybe the next time you have a free weekend, you can give me a call?" he suggested easily.

She thought about it for a second and then shook her head. "As much as I don't want Luca to become attached to men who are unavailable, I don't want that for myself either."

"Got ya." Sam stood up and took his plate to the sink. "I'll get the rest of my stuff and head out."

She let out a sigh as she watched him walk down the hall. Though she was playing it cool, she had to admit—if only to herself—that she liked Sam for more than sex. She'd had fun with him at dinner the night before. But she'd known what she was signing up for and it wasn't fair to ask him for more at this stage.

As far as dates went it didn't end as neatly as she'd hoped, but last night had been perfect and well worth any discomfort now.

Sam pulled on his shirt and buttoned it while walking out of the room. Luca was standing in the hall with the white bunny looking upset.

"Um-ere," he said while taking Sam's hand and tugging him across the hall. Sam translated his words to mean *come here*.

Once inside the boy's room Luca pointed to the wall.

"A bug," he said, clutching his rabbit closer.

There on the wall, fit as you please, was a smug-ass looking spider.

Without much thought, Sam slipped off his shoe and smashed the son of a bitch. The dead body fell to the floor, and Sam put his shoe back on while Luca watched.

"Bug dead," Luca said while staring at the corpse.

"Yep. He's dead. It's safe now." Before Sam had a chance to stand back up, Luca wrapped his arms around his neck and squeezed. It was only a second and then he ran over to tuck the rabbit in his tiny bed.

He was a cute kid. Sam had missed McKenna at this age, so he wasn't sure how to relate. Not that he needed to. He'd gotten a free pass from Riley.

He still would have felt better if she would have agreed to go out with him again the next time the kid was at his dad's, but he understood. Besides, single mothers came with baggage, and he couldn't handle anymore baggage. He carried around enough of his own.

When he went out to the living room, Riley shifted her weight to her other foot and ran her hand through her hair. Somehow she was transformed back to the sexy girl he'd been with the night before.

"Thank you for dinner, and for . . . well . . . you know."

"The orgasms?" He couldn't help himself. He grinned at her and she laughed.

"Yes. Those were quite nice."

"I still can't believe you've gone years. No wonder it was so easy to flip your switch." He shook his head in disbelief.

"I'm glad this amuses you." She rolled her eyes in a playful way, not in the smart ass way his niece and his sister did it.

"Take care." He leaned down and kissed her cheek. He remembered the first time he'd seen her, how he thought her cheek would be soft. It twisted his gut now to realize how right he was about that.

"You, too." She shut the door behind him and he walked to his truck feeling both incredibly relieved and deeply disappointed. He didn't know why.

He glanced back at her place and saw the little boy and the rabbit at the window. Luca was waving at him.

Sam waved back and then drove home to his quiet apartment.

It was easy for Riley to fall back into her normal routine. She offered to work Sunday night at the hotel. And then it was back to the jewelry store on Monday morning.

Luca was going to stay with Grammy Fisher overnight, and Riley's mother-in-law frowned when Riley told her what happened with Evan.

"One day he's going to wake up and see the mess he's made of his life and it's going to be too late for him to do anything about it. If he thinks I'm going to feel bad for him, he's wrong. He's my son and I love him, but he's an idiot."

Riley went into the living room to give Luca a kiss goodbye. She ran her fingers through her son's white-blond hair. "Baby, please don't grow up to be an idiot, okay?"

Luca nodded his head as if he understood exactly what she was saying.

With a kiss and a hug she went off to work.

Anita never charged Riley to watch Luca, so Riley was fortunate not to have to worry about paying for childcare. But last year Riley's old car had died. Ian helped find her a reliable little SUV. It was used, but in good shape. It also meant she had a car payment on top of rent, groceries, and utilities. She had enough to cover everything. She tried to put some money away each week to cover the unexpected things life had to offer, but so far her nest egg wasn't much.

Thanks to Riley's brother-in-law and his legal wrangling, she was still getting regular child support payments. After Riley told Evan she wouldn't stop the garnishment, he'd petitioned the court and was turned down. Again.

At nine that night, her phone rang. It was Luca calling to say good-night.

"I love you, baby."

"And Hops?" he asked.

"Of course. I love Hops, too."

"And S-S-Sam?"

Oh shit. She didn't want her son to be confused about any man in her life. She also didn't want her ex-mother-in-law to know she'd had a date. "I love T-T-Tommy the turtle."

"Unicorns aren't real," Luca announced as if the idea was preposterous.

"That's right. Sleep tight. I'll see you tomorrow."

"Night Momma. Love you."

"He sure does love that book doesn't he?" Anita said when she got on the phone. Riley let out a sigh of relief.

"Yes. I hope he never asks for a snake for a pet. That's just not going to happen."

"I hope you have a nice shift, dear. I'm sorry you have to work so much. You're a good mother."

"Thanks, Anita." It was nice to hear every once in a while. Especially on nights like this one, when she felt like a bad mother who wasn't there to tuck her son in.

As she sat behind the hotel desk, bored out of her mind but getting paid, she thought of how things would have been different if Evan hadn't had an affair, knocked up some other woman, and left Riley shocked and alone with a three-month-old baby.

She would have finished school and gotten a good job. She would have only had to work one job, so she would have been home to put Luca to bed every night.

Somewhere in her thoughts, she began picturing Sam as her husband instead of Evan. Most likely it was because Sam was so much better in bed than Evan ever thought to be. She laughed out loud at herself, knowing that would never happen. Sam was not husband or father material. She had a better chance of going back in time and stopping Evan from turning out to be an asshole than she did of making Sam into a relationship kind of guy.

Sam shifted uncomfortably in the stuffy auditorium. He hated being at things like this. People automatically assumed he was Georgie's husband instead of her brother. As if the thought of being someone's husband didn't already twist his gut. He and Georgie looked nothing alike so it was an easy mistake to make, but no less disgusting.

"There she is." Georgie smacked his leg and pointed.

"Where?" Sam looked down in to a sea of moving graduates.

"The tall one in the white gown."

All of the girls were wearing white gowns. More than a few of them were tall. Then he saw McKenna turn and wave up at them. His chest tightened. How many times had this girl made him feel grounded when his head was swimming with bad thoughts? So many he couldn't count. It was hard to feel sorry for himself when a preteen was painting his fingernails pink and telling him about her day.

"I can't believe she's an adult," Sam found himself saying. He knew he sounded like an old person, but he couldn't help it.

Georgie chuckled through her tears. "I wish Isaac could have been here to see this."

"Me too." Isaac was Georgie's husband and McKenna's father. He had been in the army. Sam never saw him in Afghanistan despite the fact they were both there at the same time. It was a big country and there were a lot of people there.

Isaac made it home from the war only to be killed in a car accident down the street from their home. No doubt both Isaac and Georgie thought the worst was over when he arrived home. They thought they had their whole lives ahead of them.

Sam had been honest when he said he wished Isaac could have been there to see McKenna graduate. He should have been there instead of Sam.

Sam knew the signs of survivor's guilt. He'd been told all about it as he recovered in the hospital in Germany. Anytime something big happened in McKenna's life, he felt the guilt tugging at him.

But it was nothing compared to the guilt he felt when he thought of the men—his men—that were lost on that hill. They'd all been shot, taken over by insurgents, but while Sam woke up with no more than a scar, the other men never did.

"Are you okay?" He heard his sister ask. She sounded so far away, even though she sat next to him.

He swallowed down the pain and nodded. "It's so hot in here."

"It's June in Virginia," she told him flatly. As if he didn't know. They were inside because a storm had been moving in before the ceremony. Sam hoped it would hit soon to relieve the pressure and humidity.

It felt like hours later before the group of students tossed their hats in the air and started merging toward the exits. Sam waited patiently in the lobby beside a wall of glass as the storm hit. Large drops of rain came down speckling the concrete before picking up momentum.

"Ready to go?" his sister asked.

Just as Georgie and McKenna stepped out of the auditorium, it became a full-out deluge.

Along with the survivor's guilt came the knowledge that everything in life came down to timing. Sometimes a matter of seconds meant the difference between life and death. And sometimes it just meant you were going to get wet.

At the restaurant, after dessert, Sam presented McKenna with the charm bracelet. Of course he wanted her to like it, but when she actually burst into tears, he wished she hadn't liked it quite so much. There wasn't much a man hated more than a female in tears.

"I love it!" McKenna said.

"The girl who made it said you'd be able to add other charms if you wanted. For other events in your life." Thinking about Riley made his heart squeeze a little. He shook it off and asked the waitress for more napkins since Georgie was crying now too. *God help me.*

Riley was still smiling the next week at work which caused Pauline to frown at her.

"What is going on with you?" the owner of Valley Jewelers asked.

"What do you mean?" There was no way she was going into sexual details with a sixty-seven-year-old woman who spent most of her free time with three cats named after the Stooges.

"You're smiling." Pauline pointed, although Riley knew she was still grinning.

"Can't a person smile when they're happy in their work?"

Pauline's only answer was an unladylike snort of disbelief.

Riley didn't blame her. It surely wasn't that Riley was happy in her work. It was still that night with Sam.

It had been the perfect date. From the way he'd helped her into his truck, to the three major orgasms, right up to the kiss on her cheek when he'd said good-bye and walked out of her life.

She'd gotten exactly what she'd wanted out of the relationship. Sure, it only lasted for roughly fourteen hours, but she was calling it a success. She went out on a date, like a grown woman and she'd had sex . . . like a real grown-up woman.

When her shift was over she stopped by her sister's house before going to pick up Luca. Roslyn tilted her head to one side and then said, "Ooh, what's got you smiling like that?"

"I told you I had a date last week," she reminded her sister. Roz knew what was best, and most days Riley stayed quiet as if that were true.

"Last week? And you're still glowing like that? It must have been good." Roslyn cut Maddy's hotdogs into perfect semi-circles and put them on the tray in the high-chair. Maddy picked them up one by one with her delicate fingers and looked at them before putting them in her mouth and chewing slowly.

Riley shook her head and the difference between her niece and her son who would have hogged down all the pieces in one giant bite.

"It was a very good date."

"Who is he? When will I get to meet him?" Roz pushed and the smile fell right off Riley's face.

"You're not going to meet him. It was just a one-night kind of thing."

The look of disapproval that Riley expected took over Roslyn's face. "You're a mother. Mother's aren't supposed to be having one-night kinds of things. You need to find a—"

"Father for my son, yes, I know." Today was not one of those keep-quiet kind of days. "Because the world is overpopulated with men who love responsibility so much they look for opportunities where they can take care of some other guy's child. Don't worry, I've sent off for the Super Daddy catalog, so I'll be picking one soon. He should be arriving in time for Christmas."

"Do you say stuff like that on your dates? Maybe that's why you can't find a suitable guy."

Riley wanted to argue, but the truth was she did say things like that on dates. Although Sam had laughed at most of her smart ass comments. She laughed at her sister and kissed her niece as the smile of contentment eased back into place. No one was going to steal this moment from her. She'd had a great time, and now had enough fodder for months' worth of fantasies.

Life was good.

It had been a few weeks, but Sam still found himself thinking about Riley every once in a while. The way she laughed, the way she didn't play games . . . the way she'd lied. Except she hadn't really lied, she just chose to keep some part of her life to herself. Could he begrudge her that? He'd done the same thing.

He knew if he told a woman about waking up with night terrors, sweaty and shaking, or the reason his girlfriend left, he would most likely be turned down time and time again. So he kept that hidden. And luckily he hadn't had an issue the night he stayed with Riley. Sleeping next to her allowed him to sleep more soundly than he had in years. It could have also been the fact that he was worn out from all the sex.

"What's going on with you?" Audrey asked as he stood by the coffee pot in the office. Though she was Dalton's older sister, she still bossed Sam around as if she were his own.

"Nothing."

"Uh-huh. You're thinking about something."

"So?" He held out his hands, waiting for the insult that would no doubt be coming.

"So, you never think." There it was.

"Thanks."

She laughed and didn't press for more. But he understood what she was getting at. He certainly didn't normally think about women this long after he'd been with them. But for some reason he couldn't shake the images of Riley.

"Do women ever act like they're not interested in more when they really are?" he asked her.

"Are you kidding me?" she said with a laugh. "You guys are never happy. You don't want women to be clingy, but then the minute they won't give you the time of day you figure out you don't want that either. You always want what you can't have."

He thought over her words and was shocked at her theory. "Audrey, you are brilliant! Of course! That's exactly what my problem is." He gave her a big lip smack on the cheek and left for the warehouse, happy to have his mystery solved.

The allure he felt toward Riley was simply because he knew he couldn't have her. She had a kid which made her off-limits to him. For some reason in his messed up head, that made him want her even more.

Now that he knew the cause, he could finally get over it and move on.

At least he hoped so.

Chapter 4

Sam had a date on Saturday after he got back from a business trip in Cleveland. It was with a little flight attendant he'd flirted with on the plane. She was giggly and sweet and had high hopes he wasn't going to live up to. He'd asked her out in an effort to move on and stop thinking about Riley. It was better if he didn't have time to think.

By the end of dinner he was thinking over how he wanted to handle the rest of the night. Yes, he wanted the distraction. No, he didn't want to be with this girl who wasn't Riley.

Christ, what was happening to him?

"So do you want to come in?" she asked when they arrived at her door. She'd had a drink and was even more giggly now as she trailed her perfectly polished fingernail down his chin. Riley didn't have long nails and they weren't polished. Probably because she was a single mother working two jobs and she didn't have time for such frivolous things as painting her nails.

And why in the hell was he thinking about this girl's fingernails?

"Yeah. I want to come in." He stepped past her into the room. He needed to get Riley out of his head once and for all, and maybe this girl would make that happen. But when she stepped closer and leaned up to kiss him, the sense of wrongness that hit him nearly knocked him over.

He tried to forge on. He pretended to check the lock to gain a moment. He hadn't even kissed her yet, and he already wanted to run from the room. When she moved her hand from his chest down to his waist he had to step away again.

It was becoming very obvious this wasn't going to work.

"I'm sorry. I really am, but I have to go," he finally said in defeat.

Even if he could get his head in the game, a very important member of the team was apparently on strike.

"Are you married?" She frowned but didn't stop moving her hand lower. He seized her wrist, stopping her descent and deliberated on the answer.

"Yes," he answered because it was the easiest thing to say. He couldn't explain the actual problem, because he didn't know what it was himself. Saying he was married would get his face slapped and kicked out of her room. He'd accept that gladly.

"And you're having second thoughts about this?" She started to unbutton her own shirt. "I can help with that." What? Couldn't anything go right?

"No. No, you can't. I need to go. This is wrong. I'm sorry." He backed away and fumbled with the stupid locks he'd just checked before he dashed out into the hall. It was ridiculous to be running from a flight attendant as if she was chasing him down with an AK-47, but he felt like he was fleeing for his life. By the time he got back to his truck he was sweating and panting.

What he needed was some time alone at the lake. Surely that would fix everything.

"Can I have the cabin this weekend?" Sam asked Ian from the airport in Dallas the following week. He was on his way home and while he knew going on a date was out, he also didn't want to be alone in his apartment.

"No. Sorry. Someone's using it this weekend."

"Shit."

"What's wrong?" Ian asked.

While Ian would understand, having gone through his own kind of hell a few years ago, Sam still wasn't sure what exactly was wrong. And he wasn't ready to talk about it. "I just wanted some time by the lake. Fishing therapy."

"If you just want to fish you could probably do that. I don't think they fish. You just can't stay at the cabin."

"I could put up a tent at the lake, and I'd stay out of their way," Sam promised.

"Sure. Go ahead."

"Thanks, man. I owe you big time."

"No problem."

Sam felt relieved to have a plan as the plane touched down. He wasn't going to spend the weekend trying to hook up with someone he wasn't interested in. He could sit by the lake with a pole in his hand and think about fish.

Yes. Fish.

"Life is hard," Riley said when she sat down at the bar. Luca was with Lexi's kids on a playdate. Lexi and Nichole gave her a sad smile.

"Oh, little sister, tell us," Roslyn said with a pout.

"Remember the guy I went out with the other week?"

"The guy that made you so smiley?"

"Yeah. We had a great night. I only wanted it to be for the night. I don't want Luca involved with guys who could end up leaving and hurting him. But now, I'm still thinking about him. How pathetic is that?"

She thought the fantasies would be a good thing, but they started morphing from sexual scenes into cuddling together on the sofa with a bowl of popcorn, or Sam with Luca on his shoulders. Her perfectly safe daydreams had become extremely unhealthy.

"How good was he in bed?" Nichole asked.

"Pretty damn good."

"So maybe you're shell-shocked, and it's not a matter of falling for him," Lexi suggested.

"I guess so. It doesn't seem like it's my body that's causing the problem, though. It's definitely my heart."

"Crap," Nichole said.

"Yeah. I know. He's completely off limits." Riley sighed and rubbed her temples.

"You need to meet a nice guy who wants kids."

"Yes, Roz. I know. The issue is that instead of putting in the store at the mall that carries *nice guys*, they put in another Target."

"I love Target," Lexi said.

"Let me buy you a drink," Roz said. "That will make it better."

Riley felt even worse when her great horde of friends weren't able to offer better advice than drinking away her problems. Was her future this dismal? "Lex, you said I could use the cabin this weekend, right? Is that still okay?"

"Oh, sure! I almost forgot." She searched around in her purse and pulled out a set of keys. "Here you go. Have a great time."

"Thanks. I think Luca and I just need to get away for a little while. Just us and nature. Maybe we can work on the potty training."

"Sounds like a perfect vacation," Roz joked.

After the eighth trip to the car, Riley was pretty certain everything she and Luca owned was now inside the cabin. It was just a weekend, but with a toddler it meant a lot of "necessities."

"Luc, look what I brought," she said with more excitement than a tiny potty deserved. "It's your cool big boy potty. Do you want to try it out this weekend?"

"No," he said.

"You could at least pretend to think about it," she muttered as she dropped the bag of towels by the door.

After Luca was set up on the rug with a stack of coloring books and crayons she went to the kitchen to unload the cooler.

She tucked Luca's juice boxes in beside the bottles of wine already in the door of the refrigerator.

How nice it would be to kick back with a glass of wine on the deck. Except she needed to be responsible. What if Luca hurt himself and she needed to drive him to the hospital? She was it. Everything fell on her shoulders. With a sigh she moved on to lunch meat and cheese.

Ten seconds later Luca was standing in the kitchen saying, "Fish."

"Buddy, there's no television here. No movies."

Luca blinked at her as if he'd never heard of such a thing. He hadn't.

"Look, we're poor which means this is the extent of our vacation. At least we're not at home with the air conditioner that only works half the time." More blinking.

"Fish?"

They'd been there all of twenty minutes and he was already bored.

"Why don't you go draw me a picture of a fish, and then when I'm done unpacking, we can take a walk out to the lake and maybe we'll see a real fish?" He was gone before she had the entire sentence out.

She took a breath letting out the tension, until she heard the sound of tiny sneakers on hard wood.

He held up a piece of paper with an orange blob on it.

"Fish," he said again, and Riley wondered why she thought this was going to be a good idea.

After checking the deck twice to make sure Luca couldn't squeeze through the railing and fall to his death, she let him play out there while she picked up one hundred and fifty-two crayons up off the rug.

"Why does a two-year-old need six shades of gray?" she cursed her sister for buying them. She left the door open to the deck since a cool breeze was blowing in off the mountain. Also so she could hear Luca if a large raptor swooped down to take him off the deck.

She laughed at that thought. Surely he was heavy enough now that she could finally put that fear to rest. There were so many other fears to cause worry in a mother's mind.

"Luca, please don't put your head through the railing. If it gets stuck, we can't go to the lake."

Luca laughed and then said the one word she never expected him to say.

"S-S-Sam," said a little voice from the deck above his head. Sam looked up into big brown puppy-dog eyes shaded by a fringe of white blond hair. *Luca?*

"Do you see a snake, Luca?"

He heard Riley's voice coming closer. For a second he didn't know whether to climb up the deck to her or hide behind a tree. Unable to decide he just stood there looking like a stalker with a fishing pole.

"Sam?" she said in surprise. Of course she was surprised. He surely was.

"Yeah. What are you guys doing here?" he asked, though it was obvious they were there first so it was he that looked like the crazy person.

"The owners let me have the cabin for the weekend."

"You know Ian?" he asked.

"Yeah. Lexi is one of my best friends. She works with my sister."

"Huh." He considered that for a moment. Lexi had told him to look up her friend at the jewelry store. He hadn't realized they were that close. He wondered why Ian and Lex had never fixed them up.

"Wait, are you the Sam that works with Dalton?" she asked.

"Yeah."

"Oh." He couldn't tell a lot from the tone of that one word, but it didn't sound promising. "I went out with Dalton once."

So Ian had fixed her up with Dalton? *Thanks a lot, Ian*, he thought to himself.

"I see." He wasn't sure why he felt a twinge of jealousy. Obviously they hadn't hit it off, or Dalton would be standing on the deck next to her. Plus she'd said it had been years since she had sex, so . . .

"It wasn't that kind of date," she stated, and he felt better. "Other than the occasional girl's night, I don't get out with the group very often so we must have missed each other," she explained.

"Fish. Walter," Luca said. "Fish." He pointed down at Sam.

"Yep. I'm going fishing," Sam told him.

With that Luca was running toward the steps that led down to the yard.

"I come too," he repeated three times as he got to the first step and was swept into the air by his cautious mother. She propped him expertly on her hip and came down the stairs, her flip-flops making loud smacking sounds on the wood as she descended.

As soon as she was down, Luca wiggled and squirmed out of her arms to the ground so he could run over to Sam.

"Please," he said, unleashing the full force of his brown eyes, and long lashes. *Damn.* Sam thought his dimples were a gift, but this kid had him beat with the lashes.

"Do you want to come out?" Sam asked Riley, knowing this was her decision, not his. He tried not to hope, but his heart was pounding in a good way for a change. This was a disaster waiting to happen, but yet he couldn't stop.

"I wouldn't want him to mess up your peace and quiet."

"I have tons of peace and quiet. Plus, fishing is kind of boring until something happens."

"You don't mind?" Riley asked.

Sam shook his head.

"Do you know how to fish?" he asked Luca.

Luca nodded while Riley shook her head.

"Walter," Luca said.

"Who's Walter?"

"*Willy the Whale.* It's a cartoon I hope you never have to see. Willy is actually friends with a fisherman named Walter who is really a walrus dressed in clothes. I don't get it. Why would the walrus be able to walk around in clothes, but the whale is still stuck in the ocean? And why would a whale be friends with a fisherman? The nets? Harpoons? Hello?" She shook her head as she walked back up the steps. "Stay there Luca. I'm going to get a blanket."

She got more than a blanket. She had a small cooler bag with her when she came down a few minutes later. While they were waiting, Luca stared excitedly at the fishing rod while Sam waited for him to do something like run away or ooze some kind of fluid.

He hadn't been around when McKenna was this small. Give him an eleven-year-old and Sam was fine. He knew how to deal with a smart mouth and an eye roll. He didn't know how to handle a toddler. They didn't seem to know how to handle themselves yet, so that made them an unknown.

"I brought snacks," Riley said as she picked up Luca. With the cooler over the opposite shoulder and the blanket, she looked like she would fall over.

"Here, let me take something." When Sam held his hands out, he was expecting to get the cooler, but instead Luca raised his arms and practically leaped into his open arms.

The kid was like a monkey. He quickly clamped down around Sam's neck and waist like he would never come off. He was surprisingly light, and Sam didn't need to do much to keep him in place as he walked.

"I can catch a big fish," Luca said, surprising Sam by stringing together an entire sentence.

"They have a fishing game at school. It has plastic fish with magnets in their noses," Riley told him.

"Blue fish."

"The blue fish is the biggest one," Riley interpreted for her son. Sam didn't think she even realized she was doing it. It seemed like second nature.

When they got to the lake, the sun was glinting off the surface of the water. The green trees looked like a postcard against the flawless blue sky. It was a beautiful sight and the perfect place for peace and quiet. But he found he didn't want peace and quiet.

He liked the excitement of the little boy holding on to him as he pointed to the bird in the lake and shouted, "Duck! Duck. Duck." Luca squirmed to get down and took off to go take a closer look.

"Shit," Riley said, setting down the cooler so she could run after him. "Luca! Stop!"

It only took a second for instincts to kick in and Sam was chasing after the boy. Sam's long strides caught up to him right before he got to the bank where he could have slid into the water.

"Duck," he said again while pointing.

"I see the duck, but you can't touch him. They don't like that kind of thing. Plus you'll get all wet. You need to stay back from the water okay? It's not safe," Sam explained.

"Ouchie?"

"Yes, you could get an ouchie," Riley said as she came up next to them. "Good catch." She was standing so close he could smell her hair. Memories of their night together swarmed his thoughts for a second.

He was in big trouble. He knew it as sure as he knew his own name, but he could only smile at her as he held Luca a safe distance from the water fowl.

Riley felt bad that Sam wasn't getting much fishing done. Instead he was lying on the blanket tickling Luca and drinking out of a juice box. She would never say how that scene warmed her heart.

She loved hearing Luca giggle and say "stop" until Sam stopped. And then a second later he would say, "Do it again."

Sam had let Luca try his turn at fishing. He held Luca's hands in place as he cast out the line. The line bobbed in place for only a moment before her son lost interest and came running back to the blanket.

They stayed out at the lake all day. She shivered as she packed up their things. The nights in the mountains brought cooler temperatures.

"I'll walk you back to the cabin. I need to get the rest of my supplies."

"Where are you staying?" she asked.

"When Ian told me the cabin was occupied for the weekend I asked if I could camp by the lake, so I have a tent in the truck."

"Won't you be cold?"

"Nah. I'll be fine." Right. He was a soldier. Surely he'd been in worse places than a lake in Virginia in June.

Luca, having run himself ragged all afternoon, was drifting off as Sam carried him back to the cabin.

"Where should I put him?" Sam asked when they stepped inside.

"He's in the Rose Room. It's the one at the top—"

"I know where it is. I helped do the master bathroom." He nodded toward the stairs.

"I love the tub. You did it?"

"I did the work. Dalton drew up the plans."

"It's really amazing."

She followed them upstairs. By that point Luca was hanging limp in Sam's arm with his mouth hanging open.

Sam shouldered open the door and put Luca on the bed. They each took a foot and removed his shoes. Sam stepped out in the hall while Riley kissed Luca on the forehead and covered him with a light blanket.

"Night, baby," she whispered, and left the small light on next to the door just in case he woke up and was scared.

Then she went out to face Sam.

"Thank you—" Her appreciation was cut off by his lips coming down on hers.

She wasted no time catching up. Her arms came up around his neck, trapping him to her lips as he pushed her back against the wall.

"Stay," she said, taking a chance.

His only answer was to pick her up so she could wrap her legs around his waist while he carried her across the hall into the other bedroom.

"Riley," he said as he hovered over her on the bed. His expression was so serious it scared her for a moment. "I don't know where this is going. I'm not good at this. But maybe we could try."

His words frightened her even worse than his expression. It wasn't safe for her to let him in her life. Into Luca's life. But she wanted it. She wanted him.

"Okay. No promises," she answered, and whether she meant from him or from her and Luca she wasn't sure.

He stripped her slowly, differently than the last time. He was taking his time and she was fine with that. She didn't have the urgency she had the last time either, the pure sexual need; this was about more than the physical. This was important.

Sam—the big tough soldier—seemed unsure of himself as he touched her face and let out a shaky sigh. "I've been thinking about you since I left your place. You got in my head and I can't seem to get you out. I tried, but now I realize I don't want you out. I want you right here, like this."

God, he was saying all the right things to tear down every wall she'd built.

"I want you, Sam."

* * *

Sam was no stranger to the things that happened in the bedroom, but he was out of his element this time. He was making love to Riley. This was way more than a romp in the hay. It was real. It was bodies and feelings and need. A place he'd never dared to go since his last relationship had ended in disaster.

He took his time appreciating every nuance of her body and she let him. She didn't struggle to get him to hurry, she allowed him this time to do what he wanted to her.

He moved down her body, tasting her sweetness and enjoyed watching her climax from his touch. He had the power to make her feel good. He knew he also had the power to break her heart or cause her pain, but he pushed that thought away for now.

Seeing her lust-filled eyes looking down at him caused him to move back up her body, hovering over her, ready to take her. He'd restocked his wallet with three condoms hoping for a miracle that would get him out of his rut.

Here was his miracle. She was lying under him and as he rolled on the condom and slid into her, he knew he was where he belonged. There was none of the panic he'd felt before. This was right.

When two of the three condoms were spent he collapsed next to her, sucking in vanilla-scented air as he caught his breath inches from her skin. When he could move again, he pulled her against him and fell asleep almost instantly.

Unfortunately, he didn't stay that way all night . . .

It was cold. So cold he could see his breath as he looked down from a craggy rise. Desmond and Simmons were behind him, waiting for his command, but he wasn't sure what to do.

He'd been trained for this moment, he knew the goal should be to get to higher ground until a helo could do an extraction, but now they were trapped. The chopper was still ten minutes out. No matter what scenario he worked out, it still ended the same way. They weren't going to make it.

Insurgents were moving up from all sides and they were getting low on ammo.

"Save a round for me," Simmons said. "If they get too close, I want you to take me out. I don't want them trying to use me to get intel."

Sam wouldn't be able to shoot his own men, but he understood the concern. He would rather be put out than taken prisoner.

Another round of cracks came from their left and the ground sprayed dust and pebbles as searing pain shot through his left arm. He gave in to the heat in his arm for a few minutes. Footsteps brought him back to consciousness just in time to see who was coming closer. It wasn't one of his men. It was a young boy.

Sam wasn't able to get away, and he couldn't reach his gun. Behind him he heard Simmons yell, followed by a sharp pop. The young boy running toward him raised his weapon.

"Sam! Sam! Wake up." Riley shook his shoulder a little more firmly. He was thrashing around in the bed, covered in sweat. "Sam!"

With a loud gasp he sat straight up, his chest heaving as he tried to catch his breath. She rubbed his back, and said, "It's okay. It's just a dream. You're fine."

He choked and coughed as he struggled to breathe. Then without warning he latched onto her, his arms winding around her waist, pulling her tight against him.

"I'm sorry," he whispered.

"Shh. You don't need to be sorry. Would it help to talk about it?" she offered, knowing his past was probably not an easy place to visit. Even so, she wanted to help him some way.

He shook his head. "I'll be fine."

She wasn't so sure.

Despite the fact it was only three in the morning he got up and went to the huge bathroom to take a shower. He had told her tonight he wanted a chance. She wanted him to give her a chance as well.

She got out of bed, and after checking on Luca, she went in the bathroom to join him in the shower.

"Tell me," she said as she ran her hands over his wet shoulders. He turned and kissed her in an attempt to distract her, but she didn't let him. She pulled back and picked up the soap, turning him around to wash his back in a more clinical way. She didn't want him to brush off his issues with sex. It wasn't healthy.

"I already know it wasn't a picnic over there," she said as her fingers grazed a scar on his left shoulder.

"I got shot. My men got shot. It was an impossible situation, and it didn't end the way it was supposed to. That's it." He shrugged it off, but she knew there was so much more.

She didn't want to push him too hard. She knew it would take time for him to open up. She rewarded him for sharing by stepping closer and winding her arms around his waist. Her breasts pressed up against his strong back as her hands moved lower and lower until she wound her fingers around his length.

He twitched and moaned in pleasure, making her smile.

They rinsed quickly and barely dried off before he was picking her up and rushing her to the bed again.

"I can walk, you know."

"Your legs are so short, it takes too long," he teased and kissed her before reaching for his last condom. She hadn't brought any with her, why would she? She surely wasn't planning to jump into bed with anyone out here in the middle of nowhere, while spending the weekend with her little boy. Fate had given her a pleasant surprise for a change.

Sam was not slow and loving this time, he seemed desperate as he pushed inside her. He held onto her so tightly she had difficulty breathing, but she didn't complain. She loved every second. He needed her. She could feel it in the tension of his body and the urgency of his kiss.

She wanted to take away the ghosts that haunted him in any way possible. Sure she knew sex wasn't the answer. But he'd told her a small part of his past. The rest would take time and for now she could comfort him with her body. When he collapsed on her and his breathing steadied, she hoped he would have peaceful dreams.

Chapter 5

Sam felt like he was being watched. The fear that it could be an enemy intensified until he had no choice but to open his eyes and look.

Sure enough, someone was watching him.

Four sets of brown eyes stared at him as he blinked away sleep. One set was plastic and belonged to a dingy white bunny. The other set blinked back.

"Hey Luca," Riley said from behind Sam. "Are you okay?"

Luca nodded and rubbed his eyes as if he learned the technique from some kind of Cute Kid Handbook.

Without answering he crawled up on the bed and climbed across Sam to get to his mother. Sam felt a moment of terror as Riley raised the blanket on the other side of her to let him in. But then he saw she was dressed. Shorts and a tank top.

Sam, however, was buck naked under the sheet.

"Uh, Ri?" He cleared his throat. "I need pants."

"Oh. Okay. I'll distract him and you get them." This didn't sound like the best plan, but as she tickled Luca and he began to giggle he felt it was his only shot. He darted out of bed, found his boxers and slipped them on before Luca had even started begging her to stop.

He climbed back under the sheet as Luca recovered from his fit of giggles. When he could breathe, he reached over his mother and began tickling Sam's ribs. His tiny little fingers didn't do much since Sam wasn't ticklish, but Sam laughed and pretended so Luca wouldn't feel dejected.

"Let's get Mommy," Sam suggested when Luca finished his assault on Sam. Together the two of them attacked from either side, causing her to scream and twist with laughter.

"Stop it! Stop! Or I'm not going to make you breakfast!"

Luca slowed down for a second, and Sam said, "It's okay, Luca. I know how to make breakfast." Luca gave an evil little chuckle and continued torturing his mother.

When it was apparent Riley was either going to suffocate or wet herself, they stopped, although no one made a move to get out of bed. Riley told stories about when Luca was little, and he listened to his own history as if she were telling the tale of a fictional character.

"And when you were in Mommy's tummy, I ate Popsicles every day. And what do you like to eat?"

"Popsicles!" Luca said.

"Yeah, but that could be a coincidence. I love Popsicles and I spent no time in your tummy," Sam noted with a grin, causing Riley to roll her eyes.

"I wanna Popsicle!" Luca announced.

"You can have waffles," she said.

"Waffles?" Sam asked, impressed.

"From a box. Don't get too excited."

"I can get adequately excited over waffles from a box," he said as Luca jumped off the bed and ran out of the room.

Sam pulled on a shirt before following Riley downstairs. She hadn't changed or bothered to put on a bra so every step she took down the stairs made her breasts bounce in a very appealing way. The shorts she was wearing were tight and thin and he was having visions of peeling them down her thighs when a white rabbit cut off his fantasy.

"Hey, bunny," Sam greeted the stuffed animal, happy for the distraction.

"Hops," Luca said, making it sound like Sam had insulted him by calling it a bunny.

"How do you do, Mr. Hops?" Sam shook the rabbit's paw and bowed, making Luca giggle and run off.

"Are you okay with this?" Riley asked. She bit her lip as she opened the box of waffles, and glanced at him.

"Sure. I'm telling you, the kind from the box are just as good as real ones." He was pretty sure she wasn't talking about the waffles.

She laughed and let it go. He was grateful, because he didn't have an answer.

He was having the best time with her and he even liked playing with Luca. But he knew himself, and he was sure something would go wrong at any minute. She might want to talk about what happened the night before. Not the sex, but the way she woke him up as he was sweating and gasping for air. She might want to talk about it, and what could he say? To tell her it was a fluke would be a lie.

He wasn't cut out for this kind of life, nor did he deserve it. But boy, did it feel nice at the moment.

Despite all the great sex the night before, Riley was tense as she made breakfast. She was worried the reality of being with a kid would cause Sam to freak out and run screaming down the mountain. So far he was handling things fine. Even when Luca missed his mouth and dropped syrup down his shirt. "Uh-oh," Luca said, wiping at it with his sticky hand, making it worse.

"Here." Sam whipped Luca's shirt over his head. "Guys can go skins at the table for breakfast." He reached over his head, grabbing the collar of his T-shirt and pulled it over his head so he was "skins" as well.

Riley looked him over—his caramel skin and rippling muscles—and decided she liked this rule very much.

"Pretty," Luca said, pointing to the artwork on Sam's chest. A dragon curled itself along his pectoral and wound down to his ribs. In its claw was the insignia for the Marines.

"No one has ever called my ink pretty before." He smiled, but didn't seem insulted.

"You like the colors?" Riley asked her son who nodded. It was very colorful, and dare she say . . . pretty. In a tough soldier kind of way, of course. "Me too."

"Boo boo," Luca said, pointing at the scar on Sam's left shoulder.

"It's okay, it doesn't hurt anymore," Sam said.

"All better?" Luca said.

"Yep. All better." Riley knew this wasn't true. Yes, his skin had healed, but after seeing Sam in the throes of the nightmare the night before she knew he was far from *all better.* He had demons. But didn't most people?

Riley lived behind a fortress of protection from men. She would not get close enough to be harmed, and she surely wouldn't let Luca get close either.

At least that was the goal at breakfast.

But by the time they were eating ice cream in town after dinner, things were already shifting. Sam had slipped away for a few minutes. When he came back he smiled and held up a bag from the drugstore. Condoms.

"So are we ready to go back?" he asked as he wiggled his eyebrows. "Do you think he'll go to sleep early again?" He didn't even attempt to hide the hope in his voice.

After a game of tag, and an hour at the park, Luca was already leaning to one side of his car seat with heavy lids. He would probably be asleep before they reached the end of the parking lot.

"You've thoroughly worn him out," she said as Sam drove them to the cabin. "Was that the plan?"

Sam shrugged. "I wanted him to have fun today, and I want us to be able to have fun tonight." That seemed fair enough.

At the cabin Sam reached in for a sleeping Luca.

"I can get him," Riley said.

"It's okay. You're on vacation. Take a break from lugging him around." Sam winked.

"He does get a little heavy sometimes."

"I've carried you both, and I'm pretty sure he's heavier," he joked as Riley got the door.

Sam took him straight up to the pink room and put him in bed. Riley got his shoes and watched as Sam leaned over and kissed Luca's head. Her heart squeezed at the sight. She couldn't remember a time she'd ever seen Evan do that. Even when Luc was a baby.

The fantasies she'd had before came back in a rush, and she tried desperately to keep them at bay. This was not real. This was a weekend. It was fun.

Before she could worry too much, Sam took her hand and led her out of the room and across the hall. He was shedding clothes as he went, his shoes, her shirt, by the time they got to the bed they were, for the most part, naked.

She couldn't help but think this was how life was meant to be. With someone to help when things got heavy and someone to hold her and make her feel amazing at night. It seemed so simple, and yet it was so far out of her reach.

After another intense sexual experience with Sam, he fell in a heap next to her, out of breath. She wasn't exploding into an orgasm as soon as he touched her like the first few times, but he was still able to make it happen fairly easy. He'd said he thought it was sexy as hell, but she still felt vulnerable. Surely it wasn't safe for him to know the power he had over her.

As his breathing evened out he reached for her and pulled her close against him as he always did. She could feel the heaviness of his arm as it rested on her hip. It felt nice to be wrapped up in a warm man.

"This is so much better than being in a tent alone," he murmured by her ear.

"Are you only sleeping with me so you don't have to sleep outside in a tent?" she joked.

"Ah, hell. You figured it out." He nipped the skin of her neck, making her laugh. She'd had such a great time. Tomorrow it would be over. But she would have more wonderful memories.

"We're leaving in the morning." She couldn't help but frown at the thought of leaving their happy bubble to go back to the real world.

"Me too. And then I'm flying out the next day." Right. As if things weren't already uncertain, Sam had a job that took him out of town all the time. Even if he would be interested in more, he wouldn't be around to give it.

"I had a great time. I'm glad you were here. Otherwise I probably would have spent the whole weekend coloring and explaining why there was no television."

"I was probably going to fail at not thinking about you," he said with more honesty than she had given him. She felt his arms hold her just a little bit closer. Maybe this didn't have to be over. Maybe things would work out for her and Luca this time.

She fell asleep with hope in her heart.

In the morning Sam was gone. The bed was empty; the only clothes piled on the floor were hers. She let out a sad sigh. Reality sucked.

Then she heard the sound of Luca laughing, and a deep rumbling voice coming from downstairs. He wasn't gone, and from the smells of bacon wafting up the steps, Sam must be making breakfast. She pulled on some clothes and scurried down to the kitchen where she found Luca standing on a chair pulled up to the counter.

"Stir it harder. Put some muscle into it," Sam instructed Luca who had a wooden spoon in a bowl of yellow paste. Neither of them was wearing a shirt, but aside from that they couldn't have been more opposite.

Sam was all dark and bulky and Luca was pale, blond, and bony. She couldn't help but laugh at the unusual cooking duo.

Her giggles prompted Luca to turn toward the sound, the batter dripped off his spoon onto the chair as he smiled.

"Momma! I'm makin' breffast for you," he said proudly.

"You are? It looks like you're dropping it on the chair." She picked up a paper towel and wiped the drips from his leg and the chair.

"Stir Luc. Stir."

Luca's tongue twisted out of his lips with the effort he was putting into it.

"He's stirred the bejesus out of that batter, but he was having fun so I hope you like really flat pancakes."

"I do. They're called crepes."

He smiled and then after glancing over to Luca who was occupied with his task, Sam leaned down and kissed her followed by a very sexy, "Good morning."

"Good morning. What can I do?"

"Nothing. Sit over there and let us take care of you," he ordered.

"I don't know how to do that."

"It's time you learned." He pointed his spatula at her and went back to the stove. She was impressed with his set up. Luca was positioned close enough to Sam that he could reach him, but not close enough to the stove that he could get burned or spattered. She guessed he was accustomed to thinking things through in a logical manner, planning every step out. It was necessary both in the military and at his job now.

For the next few minutes she enjoyed watching Sam work and listening to Luca giggle. Then Sam lifted him from the chair and set him on his feet. Sam handed Luca a plate and crouched down to whisper in his ear.

Luca carried the plate over to her with a giant grin on his face.

"I love you, Momma," he said. It didn't matter that it was prompted, silly tears sprang to her eyes as she took the plate. She pulled him up on her lap and hugged him until he squiggled away.

"Thank you," she told Sam as he sat down next to her with his own plate.

"Knowing how to make the ladies melt is a skill you're never too young to learn," Sam said, making her laugh.

He had certainly made her melt. He'd also given her a multitude of new fantasies she shouldn't have in her head. Even as they packed up to leave, she was trying to gather enough courage to invite Sam to their home when he got back from his trip. Riley knew better than this. She never wanted her son to grow attached to a man who would end up leaving a hole when he got bored and moved on. She wasn't sure if Sam was that kind of man, but it was obvious Luca was already attached.

As she watched Sam throw Luca in the air and catch him before tossing him in his car seat upside down, she tried not to let her heart get ahead of her brain. But hearing Luca's laughter had her hoping and wanting things that probably weren't possible with a guy like Sam.

And it wasn't Sam's fault. He hadn't tried to trick her or pretend to be more than he was. He was open and honest and had just wandered into their weekend getaway and their lives by accident.

But he was there now and she didn't know what she and Luca would do when he wasn't.

The silence of Sam's apartment as he unpacked felt foreign to him. He'd just spent the weekend in non-stop noise and chaos, but he already missed it. He wasn't expecting that. He'd told Riley he was willing to try, but he wasn't entirely sure how he was going to pull it off. Hanging out on the edge of their lives wasn't a long term plan, but he wasn't ready to jump in any further.

Instead of worrying about it, he did laundry and repacked for his trip the next day. He called Dalton to check in.

"How was your weekend at the lake?" Dalton asked. "Did you catch anything?"

"I had a good time. Very relaxing." He looked around his quiet apartment.

"Which means you didn't catch shit."

Sam laughed. It was better to let Dalton think he was a poor fisherman, than to tell him what really happened. Which reminded him of something. "Hey, did you go out with a girl named Riley Fisher?"

"Riley?" How could Dalton not remember her?

"Roslyn's sister."

"Oh! Yeah. Really short? Kid?"

"Yes."

"Yeah. I remember. It was a fix-up thing. She's not my type." Sam knew Dalton's type was the girl from high school he was still hung up on. Dalton had poured out his sad story one night when he was drunk.

"She's not mine either." This was very true. Sam would never pick someone like Riley. She was so small and almost seemed breakable. Although at this point, he knew she was far from breakable. He'd been a little rough with her, and she kept right up with him. Not to mention how flexible she was.

Hell, now his jeans were tight.

"Why? Are Ian and Lex trying to fix you up with her?" Dalton sounded doubtful. "She has a kid. She's looking for a serious thing."

"No. I ran into her and she mentioned you."

"Oh. Well, if I were you, I'd stay clear of that."

"Yes." Sam should definitely stay clear of that.

His trip was short that week. He only needed to set a pre-Civil War door from Atlanta in a house in Chicago.

As he pulled in at his apartment, he felt the chill of awaiting silence. He knew he would sit there either thinking of things that weren't fun to think about or he'd think of things that were too much fun to think about. Neither would be safe.

He looked at his phone. It was only seven. Riley would be home and Luca wouldn't be in bed yet. He should have called to ask if he could come over, but that would have given her the option to say no, and he didn't think he could handle it. Instead, he drove over to once again barge in on her life and her plans.

"Sam! Sam!" Luca came running to the door as soon as Riley opened it.

"Hey. I just got back. Is it okay—" His words were cut off by Luca tackling his legs. He picked him up as Riley opened the door wider to let him in. He couldn't tell what she was thinking. She looked sort of mad, but she didn't say anything as Sam held Luca upside down by his ankles making him laugh hysterically.

"Luca, why don't you show Sam the picture you drew at Grammy's?" Riley folded her arms across her chest, making his attention go to her breasts. When his gaze moved up to her face, he saw she didn't look very happy. He definitely should have called first.

He put Luca down and the little boy tore off down the hall. Before he got the chance to ask what was wrong, Luca came running into the living room with a large piece of paper flapping in the wind caused by his speed.

Sam bent down to help him unroll it. "What did you draw?" he asked as he looked at the mess on the page.

"You, me, and Mommy," Luca said proudly. There were three distinct blobs of color in a large box-like thing. Maybe the cabin?

"What's this?" Sam asked Luca while looking up at Riley.

"We in bed," Luca told him.

"This is us in bed?" Sam tried to swallow and couldn't.

"Yep," Luca said with a happy nod.

"Yes," Riley said. "And what did you tell Grammy? What did Sam do to you when we were all in bed?"

"He getted me." Luca smiled before adding, "In my funny places."

"Oh, no," Sam whispered. It was all very innocent. When Sam was tickling him, he told him over and over, "I'm going to get you." But now . . .

"Yeah. Grammy had a lot of questions when I came to pick him up today. Especially since I hadn't even mentioned you."

"Should I go meet her? So she knows I'm not a deviant?"

Her frosty look seemed to mellow slightly. "You would be willing to do that?" she asked, disbelieving.

"Of course. I mean, I didn't do anything horrible to him. Maybe if I explain, she wouldn't be so worried."

"Why would you care what she thinks of you?" Her eyes were huge.

"It's a good thing to have someone looking out for your kid, Ri." He stood up and tousled Luca's soft hair. "I'd like her to know the difference between an upstanding member of society having a tickle fight with her grandson, and whatever kind of loser you might date after me doing something indecent."

"Why would you automatically assume the next guy would be a loser?" She was smiling.

"Probably because the guy before me was."

"Good point. I have no argument there. However, you'd do better with Grammy if you didn't mention how you think her son is a loser."

"I thought you said she knew her son was a loser."

"She's still not going to want to hear it from you."

"Probably not." Blood made people see what they wanted to see.

She stood on her tiptoes and kissed him.

"Thank you for offering to help put her mind at ease. I think she believed me."

"Think." Sam sniffed. He could only imagine where the woman's mind had gone.

Sam stayed while Luca got his bath. He stayed while Riley read him a story. And he stayed when Riley turned off the light and quietly walked out in the hall when Luca was sleeping.

He knew it was time to leave. He hadn't come there for sex. He didn't want her to think it was a booty call or something. But it wasn't as if he was innocent. He'd come there to use her and her son so he didn't have to sit at his place alone.

It wasn't that he had a problem being alone. Alone was fine. Alone was safe. But this, with Riley and Luca was . . . better. There was no time to be caught off guard by thoughts he tried to keep away.

He moved toward the door.

"I guess I should be going. You have to get up early in the morning, while I have the day off to laze around."

"Are you rubbing it in?" She propped her hand on her hip.

"Yes. Wouldn't you?"

She laughed and reached up to his shoulders. He obligingly leaned down so she could kiss him. He assumed it would be a kiss good-bye, but her tongue slid into his mouth and her fingers grasped him tighter. Her lips moved to his jaw and up to his ear. "Stay," she whispered like she had before.

And like before, it had the same effect on him. He tried to be patient as he walked her backward toward her bedroom, but when she tripped, he caught her in his arms and just carried her the rest of the way. Allowing her to walk to the bedroom was something he was going to have to work on.

Taking her clothes off and lying on top of her felt like the most natural thing in the world. It was home. It was safety.

And when they were both completely satisfied, he was able to fall into a restful sleep. Something he rarely found outside of her bed.

He woke in the morning to the sound of loud whispers outside the door and sunlight coming in through the curtains.

"Sam is sleeping so be quiet, okay?" Riley said.

"Sam sleeping?" Luca verified loudly. Sam smiled and rolled out of bed, pulling on his jeans.

"Shh. Come on. He's tired. He was on an airplane yesterday."

"Airplane?"

Sam ripped open the door making them both jump.

"Who's making all this noise out here?" he bellowed with a smile on his face. "I'm hungry. Where's my breakfast?" He grabbed Luca up. "This will do." Sam made chomping sounds at Luca's belly while the boy squealed and kicked.

Riley rolled her eyes.

"Great. Now he'll tell his grandmother you *ate* him."

Right. He let Luca slide to his feet. Sam needed to assure Luca's grandmother that he wasn't a danger. Although while Sam wasn't a danger in that way, it still didn't mean Sam was safe.

"So where does Grammy live?" Sam asked as he helped Luca wrestle the last piece of cereal out of his bowl.

"Why?" Riley asked.

"So I can meet her."

"You don't have to do that."

"I want to. I don't want her to worry."

Sam followed the directions to Mrs. Fisher's house and knocked on the door later that morning.

The woman opened her door cautiously, as was expected when someone like Sam was at the door.

"Mrs. Fisher?" he said.

"Yes."

"Good morning, ma'am. I'm Sam Brooks."

"Oh." Her look of surprise said more than that one word. She was no doubt thinking he was much different looking than her son. It was true. He'd seen a photo of Luca and his dad sitting on the stand next to Luc's bed.

Evan Fisher was thin and pale. Sam was the opposite of those things.

"Do you have a moment? I wanted to explain the situation regarding the picture Luca drew."

"Come in. Riley mentioned you might stop by. To be honest, I didn't expect it." She glanced over her shoulder as she walked down the hall to make sure he was following her. In the kitchen, two little boys were playing at the table. One of them was very familiar, and Sam couldn't help but smile when he saw Luca's face light up.

"Sam! Sam!" Luca slid off the chair and came running, arms up.

"Hey, buddy." Sam picked him up as the blond boy in his arms pointed to the little boy at the table.

"Christian," Luca said. The other boy, who looked older than Luca waved.

"Hello, Christian."

Luca did his wiggly porpoise move which meant he wanted down. Sam put him on his feet and watched as he ran off to the toy box, pulling things out to show him.

"He prayed for you at breakfast," the woman beside him said.

"Oh. Well, I guess that can't hurt," he said, not being a religious man. The woman frowned and he tried to recall something from his bible school days, but nothing came. *Thanks a lot, God,* he thought. "So about the picture. We were having a tickle fight."

"In bed?"

"Uh." Christ. He hadn't come up with an answer for that. "Yes."

"So you and Riley are ... dating?" She seemed uncomfortable with the word. So was he.

"Uh." He looked over at Luca, hoping he would do something cute to distract them from this horrid conversation. The little slacker was building something with Legos. "We've gone out. I respect her a whole lot." That was true.

The woman frowned.

"Riley is a mother. I know your kind, with the manners and the good looks." She pointed her finger at him as if manners and good looks were the work of the Devil himself. "She's been through a lot. And I hate knowing it was my own flesh and blood that did it. I assure you my son was not raised to be the person he's become. Cheating on his wife and having a child out of wedlock." She shook her head. "He's a disgrace."

Sam said nothing. It was clearly a trap. If he said anything in agreement she would hate him. Only a parent could criticize their child and get away with it.

"But Riley never did anything to deserve what happened. She was a good wife and mother. She's a great daughter-in-law too. She should have a man who will take care of her and will stick around. Are you that kind of man?"

"Uh." It seemed to be the only noise he could make in this woman's presence.

"I didn't think so." She actually made a tsk sound at him and he hung his head. "That little boy thinks you hang the moon. Are you going to walk away and break his heart?"

Sam looked over at Luca and, of course, Luca looked over at them and gave Sam a huge smile as he held up the tower he made.

Was he going to hurt Luca when he moved on? He thought the kid was small enough to forget he was ever there, but maybe not. He'd drawn Sam in a picture and he'd been happy to see him. *Shit.*

The last thing he ever wanted to do was hurt Luca and Riley.

"Ma'am, I'm not a husband or a father. I know I can't do right by them in that regard, but Riley told me she wasn't looking for either of those things, so I assure you I'm not overselling myself and setting her up for disappointment."

The woman waved her hand as if what he just said was the most ridiculous thing she'd ever heard.

"Fine," she said. "Thank you for stopping by and letting me see what a respectable man you are." He knew sarcasm when he heard it.

"My main concern was that you didn't think I had done anything inappropriate with Luc."

"Other than sleep with his mother."

"Uh." Why had he offered to come to this hell?

"So what kind of family do you come from?" she asked. Was that a trick? "Do your parents live in Roanoke?"

"Oh. No. My parents have both passed. My father died in a work accident when I was young, and my mother had cancer. She died while I was overseas."

"You were in the military?"

"Yes."

"My Roger was in the Navy." She nodded to an old picture of a young man in his Navy whites.

"Marines."

"Well, that's something."

"My sister and niece live in Roanoke." He got back to her original question about family.

"Luca, Sam needs to go. Come say goodbye." Okay. She was apparently through with the questioning.

"No!" Luca said as he ran over and wrapped his arms around Sam's thigh. "Come see." He pointed.

"Okay. For a minute, but then I need to go."

He sat on the floor while Luca babbled on about the blocks and then showed him the annoyingly loud buttons on a fire truck.

Christian came into the living room and sat in front of the television. Soon Luca was distracted by the cartoons as well. Sam patted Luca on the head and with a wave to Mrs. Fisher he slipped out the door and took a deep breath.

He'd survived. Kind of.

Chapter 6

When Riley picked up Luca that evening Anita told her Sam had stopped by. Sam had said he was going to, but Riley was still surprised he'd followed through. It must have been awful. She smiled at the thought of big, tough Sam cowering under Anita's sharp gaze.

"He seems like a respectable guy, but I don't think it's a good idea to set your sights on him," Anita warned.

"Yes. I know." Riley nodded. "I don't want Luca to get attached, but then part of me thinks he still needs a male role model in his life. Even if it's only for a short time, right?"

"He has a father," Anita said and then frowned as if she knew Evan didn't really count.

Riley nodded again. "Evan dropped Luca off early from his last weekend with him, and he texted me today to say he's not going to make it for the next one. Luca already has a man who comes and goes in his life. I'd love to have someone steady, but until that happens . . ."

"Well, this man obviously cares to some degree, if he came to set things straight with me. I'll talk to Evan about his priorities." Riley nodded, but didn't think a lecture from his mother was going to miraculously turn Evan into a great father.

Sam was out of town for the rest of the week and the weekend. They had sent some funny texts, and some sexy ones. When she got the text asking if he could come over that night, she nearly squealed like a teenager. To him, she typed a simple: *yes*.

It was perfect timing since she was off work the next day. They'd be able to stay up late. But her plans fell through when he came in the door. He looked exhausted.

"Hey," he said with a smile and pulled her into a hug. At the sound of his voice, Luca had come running and was jumping around at their legs. "Do you hear something?" Sam pretended not to notice Luca.

"It's me!" Luca yelled. "Luca!" Her son was hanging on Sam's leg like a koala on a tree.

"Holy crap! There's a Luca on my leg! How long has that been there?" he said as he picked Luca up and tossed him in the air.

"Be careful, he just had chocolate milk," Riley said quickly.

Sam made a frown and held him in the normal fashion.

"What have you been up to?" Sam asked. "Have you drawn any-more pictures?" Luca nodded but didn't make any effort to get down to show him. Instead he wrapped his little arms around Sam's neck as if he could hold him there forever.

Riley felt a tug in her heart at the sight. She too wished there was a way to keep Sam with them. She was disappointed by this fact. She'd depended on the stupid flimsy walls she'd built to protect her from this moment. They'd let her down big-time.

Sam stayed the night, but they just slept. It felt nice having his warmth pressed against her back as she fell asleep. But despite the peaceful start of their slumber Sam had moved away from her at some point in the night.

She was awoken by him thrashing around, mumbling something about "getting down and taking cover." She put her hand on his chest feeling the sweat and the pounding of his heart.

"Sam," she said while she pushed him. "Sam!" She turned on the light and gave him a pretty good shove for a girl her size and he woke like he had the last time, coughing and gasping for air.

"Christ!" he said as he rubbed his hand over his face. "I'm sorry I woke you. Are you okay? Did I hurt you?"

"I'm fine, are you?"

He shook his head.

She understood. He wasn't fine. His head was filled with awful things that came out when his consciousness wasn't there to fight them away. She swallowed and ran her hand along his cheek.

"Let's go take a shower together," she suggested. "We'll wash the bad dream away."

He wrapped his arms around her, and pulled her tight against him. His heart had calmed slightly, but still hammered against her breasts. He held her for a long time and twice she felt his body shudder. If he had been crying, he did a good job of hiding it when he rolled out of bed to take her up on her offer.

In the shower he washed her hair and rubbed her shoulders. "I'm sorry I woke you up," he said again.

"I'm sorry you don't have better dreams." She smiled as she turned and ran her sudsy hands up his chest. "Maybe I can give you something nice to dream about."

"You're pretty amazing for a short girl," he said as he pressed her back against the wall and kissed her.

It was Evan's weekend to take Luca, and Sam wasn't sure how to play it. Riley seemed content to pack Luca's things, and fill the boy's head with tales of great adventure he would have with his father, but Sam frowned and tried to swallow down his protective urges.

After all, this was Luca. He was small and needed his mother. But she was forced by the court to give him to his father who had proven to be an asshole many times over. Sam didn't have a lot of experience with this kind of arrangement, but he thought overall the program sucked.

"You're sure he's going to be okay?" Sam asked Riley as she set his bag by the front door.

Riley pressed her lips together and forced a smile. "It will be fine."

Sam couldn't pretend to know everything about this girl, but he sure as hell knew when she was lying.

When the doorbell rang, he saw her tense and then take a deep breath. He'd worked with some extremely tough men while in the marines, but they were nothing compared to the strength of this tiny woman.

"Luca! Your dad's here!" she yelled as she went to the door.

Evan walked inside as if he owned the place, and Sam wanted to punch him. He forced his hands out of fists and tried Riley's technique of taking a deep breath. It didn't work.

"Is he ready?" the man asked with a snotty attitude until he saw Sam standing there. Then he physically jolted.

"Evan, this is Sam. Sam, Luca's father."

Sam made no move to walk across the living room to shake his hand. Being that close wouldn't be good. He just gave him a wave instead.

When Luca didn't appear, Riley yelled again.

"I'll get him," Sam offered as much to help move the situation along as to get away from temptation.

Sam stepped into Luca's room and didn't see him at first. "Luca?" he said toward the blob of sheet in the corner. The blob moved, but didn't say anything back. "Hmm. Where could Luca be?" Again the blob moved.

Sam snapped the sheet off of him in one quick movement like a magician which made Luca jump and laugh. "I thought I smelled a little boy under here. I'm hungry," Sam said while rubbing his stomach.

"Oh, no!" Luca giggled while he jumped up and ran out of the room. Sam followed close behind making hungry monster sounds, but when they got to the living room, Luca turned and ran back toward him. Instinctively, Sam lifted him into his arms, where Luca latched on and shook his head.

"I don't want to go!" he said, digging into Sam's ribs with his surprisingly strong little legs.

"Hey, champ! Don't you want to go see your little sister?" Evan asked.

"No!" Luca shot that down pretty quickly.

"Well, we need to get going. Celia's waiting in the car."

"No!" Luca's lip trembled before he started crying and he somehow managed to hang onto Sam even tighter. "Please, Sam." *God.* Why didn't the kid just take Sam's heart and tear it into tiny pieces? It would have been less painful than this.

"Put him down," Evan said, with annoyance.

"What am I supposed to do?" Sam snapped at the man, not liking him or his tone.

"Luca," Riley intervened. "Come here."

"No!" He screamed when she put her hands on his sides to pull him off Sam. "No!"

"Can you just give us a minute?" Sam said as he turned to walk back to the hall.

"I don't have a minute," Evan said with a huff.

"Everyone has a minute." Sam ignored whatever else the asshole was going to say and took Luca back to his room.

He was able to get Luca off and toss him playfully on his bed.

"So? Why don't you want to go with your dad?" Sam asked him.

"I wanna stay with you," was the answer.

"I'd like you to stay here with me too. Believe me. But unfortunately we have to take turns. You know about taking turns, right? You have to take turns with Christian at your grandmother's house." Luca nodded.

"Well, it's the same thing with your mommy and daddy. They have to take turns with you. And it's your dad's turn."

Luca pouted and said again, "I stay with you."

"You're killing me, you know that?" Sam said while ruffling Luca's hair. He changed up his game plan. "It's only going to be for two days. That's really quick. Then when you get back, you and your mommy and I will go for ice cream. But we have to wait until you get back from your dad's to go." He'd discovered bribery was a great tactic with toddlers. Unfortunately ice cream wasn't enough of a motivation.

"You know how I have to go away to work sometimes? And I'm gone for a couple of days?" Luca nodded. "It's not fun, and I'd rather be with you, but I don't have a choice. I have to do it. This is kind of like that. You have to go with your dad now. But you'll get to come back home and we'll all be together. Just like when I go away and I come back. Can you be like me and go to work for a couple of days? And then come back?"

Luca blinked while he thought it over. For some reason the kid thought Sam was great. He jumped at any chance to be like Sam or do something Sam did.

Reluctantly Luca nodded.

"Okay. Good. Let's get Hops and your stuff. And I'll see you in two days when you're done working."

Luca nodded, a little more agreeable.

Sam hugged him but didn't let him latch on, just in case. He took Luca's hand as they walked out of his room.

When Luca stopped before they got to the living room, Sam was prepared for a retreat, but instead Luca looked up at him and said, "I love you." *Ah, hell.*

"Yeah. I love you too." He might have said it quickly and quietly so no one else would hear, but it didn't make it any less true. For some reason it was easier to share his feelings with Luca. He didn't seem to have any expectations.

Luca walked out into the living room and picked up his backpack full of books as if he was heading off to the mines.

"I go to work," he said with an exasperated sigh.

Riley's brows pulled together and she looked up at Sam who just shook his head.

They said their goodbyes and she watched while Evan buckled Luca into his car seat and drove off. Then she turned around to face Sam with tears on her cheeks. "I don't think I'm ever going to get better at this," she said through her sobs.

"It's okay. He's going to be fine. He'll be back tomorrow night. Probably earlier, because let's face it, Evan isn't cut out for this. He'll be back before you know it. And in the meantime, I'll be here to distract you." Sam lifted his eyebrows, hoping to make her laugh. When it didn't work he just pulled her into a hug and let her cry it out.

"I wish he'd just sign off his rights so I didn't ever need to send Luca away with him."

"But the support—"

"I would find a way to do it without the support if I knew he would agree to sign over his rights." She wiped her cheeks with her palms.

"Have you asked him?"

"Yes. But he refused. Probably more because of what his mother would say than any real devotion to his son, but he still said no."

Sam frowned. He could kind of see Evan's point. If Luca was Sam's kid, he wouldn't want to give up his rights to see him. Of course, he hoped he would be a better father than Evan.

Riley was embarrassed by her breakdown, but Sam handled it like a champ. He didn't try to fix it, which would have been impossible. Instead he let her cry while he rubbed her back.

Sam seemed surprised when she moved on from being the sad mother who was missing her son, to the seductress who had the house to herself with her boyfriend. She didn't blame him. It was a huge divide. She laughed at his expression when she undid his jeans in the kitchen and knelt down in front of him.

"Uh, Ri?"

"Yes?" she purred, or attempted to, as she freed him from the confines of the denim.

"We're in the kitchen."

"Yep."

"Window's open."

"Yep." She licked over him, making him moan. Apparently, he

didn't feel the need to point out any more obvious facts as he braced his hands against the counter and let his head fall back.

She worked him with her mouth, and used her hand too, since he was too big to fit without choking. He said her name like a curse a few times and clenched his heavy hands in her hair. Never did he try to maneuver her, he merely held on as she moved.

When she finished him, she tucked him back into his pants and stood up.

"God, girl," he said, breathless.

"I don't have any responsibilities today, so I'm being reckless."

"Sign me up." He smiled at her and pointed. "I think you have a Fruit Hoop stuck to your knee."

She looked down, and sure enough the piece of cereal mocked her. Then she noticed what she was wearing. An old stretched out T-shirt and faded denim shorts. From her reflection in the microwave, she could tell her hair was a mess.

"I look awful. Let me go clean up and then I can be sexy."

"Baby, I've been with my share of women, and none of them were as sexy as you are right now."

"With the cereal and the messy hair?" she challenged.

"Your hair is messy because I was tugging at it."

"Oh. Right."

"There's really no sense to fix it. As soon as I catch my breath I'm planning to carry you over to the couch and mess it up some more. As far as what you're wearing, you won't be wearing it for long."

"You're quite the problem solver."

"Trust me, you're not a problem." Sam moved in closer. He wasn't as tall as Evan, so she never felt like Sam was looming over her. When he picked her up she wrapped her legs around his waist and bent to kiss his ear.

When they got to the sofa, he lowered her onto the cushions, tossed a book to the side, and then a car before he started working on her shorts.

She arched up so he could move them over her hips. They came off with her panties in one sweep. She sat up only long enough to pull off the shirt which Sam took from her and threw over his head with a naughty smile on his face.

"We'll have to clean that up later," she told him.

"Shh. We're being reckless right now."

"Oh, right." She giggled as he yanked his shirt over his head in the same fashion. He stood and kicked off his sneakers and tugged off his socks. Then slowly—torturously so—he unzipped his jeans and slid them down inch by inch.

"You know we only have so long, Sam."

"We have all night, and all day tomorrow. Be patient."

"Easy for you to say." He'd already been satisfied. She was going crazy. She started to say that, when he dove between her legs and took a swipe of her with his tongue. That shut her right up. Instead, she moaned and arched her back, trying to get closer to him. He chuckled against her damp flesh, which added to the pleasure.

When he'd taken her right up to the edge with his mouth, he moved over her and slid home, causing her to cry out in release on his first full stroke. She would have been embarrassed with how easily she'd climaxed except it seemed to turn Sam on. And it wasn't anything new.

They moved and changed positions a few times, utilizing the entire apartment while they had the opportunity. Eventually they ended up in her bed, spent and smiling.

"Wow," she said with her eyes closed.

"Yeah," he agreed before he pulled her close and rested his head on her chest. She played with his hair while he fell asleep. She didn't fall asleep as easily. After the high of her third orgasm melted away she was left again with worry.

Luca was in the next town with his father. If he cried in the middle of the night she wouldn't be there to soothe him back to sleep. Evan or Celia would do it. A woman Riley barely knew was currently in charge of her son's happiness and well-being. She felt so helpless.

"Ri?" Sam lifted his head. "You okay? Your heart is pounding in my ear."

"I'm sorry my heart woke you," she joked.

He propped his head up on his elbow. "You're worrying?" he guessed correctly. She nodded as he brushed her hair back from her face. "He's fine. I'm sure right now he's telling them all about how they're not tucking him in right, and how their bubble stuff is all wrong."

She laughed at that.

"Why did he say he was going to work?" she wondered.

"He didn't want to go with his dad, and I told him it was like work."

"You're kidding," Surely this technique would be frowned upon in some parenting magazine. Though she had to admit the similarity between going with Evan or going to work was fairly accurate.

"Hey, it worked. Don't mock my ways if they have the desired effect."

"Okay." She continued to laugh. "He looks up to you."

"Is that a problem?" She could feel the tension in Sam's body as it partially covered her own.

"I don't think so," she answered honestly. Whatever came next, she and Luca would handle it. Sam relaxed and kissed her stomach.

"So I guess I need to try to distract you again," he said as he moved up, teasing her breast with his tongue.

"Sam. I don't think I could possibly—"

"Let's find out."

They slept like the dead after that. No worries from her and no nightmares from Sam. In the morning they were awakened by the sun and the sound of someone yelling from across the street.

She never slept this long when Luca was there. If she tried he would come in and stare at her until she opened her eyes. The thought of him not being there made her heart squeeze with anxiety.

"Morning," Sam said beside her.

"Good morning." She tried to smile, but she could tell it wasn't her best work.

"Yeah. I miss him too," Sam said, surprising her.

"What?"

"It's Sunday. He usually comes in to snuggle and tickle us on Sundays. Then we have pancakes." Sam shrugged. "I miss it."

She knew she liked Samuel Alvarez Brooks more than was safe, but she'd never been more in danger of falling in love with him than at that moment. It wasn't a romantic gesture or fancy words that elevated his status in her heart. It was simply that he missed her son and wasn't afraid to admit it.

"What?" he asked when she wasn't able to make words.

"I think you're amazing."

He smiled. "Do I still get pancakes?"

* * *

He'd guilted Riley into making him pancakes, and watched her as she mixed the batter. She wasn't huge in the chest department, but when she stirred, the action made her breasts move in the most appealing way. He could only stare.

"So have you been invited to this party at Lex and Ian's?" she asked, hinting.

He knew hinting from a mile away. He stopped looking at her chest so he could make eye contact. A smile tugged at the corner of his mouth as he nodded. "You mean the party where they subject their newly adopted children to their friends? Is it not terrifying enough for three little kids to be flown from another country to one where they don't speak the language, just to wind up at a picnic with a bunch of strangers gawking at them?"

"Well, when you put it that way it sounds like torture. I think the idea is to let them meet a bunch of other kids so they can play and have fun."

"Oh. I guess that's not so bad then," Sam agreed.

"So are you going?"

He bit his lip, stalling. He liked Luca. He was a cool kid. But that didn't make him a kid person. Besides, no one in their mixed group of friends knew about them, except for Cooper and Roz. This would be an announcement of sorts.

This would also give everyone the opportunity to lecture him about dating a mother and the seriousness of that. He was well aware of the seriousness.

"Yeah. I guess I'll be there," he said, though he wasn't sure it was a good idea. "Do you want to go in together on a gift? Maybe I buy and you pick it out?"

"Seriously?" The way she was looking at him made it quite obvious that this went far beyond what he intended. He had meant it to be a convenience. She was seeing it as some kind of commitment. *Crap.* He just kept digging a bigger and bigger hole. He was never going to be able to crawl out.

Since he was already up to his ears in commitment, he suggested they ride together. Again, for the sake of convenience. She agreed with a smile and he hoped she wouldn't hate him someday.

Luca came home later that night. The minute his father put him down he ran to Sam with his arms up. Sam held him while Luca whispered in his ear, "I'm home from my work."

Evan was complaining to Riley about diapers and wipes so Sam took Luca back to his room to unpack. If he'd stayed he couldn't promise Evan would have left in one piece. He only had so much control.

As promised they went for ice cream. Sam noticed how closely Riley held her son, despite how much Luca tried to squirm away. It seemed like there wasn't enough kisses and snuggles to make up for the time Riley missed.

Sam went to Sacramento for three days. He checked in with Riley twice. Not that she'd pressured him to check in, but because he had legitimate questions regarding the party. When he got back in town they went out to eat at a kid-friendly place. They chatted about his job and both of hers. Along with Luca's antics.

He dreaded the party on Saturday for multiple reasons. First, because it meant lost time with just Riley and Luca at the house having fun. Second, because it was a kid's party, which meant there would be kids there. And thirdly, because there was a very real possibility that someone might spook Riley about him and he might lose her and the arrangement they had.

She picked up the gift from the backseat while Luca turned his shy on and put his arms up to be held. Sam obligingly leaned down, and the monkey-child clung to him as expected. "Don't think for a minute I don't know you're going to be wiggling down about two seconds after you see the kids. You're not fooling me," he told the boy.

As if trying harder, Luca laid his head on Sam's shoulder and held on tighter.

It turned out to be more like twenty seconds, but before Luca did his squiggling exit, all the adults in Lex and Ian's kitchen were staring at Sam. Roslyn was the only one smiling. Cooper looked skeptical and everyone else had their mouths hanging open in shock.

"Um. Hi," Lex said as she glanced between him and Riley. "I didn't realize you two knew each other."

"Yes. We do." Very, very well. Though he doubted Riley was going to elaborate. At least not while the menfolk were still in the kitchen. "Remember when you suggested I stop in at Valley Jewelers when I was looking for something for my niece's graduation?" Sam said. "We met then."

"Oh." Lex glanced around the circle of their friends as if worried she was going to be held accountable for this atrocity.

Before too long, the party split into two sections as most parties do. The men went outside to assist Ian with the task of combining meat and fire. While the women stayed in the kitchen. This had been Sam's apprehension about attending.

He wondered what stories they were sharing about him.

"Dalton didn't make it?" Sam said as he looked around the patio.

"No. He's in . . . Someplace really hot," Ian said with a frown.

"Oh! Albuquerque." Sam forgot about that job. No doubt Dalton went over the weekend so he had an excuse to get out of the party. Why hadn't Sam thought of that?

"Yep. That's it," Ian said at the reminder. "So what's going on with you and Riley?" Cooper and Tucker stopped talking so they could listen to his answer.

"Uh. Well. Just the normal stuff. We're seeing each other a little bit. Nothing serious." Frowns turned down every face. "What? She's okay with it." Frowns were replaced with eye rolls. "No. Really. She got burned by her ex. She said she's not looking for anything complicated."

"She has a kid," Tucker said.

"Right. I know. Luca and I get along great," Sam pointed out.

"For now." Ian's brows knit.

"Yeah. For now. You know it's not like any of you haven't screwed up before." Sam pointed at Ian who had divorced Lexi even though he still loved her, and Tucker who had nearly botched his relationship with Nichole because he couldn't handle his fame.

Cooper continued to frown, and Sam didn't have any dirt on him. Cooper was also closest to Riley, being her brother-in-law. It wasn't going to be easy to win him over.

"Look. I'm not making any promises to her. And I'm sure the hell not making them to you guys. I like her. She likes me. We have a good time together and her kid is fun. That's what this is. I'm not some creep who's planning to do something bad to her. I'll try my best to be respectful. You all know me well enough not to doubt that."

They all gave a nod of half-hearted agreement. Better than nothing. The subject changed to baseball, and he was free. His drink was empty and he knew he could get a refill in the kitchen. But now that he was out of the frying pan, there was no way he'd purposefully put himself in the fire.

Chapter 7

"Every great husband and father was at one time a bachelor," Roslyn defended Sam to their friends while Riley watched Luca playing.

"No one could match Tucker for bachelordom. He had women throwing panties at him while he was on stage. Trust me when I say, if Tucker can settle down with one woman, anyone can," Nichole pointed out while stirring her margarita. "And we're talking about starting a family."

"Excellent!" Roz cheered. Riley gave her a hug first since she was closest. She was happy for Nichole, and glad for the subject change.

The problem wasn't that Sam was too much of a bachelor. He'd told her he wasn't good at relationships and she had assumed it was a case of not wanting to commit. But the truth was, Sam was very good at being in a relationship. And he was excellent with Luca.

No, the problem wasn't that Sam didn't want to be with her. She wondered if the problem was more that he thought he *couldn't*. Riley and her friends talked about kids and childbirth until they nearly had Nichole talked out of it. Riley noticed Sam out on the patio with the men, the same empty bottle in his hand. She smiled knowing he'd rather die of thirst than come inside and be subjected to Team Estrogen.

She picked his favorite beer from the refrigerator and ventured outside, confident in her abilities with Team Testosterone.

"Need a drink?" she asked as she held up the beer.

"Baby, you have no idea," he whispered in her ear as he took the bottle from her. "I was getting ready to text you."

She laughed at that and wrapped her arm around his waist.

"They're talking about umbilical cords inside," Riley told the men who all cringed in unison. "What were you guys talking about?"

"Deck stain."

"Hmm. I'm not sure which conversation I want to avoid the most," she admitted with a wince. Sam leaned down to kiss her.

"Fortunately we're about to eat, so we can all stop talking for a few minutes while we stuff our faces," Ian said as he held up a plate of meat.

They all filed into the kitchen and the noise grew while everyone filled their plates and found a place to sit.

Sam winked at her. She knew him well enough to know he was telling her everything was fine. She winked back to tell him the same thing.

"How bad was it?" Riley asked as Sam carried a sleeping Luca out to the car after the party.

"How bad was what?" He played dumb, but it didn't work.

"How much did they try to scare you?" she explained.

"Probably about as much as the women tried to warn you off me." He hoped it hadn't worked.

"Actually they said you were nice."

"Well, I don't know if I believe you. But all the guys said the same thing about you."

She laughed and got in the car as he started it to drive them home.

"I fly out tomorrow evening," he told her. He didn't want to leave them.

"When will you be back?"

"Friday night."

"I'm working at the hotel Friday night."

"I'll see you Saturday?"

"Sounds good." Except that it was an entire week away. He'd have to get over it. Maybe it would do him good to gain some distance.

The job in Ohio frustrated him beyond belief. The guys he'd hired for the demolition didn't seem to care if they ever got done. "Hey, remember how I told you this needed to be done by Friday?" Sam said on Wednesday while they were taking their third break of the morning.

"Yeah." The foreman gave him a raised brow.

"Well, we're not going to make it with you standing around with coffee cups in your hands more than you're working. I need to be home by Friday. I have a—" He stopped. He'd almost said he had a *family* to get home to. It nearly erupted out of him as if it were the truth. He blinked a few times and then angrily pointed at them. "Get back to work. You're staying tonight until that second story is down, or don't come back in the morning."

The next day, the guys seemed more motivated. Especially after Dalton called the foreman and explained that their bonus hinged on the job being done on schedule. During lunch they all came into the job trailer to escape the heat for half an hour. It only took a few minutes for them to start bitching about their wives.

Sam listened with new interest in the age-old conversation. He'd heard these same gripes before. He never paid attention, not planning to ever be in that position. But now he was curious about the realities of marriage. Obviously it couldn't be that horrible, or no one would ever do it. Marriage would be extinct by now if it was that bad.

"The old lady thinks we need a new sofa." This from a bearded guy who was unwrapping a sandwich. "As if I'm out here working my ass off for some floral piece-of-shit sofa."

"Maybe you wouldn't need a new sofa if you hadn't worn yours out from sitting on it all the time," one of the others teased.

"My wife is always yapping about needing this or that for the kids or the house. She stays home all day and then complains when I get home and want to relax."

"I hear you," said another. "When I get home, I'm tired. Is it too much to ask that I be left to recoup from my long day? Maybe a nice dinner? Maybe get the kids to keep it down?"

Sam couldn't take anymore. It was ridiculous.

"When I was in Kandahar, I was with two guys who missed their wives and kids. They had to make do with phone calls and the occasional Skype. They died over there, and never got to come home to bitch about dinner or about buying a new fucking sofa."

No one said a word.

The guys finished up their lunch in silence, and left the office eight minutes before their time was up. Win. Win.

That night when he went back to the hotel room, he called Riley.

"Hello?"

"Hey, you busy?" he asked, as he relaxed at the sound of her voice.

"I'm heating up pasta-Os." The girl never bought anything name brand. "What's up? Are you okay?"

"I guess so."

"What's wrong? You never call. You just send sexy texts."

"Well, I wanted to talk to you tonight. Is that okay?" He rubbed his forehead not sure why the need was so crucial all of the sudden.

"Yeah. It's fine."

"What do you think of your sofa?" he asked.

"What?"

"I noticed it wasn't floral."

"Why would I want a floral sofa? I like this sofa. It's easy to clean and we've had sex on it. Good memories. Why are you asking about my sofa?"

Sam couldn't help but smile. "No reason. I'm just working with a bunch of assholes. I can't wait to come home."

There was a long pause, and Sam—hearing what he'd said—began to panic until she said, "We miss you too."

He could have easily played it off that "home" was Roanoke, and Sam hadn't said he missed them. But Riley knew what he was thinking. He'd never had a connection like that before.

"I'll see you in a couple of days," he said huskily.

"See you then."

The rest of the week couldn't be over fast enough, but eventually he was on a plane heading east. Back to Riley and Luca.

While Luca was taking a nap on Saturday afternoon Riley and Sam were on the sofa making out, and making up for lost time. She'd told herself not to get attached, but she couldn't help it. When Sam got there he picked her up and kissed her for a very long time while Luca danced around their legs. Any distance she had managed was gone after that.

Then Sam turned his attention to Luca, holding him by his ankles and making him laugh until he couldn't catch his breath. It was no wonder why Luca was worn out.

Sam had his hand under her shirt and they were just about to move it to the bedroom when her phone rang. When she saw her sister's smiling face on the screen she almost went into a panic.

Roslyn never called her. They would text back and forth for hours, but actual conversation? No. Who did that anymore?

"What's wrong? Is Maddy okay?" was Riley's greeting.

"Yes. It's Mom. She's had a heart attack. They took her to Centra. Ken says she's stable, but he didn't have a lot of information. Should I swing by and pick you up on the way? Cooper is staying with Maddy."

"Um." Riley's mom brain kicked into gear as she quickly ticked off available child care. Anita was at bingo. Lexi was up at the cabin. And Roslyn was getting ready to drive to the hospital too. She could drop Luca off with Cooper, but that would be a lot for him to handle alone. "Let me call you right back."

"What is it?" Sam asked.

Riley was already calling her mother-in-law on the off chance she hadn't left yet.

"My mother had a heart attack. She's been taken to the hospital in Lynchburg. I need to go as soon as I figure out who can take care of Luca." Anita didn't answer so she canceled the call and started to dial Evan.

"I can watch Luca," Sam offered immediately.

"No. You don't want to do that." Evan didn't pick up either. No doubt he was worried that she was going to ask him for money. Freakin' coward.

Sam took her phone so she would look at him as he spoke.

"He's sleeping. And when he wakes up we'll play or watch a movie. I can make him a sandwich or pasta-Os."

"Are you sure?" She wasn't worried that Sam wasn't capable of taking care of Luca, but that it might make him feel trapped.

"Yeah. How hard can it be?" He shrugged as if it was no big deal. She didn't have a lot of choices.

"Don't let him out of your sight for a minute. He's devious."

"Already know that," Sam said with a grin.

"You're sure?"

"Absolutely. Go be with your mom."

"Okay." She called her sister back. "Roz, come pick me up. Sam is going to watch Luca."

"Aww."

"Don't start." Riley hung up on her match-making sister and went to find shoes.

* * *

They got to the hospital in record time, thanks to Roslyn's Nascar-esque driving.

"I thought Ken said she was stable," Riley noted as she unlatched her seat belt.

"He did, but what does he know?" Neither of them were too fond of their newest stepfather. Ken—or Number Four—as they sometimes called him could be rather cold.

After a few stops for directions they finally got to the correct room where their mother sat complaining to the nurses about how long before she could go have a cigarette.

"Where's my grandchildren?" her mother asked, dismissing the nurse.

"Her new boyfriend is watching Luca and Cooper has Maddy," Roslyn said. "How are you?"

Their mother started into the long dissertation about how close she'd been to death, and how awful they were treating her. Neither of which was completely true.

Her mother was going to be fine. She could only hope the same was the case for Sam and Luca.

Sam looked around Riley's small living room. The top two shelves on the bookcase held actual books. Some college text books, some novels. The bottom three shelves were filled with movies. Most of which had colorful covers. Why did animals wear shirts, but no pants? Something was very wrong with that.

"Princesses?" He frowned at the movie and hid it at the back toward the wall. Surely Luca didn't want to watch a princess movie.

Riley didn't have cable so he picked up a magazine which had her sister's name on the address label, and flipped through a few pages.

He was actually excited to see Luca when he wandered out of his bedroom with his blond hair sticking out in every direction. Finally, Sam would have a reason to play cars or watch the penguin movie.

"Momma," he said, his voice rough with sleep.

"Momma went to see your grandma. She'll be back soon. Are you hungry?" Luca shook his head. "Do you want some juice?" He nodded.

See? Not that difficult. He could handle this.

He poured apple juice into a spill-proof cup and topped it off with water. Riley didn't like him having fully loaded juice because it was mostly sugar.

He felt like a professional as he shook it over the sink to make sure it was sealed as he'd seen Riley do.

"There you go. Do you want to watch TV?"

He didn't say anything, he looked as though he could fall back to sleep at any second. His rabbit was tucked under one arm as he crawled up on the sofa and stared at the wall.

Sam took a while to wake up too. He'd let Luca move at his own pace.

It only took about ten minutes for the juice to kick in and Luca was up running around. He'd pulled out the Candy Land game that had no pieces and wanted to play.

"Okay. Here." Sam went to the cupboard and got out the animal crackers. "I'll be the elephant. What do you want to be?"

"Elephant!" Luca said.

"I already called the elephant. Do you want to be the lion?"

"Roar!"

"Right. Luca, the Lion and Sam the Elephant are going to take Candy Land by storm." Luca laughed even though he couldn't have understood the joke.

They managed to get three spaces before Luca ate both crackers and jumped up to go do something else.

About an hour later, Sam was exhausted and needed to use the restroom.

"Don't do anything while I go take a piss. Stay right there and don't move." Sam knew that wasn't going to work so he hurried back to the hall, undoing his jeans as he walked. He kicked the door halfway closed with his foot as he lifted the toilet seat. How did people do this? He didn't have a moment to himself.

He tried to hurry, but hurrying never worked. Maybe he could hear Luca from the bathroom and yell for him to stop whatever it was he was undoubtedly doing.

Instead, Luca opened the door and stared at him as soon as Sam had a steady stream going.

"It's not cool to look at another guy's junk."

"Taking a piss," Luca repeated. Sam was pretty sure that was not the phrase Riley would have taught him.

"Yep. I'm a big boy, so I go in a potty. Not in a diaper like a baby."

He knew Riley was trying to get him interested in the potty. To be honest, Luca's little toilet did look pretty interesting. Red, with race cars all over it. Sam might have tried it himself if it would have flushed.

Sam shook off and tucked himself back in his pants. Then he washed his hands while Luca took in the show.

"See? I'm washing my hands. No matter when you get around to being a big boy, make sure to wash your hands. A lot of guys don't."

"Piss," Luca said as he started pulling down his shorts.

"Maybe you shouldn't call it that. Maybe . . ." He couldn't bring himself to say pee-pee. He was a fucking marine. He'd been shot. He would not say pee-pee.

"Piss," Luca said again. Pointing down.

"You have to go now?" Luca nodded emphatically so Sam assisted in getting his shorts down, and the diaper somewhat out of the way. He wasn't sure how he was going to put that back the way it had been.

Instead of sitting on the seat with the weird little deflector shield, Luca raised the seat like he'd seen Sam do.

"Make sure to aim. You don't want it all over the wall. Your mother will have a fit."

Sam helped by holding his shirt out of the way, and realized how surreal this moment was. He'd never been there for someone's first piss before.

There was a little trickle and Luca giggled at the sound it made when it hit the plastic bowl.

"Good job. Aim for that blue car and let it rip. Step a little closer, your hose is kind of short." He frowned. "I'm sure it will grow with the rest of you. Don't worry about that now." God, he'd hate to give the kid a complex.

Luca laughed some more as he finished.

"You done?" Sam asked. Luca nodded. "Okay, now shake it a little. Not enough that it comes back and hits you in the face, just enough to get the excess off the end."

"God, I wish I had a video of this," Riley said, causing Sam to jump. She was smiling by the door.

"Momma, I'm takin' a piss! I'm a big boy!"

Riley cocked an eyebrow at the term.

"He's a big boy," Sam said, trying to distract her.

"You *are* a big boy. Since you went in the big boy potty it means you get a big boy present."

Luca's brown eyes were huge.

"What about me? I went in the big boy potty too." Sam winked at her.

"You'll get your prize later." She winked back at him.

"How's your mom?"

"She's going to be fine." Riley waved away his concern. "She had a mild cardiac event, whatever that is. She's being released, and her husband is taking care of her, so she didn't really need me after all. Except to have someone to complain to."

"We need you," Sam said.

"You do?" She smiled.

"Yeah. That cool little potty doesn't flush." He pointed down at her son's urine.

"One of his big boy presents is a fire truck stool so he can reach the real potty."

"I like fire trucks. Do you think I can—"

"No. It's for kids."

Riley was still laughing as she followed her excited son down the hallway in anticipation of his presents. She'd hidden them on top of the refrigerator, and since Sam was there she wouldn't need her own stool to retrieve the stool for her son.

"You're pretty handy to have around," she joked as he handed her the packages.

"Does that mean you might be willing to keep me?" he asked, his tone serious.

"Is that something you would be interested in? I thought . . . ?"

He shrugged. "Things change. People change."

Riley was well aware of how people could change. Her perfect husband had changed into the kind of guy who cheated on her and left. And then she had changed from the happy girl who saw the best in everything to a hardened shrew of a woman.

If Sam was changing into a relationship kind of guy now, what would he turn into next?

Now was not the time to ask. Not with Luca hanging on her pants.

"Momma! I'm a big boy."

"Okay. Here you go, big boy." She handed him the two wrapped packages and watched as her baby opened up his Disney character underwear and the fire truck stool.

Right there in the kitchen he proceeded to tug off his pants and the disheveled diaper so he could put on his briefs. Backward.

"Hey buddy, turn them around," Sam instructed and bent down to help. When Luca ran off to go put his stool in the bathroom, Sam looked at her.

The serious expression was on his face again, and she worried he'd already changed his mind about sticking around.

"His junk *will* grow, right?" Sam winced as he whispered.

Riley burst out laughing and all of the tension in her body escaped.

"I'm ready to keep you around, Sam. And not just to get things I can't reach."

He wrapped his arms around her waist and pulled her closer so he could kiss her.

"It's the orgasms too," she teased, making him chuckle against her lips.

She invited him to stay the night. He needed to leave for another trip the next morning, but his flight wasn't until ten, so he told her he could run home and pack before he went to the airport.

With her big boy snug in his own bed, she was free to snuggle in with Sam. She imagined what it would be like if this was a normal thing. She liked having a man in her bed, and in her life. As long as it was the right man.

Sam had only been gone for ten minutes the next morning when there was a knock at her door.

Evan.

She opened the door and called for Luca who was running around in just his underwear. He'd complained when she made him wear a diaper to bed, and took it off as soon as he woke up. *After* using the potty. However crude Sam's lesson had been, it seemed to be working.

Riley noticed Luca didn't yell and run over to greet his father like he did when Sam arrived. She felt an evil twinge of satisfaction in this fact.

"What's up?" she asked, opening the door wider so he could come in.

"Your boyfriend is gone." He nodded toward the parking area in the alley. So it wasn't a coincidence that he'd arrived right after Sam. He had apparently been waiting for Sam to leave.

"So?"

"I don't like him. He seems rough."

"Rough? Is that your way of saying he's big enough to kick the crap out of you?" Luca had run back to the bathroom for his stool to show his dad.

"Look!" Luca said as he put it down and climbed up. "I'm a big boy."

"You sure are." Evan dismissed him quickly and turned back to Riley with a smirk. "Is he the kind of trash that goes around beating the crap out of people?"

"He isn't. But I'm sure he would change his mind if I asked him." She smiled sweetly at him. She didn't know how it was possible for a person to love someone so much at one point in their life and then hate them with such fierce intensity at another point, but as she glared at Evan, she knew it was possible. "Sam is the kind of guy who put himself at risk to serve his country. You know, a standup guy. Have you ever heard of this kind of thing?"

Evan rolled his eyes and sat down at the table. She fought the urge to ask him if he wanted tea. She was a southern girl who was raised with manners, but he was an asshole. Even southern hospitality didn't apply to him.

"I need to talk to you about something important," he said.

With a sigh, she sat across from him, waiting for him to ask her to reduce the child support as he'd done twice before. That wasn't going to happen.

"What is it?"

"I'm moving to Arizona," he said.

She wasn't sure how she was supposed to feel about this. Happy, was the first emotion. If he moved to Arizona she wouldn't have to see him. She wouldn't have to fight the urge to shove her knee into his crotch, and she wouldn't have to deal with his smirky grins when he talked about the guy she was seeing.

But then her thoughts turned to her son.

For a second she felt guilty that she hadn't thought of how this would affect Luca first.

She was overcome with the desire to get Evan as far away as possible. But would Luca miss his dad? Would he remember him at all?

He was almost three. She couldn't remember anything from when she was three.

Luca hadn't even wanted to go with his dad the last time. Maybe Luca was over it. He probably wouldn't mind if he didn't see his father.

Then a trickle of panic started moving through her body. According to the custody agreement, Evan was entitled to visitation rights. If he chose to enforce them while living in Arizona, it could mean sending her child across the country for longer lengths of time than a single weekend.

"What does this mean for Luca and me?" She got right down to it.

"Well, obviously it's going to take a little while for me and Celia to get set up out there. She has a job waiting for her, but we're going to be a little tight until I get a job too. So I was hoping you could be patient with the support payments."

"I still need to keep a roof over Luca's head, even if you decide you want to go on an adventure."

"Does it need to be this nice of a roof?" he asked while looking around her apartment. Her place wasn't glamorous in any way. It was small and old, but clean and maintained. Plus it was in a nice neighborhood with a small fenced-in yard, which had been the deciding factor.

Her hands balled into fists, and she moved them to her lap so he wouldn't see how close she was to launching herself across the table to attack him.

"You were the one who decided you didn't want your family. You can't just brush him aside because you have something new and shiny. Do you want him growing up in some shack with no yard?"

"No. But does he honestly need his own room? At my place he sleeps on the sofa or with his sister." Riley pressed her lips together.

"Yes. He needs his own room," she said, impressed by how calmly she answered despite the anger she felt.

"Well, if you're having so much trouble making ends meet, I could just take him to Arizona for a while." Evan looked directly in her eyes as he said this, and as she looked back she saw the threat lurking there.

"Are you implying that if I don't back off on the support you're going to push for full custody?" He wouldn't get it. At least she didn't think so.

"I have a wife and another child. We're going to be buying a house with the help of Celia's parents. You are dating questionable men. Things might shake out differently than they did the first time."

"Get out."

"Sure. I need to get going anyway." He stood and she noticed how skinny he looked in comparison to the way Sam filled the room.

"I'm a big boy," Luca told his father again.

"I know, Luca. You said that already." Evan seemed annoyed.

"He used the big boy potty for the first time yesterday," Riley informed him.

"Taking a piss," Luca supplied.

"That's great, champ!" Evan bent down to pat him on the back and looked up at Riley. "See? You won't have to spend money on diapers anymore."

If her eyes could have shot lasers, Evan Fisher would have been obliterated.

The second he was out the door, she put on a movie to keep Luca occupied and called Cooper.

"How's your mother?" he asked as a greeting. "Roz took Maddy to visit, I haven't heard yet today."

"I guess she's fine. I haven't heard anything. I didn't get a chance to call yet." Again she felt the guilt. She should have already checked on her mother this morning. "Evan stopped by."

"What did he want?"

"He's moving to Arizona with Celia."

"And?" It was obvious Cooper knew Evan had more to say than just this. Being her divorce attorney gave Cooper the opportunity to see Evan at his worst.

"He asked that I be patient with the support until they get settled out there."

"Or?" Cooper was an excellent lawyer.

"He might push for full custody and take Luca out there with him."

"That won't happen." His voice made it clear he would go to the ends of the Earth to make sure of it.

"He says I'm dating someone questionable."

"Sam?"

"Yes. I'm still seeing him."

Cooper made a noise that sounded like he was surprised.

She'd never taken the time to figure out why their friends hadn't suggested she and Sam go out before. They'd sent her on a date with Dalton once, but no one so much as mentioned Sam.

"He's a nice guy. He's great with Luca," she defended Sam, though compared to Evan, Sam was a super hero.

"Sam is a great guy, he'd do anything for anyone. He's just not the kind of guy who is good at relationships."

"I—I know that." She did know that, but hearing it made it more real. It caught her off guard. Sam had hinted that he was ready for more, but did he even know what that meant?

"Do you? Are you sure it's a good idea for Luca to get attached to him?"

This was the question she'd asked herself more than once, and still hadn't come up with the answer.

"There are worse men Luca could get attached to," she said as she considered the damage Evan would eventually do to her son.

"He was involved with someone before and it didn't work out. I don't want you to get hurt."

"What happened?" she asked, hoping she might finally hear the story.

"I'm not sure, but it went bad. Really bad. Just be careful."

"I will. What do I need to do about Evan?"

"It depends. I honestly don't think he has any grounds to take Luca from you, but do you want to get into a war with him?"

"Not really. Can't we force him to sign over custody? I mean if he's not going to pay, I'd just rather do it on my own and take him out of the equation altogether. It would be better than dealing with his threats."

"You can't force him to sign off. I'll notify Domestic Relations. As soon as he gets a job in Arizona, we'll set up the garnishment again. Until then, if you or Luca need anything, let us know."

"Thanks, Cooper."

"We're family," he said before he hung up.

Yes, they were family, but she hated the idea of needing to rely on them to take care of her son. That was her job.

She sat at the table and assessed her situation carefully. She could take more hours at the hotel for a little while until Evan got set up out there. There were always ways she could cut costs if she had to. She had been thinking about making jewelry and selling it online for some extra money. Something like she'd made for Sam's niece. She sighed and rubbed her forehead.

"Momma! Piss!" Luca said as he ran for the bathroom holding his crotch.

"I can do this. I can," she said and went to help.

Chapter 8

Sam waited to call Riley for two days. It had been a struggle not to call to check in the first night he was in Sacramento, but he was trying for her sake to keep his distance.

After that first night in the hotel, when he'd woken up drenched in sweat with the guy in the next room pounding for quiet, Sam had been reminded of why he couldn't have something long term.

The time he'd spent with Riley and Luca made him feel normal. He thought maybe he could handle things and had a chance to have a family. But he realized it had all been a dream.

He wasn't a safe bet for a single mother and a kid. But he missed them both so much. Eventually he gave in and called.

"Hello," she answered and he couldn't miss the hardness in her voice. Was she angry at him for not calling sooner? She hadn't seemed clingy before. He suddenly felt uneasy. Like maybe he shouldn't have called at all.

"How's the potty training going?" he asked, trying to keep it light.

"Good. He had one accident at Grammy's, but other than that he's doing fine." He realized the tone he'd taken for anger now sounded more like exhaustion.

"How are you?"

"I'm fine. You?"

"I don't believe you're fine. What's going on?" He hated that he was across the country. Whatever was going on with her, he found himself wanting to see her so he could comfort her.

There was a long silence before she finally answered. "Evan is moving to Arizona."

Sam was stumped by the contradiction between the words she'd spoken and the sadness that coated them.

"You don't want him to go?" *Good riddance*, Sam thought.

"I'm ecstatic that he's going. I wish he'd go to fucking Mars."

"Then what's the problem?" he asked, because there definitely was one.

"He said he would fight me on custody if I don't back off on the support payments for a while."

Sam let out a stream of curses while turned away from the phone. He had always made sure to use a condom so he wouldn't be in the position of paying child support. But he always knew if something went wrong, he would stand up and be supportive of the child he'd created. It wasn't the kid's fault that his parents couldn't work it out.

"Do you need some money? I'll be home tomorrow night. Let me know how much you need."

He heard a sniffing sound followed by another long silence.

"No. I'll be okay. I won't be home tomorrow night. I can't do this, okay?" Her voice sounded strained as if she were holding in tears. He didn't understand why his offer would upset her. He didn't mind helping out. He didn't want her or Luca to struggle. And what did she mean she couldn't do this? Did she mean him?

"Okay," he said, not really understanding.

"Goodbye," she said, and didn't wait for him to say it back before she'd hung up.

Sam decided to let it go, and by the next day he'd upgraded the decision to letting her go. Riley and Luca surely didn't need him. And if she didn't want his help, he wasn't going to force himself on her. There were plenty of other fish in the sea. The next time he went out he was going to make sure he found a fish that didn't have any little fish.

He slept fitfully that night. To his surprise his nightmares weren't so much about being pinned down by insurgents and having his men killed, but about Riley and Luca being in danger and needing his help. He saw them in a burning building and he couldn't get to them. Then they were being whisked away by a flooded river and he couldn't reach them.

All night he failed them over and over again, just to be faced with another situation in which he couldn't help them.

Riley was sitting at the hotel desk on Wednesday, working out a budget. Even without the support payments she was going to be fine.

She would add an extra shift at the hotel just to make sure, but she had enough saved to keep her afloat for a while.

Earlier she had dipped into those savings to order some supplies for her new jewelry-making venture. She saw the beads and charms as an investment. There were always craft fairs in town during the summer where she could sell them. Plus it gave her a way to make money while being at home with Luca. He liked "helping" her make "pretties."

Reassured that her situation was not dire, she was on her way to the snack machine for a celebratory pack of M&Ms when she heard the loud crunch from outside. It was a little after midnight, she hadn't seen a guest in hours.

She went back to the desk to look over the monitors, specifically those in the parking lots where she'd heard the noise. The cameras were set to look out over the guest parking areas on both sides of the building and the front door.

Nothing seemed amiss.

With a sigh, she locked up the till and went outside to investigate, phone in hand. As she'd seen on the monitor from inside, the main parking lot looked normal. She moved around the building on the way to the back lot and froze.

Her SUV was parked in the side lot, the one designated for employees.

But now her vehicle was sitting sideways with a large dent along the driver's side.

"What the hell?" she said out loud, wondering if it only looked bad because of the harsh blue glow from the parking lot light. She tried opening the door, but it wouldn't budge.

It probably wasn't the light then.

"I was just walking to my car when I heard it," a teenage boy in a fast-food uniform said as he walked up. "I didn't see the license plate, but it was a white tractor trailer."

That made sense. Only a vehicle of that size could have caused this much damage and kept going.

The Mountain Gate Hotel was conveniently located near Interstate 81 which was the main truck route from New York to Tennessee. She knew as she dialed the police that finding a white tractor trailer was going to be nearly impossible.

"At least, I'm pretty sure it was white," the boy said, dashing what little hope she'd had.

When he landed in Roanoke he was determined to go to his apartment and stay there. Riley hadn't called him, and he wasn't ever going to call her again. He could read between the lines. It was better for all of them to just let it go before someone or all of them ended up hurt.

But as soon as he was unpacked he was back in his truck, driving to her place. Her dark, empty apartment should have been enough to put him back on his original plan, but he couldn't shake the visions of her and Luca needing him. And he wanted to end things officially. He didn't want a miscommunication.

He pulled in the driveway at Mrs. Fisher's house and waited a few minutes before getting out. When the door opened, Luca was right there.

"Sam! Sam!"

Mrs. Fisher opened the screen door.

"Hey monkey!" he greeted the little boy who was already clinging to his leg, trying to get up. He lifted him, and kissed the top of his head. Noticing how holding Luca felt like the most natural thing in the world.

"How's it going?" Luca felt smaller in his arms without the bulk of the diaper. "Are you playing blocks?" Sam asked, noticing a pile of them on the living room floor.

Luca nodded and wiggled out of his grasp to go show him what he was building.

"Is Riley okay?" he asked the woman who stood next to him.

She frowned. "She's been working so much. I'm worried about her," she said.

"She's at the hotel?" he guessed, knowing the jewelry store wouldn't be open this late in the evening, it was nearly nine. "I offered to help."

She nodded. "She doesn't like to need help." Mrs. Fisher frowned again, as if this were a character flaw.

"Everyone needs help sometimes."

"And you look like the kind of man who would take an offer of help without making any trouble." Mrs. Fisher raised her brows, calling him on his hypocrisy. "It's even worse now with the car."

"What happened to her car?" he asked. Her little SUV wasn't that old.

"She didn't tell you what happened?"

"We haven't gotten a chance to talk this week."

"Two nights ago, a tractor trailer hit her car while it was parked at the hotel. Then the driver left." She frowned. "I offered to let her use my car, but Roslyn and Cooper gave her one of theirs. They offered to help with the insurance deductible too, but of course she thinks she needs to do everything on her own."

"What should I do?" he asked. He realized forcing money into Riley's hand wasn't going to work. He wouldn't like it if someone did that to him.

The woman shrugged and sighed. "She doesn't make it easy. Be supportive."

"Does Luca need anything?" he asked.

"He needs his mother." She frowned again.

"What time does she get off work?"

"Three a.m."

"And she works tomorrow?"

"Nine to six," the woman answered. Sam rolled his eyes. How did Riley think she would survive this kind of schedule?

"And while she's at the hotel she's also working on making jewelry for her new business."

He rubbed his forehead and watched the little boy on the floor. "You could probably use a break," Sam said. Since Mrs. Fisher was Luca's babysitter, extra hours for Riley meant extra hours for her as well.

"I'm getting by all right." Of course she wouldn't admit that caring for her grandson for long periods of time was a burden. She loved him. But Sam could tell she was exhausted.

"Can I take him home?" he asked. "So he can sleep in his own bed."

"You have a key?"

"I know where it is." Riley kept a spare key on the porch under a pot.

She tilted her head to think it over for a moment and then nodded. "I know Riley trusts you with our boy. I'll get the car seat."

"I'll call her and let her know he's at home," Sam offered.

She turned to her grandson. "Luca, do you want to go home with Sam?"

"Fire truck!" he said.

"Yes. You can use your fire truck stool." She turned to Sam with a smile. "God forbid my stool is just a normal stool. He brings it up every time he needs to use the potty."

"Where's Hops?" Sam asked as Mrs. Fisher went to gather his things. He tore off down the hall and came back with the rabbit a second later. He went right for the door and pointed.

When the car seat was installed and Luca was sitting in it, Mrs. Fisher leaned in and gave him a kiss.

"I'll see you tomorrow," she told him.

"Love you, Grammy," he said, cute as could be.

Sam thought about the three days off he had in front of him with no plans. "I can keep him tomorrow," he offered. "Isn't it bingo?"

The woman laughed and shook her head. "Sam, my own son doesn't care about my bingo. You are a pleasant surprise." Sam wondered what she had thought he was before, but didn't press. "Let me get you some food," she said. "I don't think there's much at Riley's house."

Sam looked at Luca, sitting happily in the backseat of his truck, chewing on the rabbit's ear. "Don't worry about it. We're going to go do some shopping before we go home, right Luc?"

Luca nodded, though Sam was sure he didn't really understand the question.

"Brave man," Mrs. Fisher said. "Have fun, boys." Sam was shocked when the woman gave him a hug. She felt frail, and Sam simply patted her back so not to break her bones. "Thank you, Sam." She released him, gave Luca another kiss, and went inside.

"Momma's car hurt," Luca told him when he started his truck.

"I know, buddy. I'm so glad you and your momma weren't inside when it got hurt." When he'd gotten home tonight he had an entirely different set of worries than the ones he had now.

At the grocery store, Luca sat in the cart and pointed to stuff, asking what it was. He was well behaved and didn't make a fuss the whole way through the store.

"Your son is adorable," the cute checkout girl said as she rang up their purchases. Sam looked down at the very white boy with the pale blond hair. His big brown eyes blinked at the lady and she smiled at him again. Other than the flirting, he and the kid had nothing in common. And yet this woman automatically assumed he was Sam's son. Sam would never tell anyone the way that made him feel—kind of warm and terrified at the same time.

"Pretty," Luca said while pointing at the woman. He was, no doubt, meaning the sparkly necklace around her neck, but the woman's face lit up and she gave him a sticker. One day the girls would be giving up other things to get his compliments. Who was going to teach him to be respectful to women? His father—the cheating asshole who was leaving him high and dry to go to Arizona? Sam didn't think that was likely.

As he pushed the cart out to the truck he realized he was having more fun shopping with Luca and teaching him how to say "artichoke" than he ever imagined. Who would have thought?

Luca was almost asleep by the time they got home so Sam carried him in first and put him in his bed. Then he put away the groceries, noticing there was plenty of room in her cupboards for his three massive jars of peanut butter.

He also noticed a pile of bills on the counter, and the fact there were no clean towels.

He ran a few loads of laundry, even pulling her sheets off the bed. He took care of the dishes in the sink and glanced over at the pile of bills again. She would be so angry if he offered to help her with them. If he was in her position he would be pissed if someone swooped in to save the day by taking over.

He put the few toys away and, knowing Luca would sleep through anything, he ran the vacuum.

When everything was in order he crawled into her bed with clean sheets and closed his eyes. He was proud of himself for not touching her bills. Though tomorrow, they were going to have a serious talk. While he would be upset if someone took over when he was trying to handle the situation, he also knew he would be grateful if someone was willing to ask what they could do to help. Maybe.

Besides, this wasn't just about her and her stubbornness. There was a child involved who needed things. She couldn't say no.

At least he didn't think so.

Riley had to focus on the road to keep from falling asleep as she drove home at a little after three in the morning. What she really wanted was to kiss her son goodnight, but he was at his grandmother's, sleeping.

Due to a plumbing issue at the hotel, she hadn't even had the chance to call to say goodnight. She missed him like crazy and worried that he would forget who she was by the time she saw him next. It seemed so long since she'd been able to read to him or hold him. She hoped he understood why she couldn't be there. Not about money and bills and things like that, but that she was taking care of him.

Her headlights swept across a familiar black truck in her parking area and she noticed a light was left on in her kitchen. She'd seen a message from Sam on her cell phone, but hadn't listened to it. She wasn't ready to deal with breaking things off with him, but she didn't have time for her own son right now let alone a relationship.

Curiosity made her more alert as she slid out of her car and walked to the door. The pot where she kept the extra key was moved. If Sam thought he'd stop by for a booty call, he was going to be disappointed. Riley's booty was dragging and not up for any sort of call.

The smell of fabric softener greeted her as she walked in the door. Her washer and dryer were in a small closet in the kitchen, and through the open door she could see a large stack of folded laundry sitting on the dryer. In the kitchen she noticed the dishes were done, and there was a brand new box of cereal on the island. She opened the cupboards and gasped at how full they were. Soup, peanut butter, pasta-O's, and snacks. The refrigerator had juice, milk, lunchmeat, and cheese. Even the freezer was stocked full of hamburger and . . . *steaks*?

Her counters were clean and it looked like someone had vacuumed the floors. Then she saw Luca's bag sitting on the edge of the sofa. The bag she had left with him the day before when she went to work. Suddenly the wonder of her clean apartment evaporated.

She moved down the hall to his room and found him sprawled out on his tiny bed. His Spiderman sandals were on the floor, and he was wearing a pull on diaper and a T-shirt. She kissed his forehead and brushed his hair with her fingers. He looked bigger than he had when she saw him the day before.

Hearing a noise behind her she turned to see the second best thing in her apartment that night. Sam was leaning against the doorway in nothing but his boxers, which quickly moved the pile of clean laundry into third place.

With another kiss on Luca's cheek, she stood and followed Sam out into the hall.

"What are you doing here?" she whispered until they were out in the living room where it was safe to raise her voice to a normal level.

"I left you a message."

"I didn't get a chance to listen to it."

"Let's not talk about it now. You need to take a shower and come to bed. I'll stop by the store tomorrow and take you out for lunch. We can talk then."

She let out a breath. She didn't have it in her to fight. And she realized she didn't want to fight with Sam.

She nodded and he bent down and kissed her.

"Shower. Bed," he instructed with a grin and walked back into her bedroom.

Following his orders she hurried through her shower. When she got in bed, she couldn't help but notice they smelled clean.

"Did you wash my sheets?" she asked.

"Mmmhmm," he mumbled his sleepy answer.

She couldn't help it, she started to cry. It was easy to keep the walls up and be strong until someone chipped their way in with kindness and demolished the whole thing.

Silent sobs shook her body and woke Sam.

His big arms wound around her and pulled her tight against his chest. She felt his lips touch her forehead.

"You're not alone, Ri. I'm here. I want to help. Please let me."

She was no longer able to stay silent as she cried, and he held her until she eventually gave up and fell asleep.

Riley was able to have breakfast with Luca before she left for work the next morning. While she appreciated the clean house and the stocked cupboards, the extra time with her son was the thing she was most grateful for.

Sam eating Fruit Hoops in nothing but his cargo shorts was, once again, number two on her list. The perfect image to get her through a long morning at the jewelry store.

Sam showed up on time to take Riley to lunch. He'd dropped Luca off at his grandmother's so they could talk without any distractions.

"How long do you have?" he asked as he opened the car door for her.

"An hour."

"Is the diner okay?"

"Sure."

Since they didn't have tons of time, he started right away as he weaved through traffic.

"I hope you're not mad about the groceries and picking up Luca."

She shook her head and sighed. "I'm not mad. I really appreciate it Sam. I'll pay you back as soon—"

"No." He shook his head.

"Sam."

"Just no, okay? No paying me back. I need to make up some karma. Just let me do this so I can see what it feels like to be a good guy. Who knows? I might like it." He gave her his best smile and she laughed. Good.

"You heard about what happened with my car?"

"Yes. I wish you would have told me." He made sure not to sound accusatory.

"I've been busy." She sighed. "I had it all worked out. I was fine without the support payments. But then a tractor trailer demolished my car and my plans."

"I want to help."

"All right. If you feel like more of a man by helping out the poor damsel in distress, then I'll play along and pretend I can't do it without you."

"Thanks. That means a lot." He threw her a wink as she shook her head and rolled her eyes. Time to move on to the next thing. "Can I ask you something that is completely none of my business?"

"You can ask. No promises I'll answer." They got out of his truck and he took her hand as they walked in the diner and got a seat by the window.

"You have a sister?" he said.

"Yes."

"She's some kind of child psychiatrist—"

"Guidance counselor," she corrected.

"She's off all summer starting like now. Why don't you ask her to help watch Luca so his grandmother doesn't have so much on her plate?" It seemed like a great suggestion. He honestly thought the problem was that Riley hadn't considered the option. He was, of course, wrong.

Her eyes got weepy, but she didn't cry, not even when her bottom lip shook. He didn't know what he had done, but he wished to hell he hadn't done it.

"You have an older sister too, right?"

"Yeah. Georgie."

"You know how they are," she said. Sam nodded. Georgie could be a little bossy at times, but she was always there. "I love Roslyn, I do. She's great. She's an awesome mother. And I like hanging out with her and the other girls. It's just . . ."

She let out a sigh and slumped down in her seat. The waitress came over to take their order. Instead of continuing, she folded her straw paper into a tiny square.

"What?" he pushed after another few seconds of silence.

"She's perfect."

"No one's perfect." At least he hadn't met them. Everyone had flaws. Some people had them hanging out for the whole world to see. Like Evan—he was an asshole, clear as day. But for some people it was more difficult to see their flaws. Sam had plenty, but he hid them down deep so that they only came out when he was sleeping.

"Roslyn is as close to perfect as you'll find. She floated through school. Good grades, boyfriends, even her hair just worked out for her. College was the same way. Never so much as a question as to what she wanted to do. No obstacles in her way. Everyone loves Roslyn.

"She got her job immediately. It was as if the local high school was waiting for her to be available. She dated perfect guys. Had a carefree lifestyle, bought her own townhouse and a freaking convertible.

"She met Cooper, the perfect guy. He was my divorce attorney, and she had come with me for moral support. While my relationship with Evan was circling the drain, she was getting busy with Cooper. They were disgustingly happy during a time when I hated anyone who was happy.

"Then they got married with the perfect wedding at the cabin. And now they have the big house and the perfect little girl, and I'm jealous, and I hate that, but I can't do anything about it." She puffed out a breath after gushing the last sentence.

"The worst part is that she thinks anyone can have everything as easily as she does. 'Riley, you just need to find a nice guy who will be a good father to Luca.' 'Riley, you should go back to school and finish your degree so you can get a better paying job.' 'Riley, surely you can save somewhere else so you don't have to get store brand diapers.' You know what? Luca doesn't know the difference if there's a name on his diapers."

She lowered her voice as the waitress set down their food. She'd ordered the Asian salad and stabbed a mandarin orange with her fork.

"And then they just *gave* me a car. I guess Tucker bought Cooper a new car so they had an extra BMW just sitting in the driveway. I'm grateful, really I am, but who has extra cars?" She shook her head. "How can I ask her for anything more?"

"Do you think she does it to make you feel bad?" Sam didn't know Roslyn that well, but she didn't seem the type.

"No. She doesn't. Which makes it worse. She's offered to help by watching Luca. I just don't want to need her to."

"Oh. I see. You're being a big, stubborn baby."

"Yes. Except the big part. I'm only five-one, while Roz is a glorious five-eight." She rolled her eyes and shoved another bite of salad in her mouth.

"Of course," Sam allowed. "What about your mother?"

"I think she's five-six."

"No. I mean to help watch Luca." He didn't roll his eyes, instead he focused on his sandwich.

"No." She shook her head. "My mother was done with responsibility the second I moved out of the house. She likes having pictures of her grandkids to show her friends, but that is the extent of her involvement. Besides, I really don't want Luca exposed to her. He could end up like me."

Sam smiled. "I think you turned out pretty good."

"I'm not so sure I want her taking care of my son. And she lives in Lynchburg. Probably so we *can't* ask her to babysit."

"I just hate seeing you do all this on your own. My sister has always been there for me. When I first came home from the service, she let me live with her until I got my feet under me."

"If you're suggesting I would endanger my child rather than ask for help, you're wrong. There's a huge difference between store brand diapers and no food. I've got this. It's not that bad." She was getting upset and defensive.

"I wasn't suggesting anything. I was just trying to come up with a way to help."

"You already put a huge tub of peanut butter in my cupboard. You've already helped more than I ever expected."

"But . . ." He didn't know how to say what he wanted to say.

"What is it? Just tell me." She took a sip of her lemonade and waited.

"It's going to sound horrible." He rubbed his forehead. How was he going to get himself out of this one?

"Just say it. There's no way it could be as bad as 'Hey, I know we are married and just had a baby together, but I've realized this isn't what I want right now so I'm moving out. Oh, and you'll have to find another place to live because I'm canceling the lease and you can't afford this place on your own.' "

Yep. Evan was an asshole. Hopefully, Sam wouldn't end up in the same category.

"I travel a lot for work."

"I know. Either that or you're one of those guys who has a secret family in another state. I saw a show about that."

"No. No other family. It's really work."

"Okay."

"Well, when I get back in town, I'd like to be able to see you. You know, like a date, when you're not working or dead dog tired."

"Oh!" Her eyebrows shot up just as the waitress came to take their empty plates and drop off the check. Sam said nothing else as he tossed the tip on the table and got up to go to the register. Riley followed silently behind him.

She didn't say anything until they were in his truck.

"You miss me," she finally said.

"What?" His brows creased. Was that it?

He'd admitted that much before, but that had been about missing having someone to hang out with for fun. The way she said it now implied much more.

He didn't know how to translate how he felt into "girl language." It could be that he missed her. He shrugged, hoping the gesture would get him out of having to admit that, yes, he did miss her. In many ways. Sexually was near the top of the list, but surprisingly it wasn't first.

"I guess I didn't realize you were getting pushed to the back of the line. That's not fair to you. Maybe this isn't a good time for us to be—"

"I'm not asking to be cut loose, Ri. Yes, okay, I miss you. It's not like I don't see how much you have on your plate. I'm not expecting anything, except maybe a date here and there. If you could work me in."

Once again her eyes got wet.

"I'm sorry, Sam."

"Please don't cry." He leaned across the seat when he parked back at the jewelry store and pulled her to him. "I didn't mean to make you cry."

"You didn't," she said, but she was crying and it was because of something he had said. He wasn't an idiot, he knew what that meant. He'd made her cry.

She quickly wiped the tears away and nodded while taking a resigned breath.

"I'm going to make time for us. It might not be a lot of time, but if you are willing to try to be with me after everything I've put you through, you sure as hell deserve a night when I can manage it. I'm sorry I didn't see it sooner."

"It's okay. I honestly don't know how you're doing this. I'm amazed."

"And you miss me." The tears were gone. She was smiling and looking a little smug.

"Do you have a night off anytime soon?" He chose to move on.

"Thursday, I work at the store until five, and then I have the rest of the night off."

"Pencil me in. We're going out. You can stop at Grammy's to give Luca a kiss before we go for dinner. Then we can pick him up when we're done. Two hours at the most. I don't want you to forget about me."

"How could I forget about you? Your giant peanut butter makes my mouth water."

"You do realize you said peanut butter, right?" he teased.

"Everyone has priorities, Sam."

"So you're cool with me keeping Luca some evenings while you're working. And you like my peanut butter in your cupboards."

She smiled at him and nodded.

"Would you also let me help with some of the bills on the counter?"

She gasped. "Did you look through my things?"

"Absolutely not. It was really hard, because I wanted to. I had to fight the urge not to take the pile and make them go away, but I didn't touch them, I swear. I respect you enough to ask."

She relaxed but shook her head. "I appreciate what you're doing. Taking Luca in the evenings gives his grandmother a break, so thank you for that. But I can't let you take care of my bills too." He let out a sigh and she put up her hand. "Before you go thinking it's because I'm being stubborn and have control issues, there's another reason."

"Which is?"

"Well . . ." She winced. "It's not a secret that everyone we know says you're not the kind of guy who stays in relationships for the long haul. They've all warned me about you at some point. I can handle it when you decide you're done here and want to move on. For the most part, I think Luca will be okay too. He's little and he won't remember you."

Sam's chest hurt. Would Luca just forget him? He'd showed him how to use the toilet and say artichoke.

"Sure it might be sticky at first, but I think he's already over his dad leaving. Kids are resilient . . ." Riley paused and took a deep breath. "I, however, can't be resilient if I let you pay for things. If I grow to depend on you and then suddenly you're not there, I will be worse off than I am now. So let me take care of my bills, because no matter what happens to you, they will still be *my* bills, and my responsibility."

He understood completely, but it didn't make him feel any better knowing she was ready to just wipe him out of her life as if he never existed. He didn't like clingy women, but apparently he wasn't thrilled with independent ones either.

She looked at her phone for the time. "I have to go back."

"Okay." He kissed her before she hopped out of the truck.

"Are we still on for Thursday?" she asked.

"Yes." He wanted some time alone with her, if for nothing else but to remember what it felt like to be out on a real date.

Before he went to pick up Luca, he decided to stop in at his sister's house.

It was her day off, but her car wasn't in the driveway. She'd asked him to look at her mower.

He pressed the code on her garage door and nearly jumped a mile in the air when she walked into the garage from the kitchen.

"Where's your car?" he asked as he caught his breath.

"I have a teenage daughter. Where do you think it is?" She cocked her head to the side.

"I told you I would help get her a car."

"I know. I'm almost willing to let you do it. It would just make me feel better if she earned it. I don't like the idea of giving a teenager big presents. It's causing a whole world of entitled people that piss me off."

Sam laughed. "You watch too much *Dr. Phil.*"

"Maybe, but we had to work for everything we have and we appreciate it. We don't expect people to hand things over."

His thoughts immediately went to Riley and he had a great idea.

"Isn't McKenna certified as a babysitter?"

"Yes." She tilted her head.

"Do you think she'd be willing to babysit in exchange for me helping her get a car?"

"I'm sure she would. If it doesn't interfere with her job at the pharmacy."

"What's her schedule?" Sam asked as she went in the house to the refrigerator. She pointed to the calendar. He took a picture of it with his phone so he could work it out with Riley. "Tell her I'll pick her up on Thursday at five. I have someone who could use a free babysitter."

"Okay. What baby is she watching?"

"My girlfriend has a little boy. He's almost three." Sam started for the door and was instantly stopped by his sister.

"Whoa, whoa, whoa! Since when do you have a girlfriend? And why are you seeing someone with a kid? Are you sure that's a good idea?"

"I'm not messing around."

Georgie's eyes got wide as a grin slowly took over her face.

"So then this is real."

"It feels kind of real. But don't go getting all wedding bells on me. That's not an option." Riley had handled a few nightmares. It didn't mean she was ready to sign up for that every night. "You know this can't be more than what it is. Don't expect things, Georgie."

"I don't know that, and neither do you. Not every woman is going to be like Jessica. A lot of women are strong enough to handle this kind of thing if you give them the chance."

"My therapist said—"

"Your therapist was an overworked bitter man who didn't want to take the time to actually help you. It's much easier to say this is just how it is, rather than work to fix it. Look at how much better you are now than when you first got stateside. You're healing. You used to jump at everything."

"Now it's just garbage trucks, and a car door the other day."

"It's not a big deal."

"I've scared Riley. I've seen the way she looks when I wake her up in the middle of the night."

"Is she angry with you?"

He shook his head. Just because they weren't angry didn't mean they shouldn't be. "No, but I'm not ready to get my hopes up."

"Sure. Sure. I'm just happy to hear you're taking someone serious."

"Are we onboard with this babysitting plan or not?" he asked, dismissing her insinuation that he was serious. Which he had to admit he was.

Chapter 9

Riley noticed Sam frown when he walked in her apartment. She'd sent him a text that said she was home. Then she'd picked up Luca and was planning to ditch on his invite to a real dinner date. Fast food would have to do.

"I thought I told you to be ready to go out," he said as a young girl came in behind him.

"I am. I thought I looked good enough for Burger Barn."

"We're not going to the Burger Barn. This is my niece McKenna. She's a certified babysitter. She's going to watch Luca while we eat. If it works out and he likes her she can help fill in for Mrs. Fisher, so she doesn't get burned out."

"Oh-kay." She didn't know what was happening.

The girl stepped forward and handed her two pieces of paper stapled together.

"Here's a copy of my certification, along with a letter of recommendation from another family I babysit for."

"Very nice." It was obvious McKenna was qualified. She'd already bent down to play with Luca and he was giggling and covering his belly. "How much do you charge an hour?" Riley asked.

"Sam is helping me buy a car in exchange for babysitting. I'm working for him," the girl said with a friendly, trustworthy smile.

"Go change into something girly. We'll talk at dinner," Sam said, borderline bossy.

"Yes, we will." She didn't like being ordered around. Even when the person doing the ordering was helping her out and smelled delicious.

She slipped off her denim shorts and T-shirt and pulled on a sundress. She let her hair out of the ponytail, and put on some mascara and lip gloss. Good to go.

Sam smiled as she came out to the living room.

"Do you have some kind of fairy godmother back there or something?"

"If I had a fairy godmother do you think I would waste her skills on my hair?"

"No. Probably not." Sam leaned down to talk to Luca. "Be good for McKenna, okay?" Luca nodded. "You have my number. If you need anything, call. We won't be far."

"No problem," McKenna said. "Have a nice time."

Sam led Riley out of the house and to his truck.

"You don't need to worry. She's a great kid," Sam assured her.

"And she's doing this because you're buying her a car?"

"I'm helping. She has money saved up. I'm going to make up the rest. Her mother didn't want her to be given a car so we've come up with this solution for her to pay it back."

"But I'm the one who's benefiting. What do I owe you?"

He wiggled his eyebrows at her and then laughed.

"I'd still be the one benefiting," she allowed, making him laugh louder.

They had a nice dinner at the same restaurant he took her to on their first date—before he knew she was a mother.

"So we're okay with McKenna helping cover the nights when I'm out of town and you're working? I'm worried about Mrs. Fisher. She's no spring chicken, you know."

"I do. Thank you, Sam. For a guy who doesn't like responsibilities, you sure are good at them."

He shrugged it off. "As long as we don't actually call them responsibilities, I might be all right."

She had something she needed to ask him. This might be the right time, now that he was feeling all in control of the situation.

"I was wondering what you were doing the Saturday after next," she said.

"Why? What's up?"

"It's Luca's birthday. I was hoping you'd be off, and maybe you could come to his party. It's not a big thing. It will be at Cooper and Roslyn's because they have a big yard. Maddy's birthday is the week before Luca's so we're going to celebrate them together. There will be cake."

"Sure. I love cake."

She swallowed.

"Everyone else will be there too. Lex and Ian and their kids. Tucker and Nichole. I think Dalton is going to come too."

"Okay." He tilted his head to the side, watching her. "Why would this be a problem? They know we're seeing each other."

"Right. They know we're seeing each other. But if you're there for Luca's birthday party, they might think this thing with us is more serious than you'd like them to think." She was trying to give him an out. It was one thing to hang out at her house, but another to spend his Saturday at an event with a bounce castle.

"If I spent a lot of time caring about what they think, I wouldn't have time for anything else."

She relaxed slightly. It was a good answer, however it didn't firm up his intentions with her at all. She frowned as she envisioned Luca with an album full of pictures of him with men who never stayed.

Sam honestly didn't care what everyone thought of him and Riley. They all had their chance to give their opinions. Besides, they all assumed he would have moved on by now and hurt her, but he hadn't. He wasn't even planning on it.

He paused at the thought. If he wasn't planning on leaving at some point, then that meant . . .

They finished their meal and got home in time to give Luca his bath and put him to bed. Sam gave McKenna a ride home while Riley read the fire engine book a second time.

"So you don't mind doing this?" he asked McKenna.

"He's a great kid. I don't mind at all."

"Thanks."

"Riley seems nice," she mentioned, clearly trying to be offhand.

"She is."

"Is she going to be my aunt someday?" Her lips were pressed together as she tried to hold back a smirky grin.

"Did your mother tell you to ask me?"

"Yes, but I want to know myself."

"Do you remember that time when I first came to live with you and you jumped out from behind the sofa?" Without thinking, he'd grabbed her and flipped her on her back, knocking the wind out of her.

"Oh, yes." She laughed. It had scared her at first, but then she had asked him to flip her over the sofa again, but not as hard.

"I'm messed up. And besides, eventually, you did ask me to stop flipping you over the sofa."

"I think you're a pretty nice guy," she said.

"That's only because I'm going to help buy you a car."

She laughed at that, but let it go.

When he got back, Riley was sleeping in Luca's bed. He picked her up and carried her to her own bed, wondering if he could ever be good enough for her.

"Thank you for tonight," she whispered as she cuddled up next to him.

"Anytime. Anything."

The next morning he dropped his bag by the front door and went to the kitchen to say his goodbyes to Riley. He was heading out for a week, but he'd be back in time for Luca's party.

He didn't want to leave them. Not for a week.

Not ever.

Sam was leaning against the counter with a glass of milk, unenthusiastic about leaving for his trip. Seeing his reluctance warmed her heart in a selfish way. She understood he had a job to do, but knowing he'd rather be with her made her feel wanted.

It was at that peaceful moment when Luca came running into the kitchen brandishing his selected toy of the day. The way he chose his toys baffled her. Some neglected toy from the bottom of his toy box would resurface to be the next best thing if only for a few hours.

Today the toy of choice was a machine gun, complete with the annoying sound effects and an orange rim at the end of the barrel to inform his potential victim that the tiny weapon wasn't real. To her, it was no more than bothersome. But Sam reacted in a much different way.

Sam didn't have the luxury of seeing the orange rim, and Riley wasn't sure it would have mattered. His back was turned to Luca as he pulled the trigger causing an irritating rat-tat-tat-tat sound to fill the kitchen.

The glass in his hand fell to the floor, sending shattered glass and milk everywhere. She didn't have a chance to say anything before Sam had grabbed her forearm and forced her down to the floor in front of him.

Fire and pain shot through her hand when she landed in the glass.

Sam reeled around on Luca, releasing his painful grasp on her arm. He ripped the toy out of Luca's hands and threw it across the room.

"What are you doing?" he yelled at her son. "You can't do that!"

Luca burst into tears, wailing for her. She had blood dripping from her hand, and trickling down her milk-covered leg. Bits of black plastic littered the floor along with the broken glass.

Sam's face changed in an instant. He was no longer angry, he looked terrified as he picked up Luca before he could reach her so he didn't get cut by the glass.

Luca screamed, and Sam handed him over to her with pain in his eyes.

"I'm so sorry," he whispered.

In a matter of seconds her moment of peace had been transformed into some kind of nightmare.

Sam continued to apologize as he cleaned up the mess and helped put a bandage on her arm.

"I'm sorry about your toy, okay, Luc?" He frowned at Luca who was still curled up in her lap, little sobs shaking his body. "I'll get you a new one."

She wanted to tell him he wasn't upset about the toy, but she was pretty sure he already knew that.

"You need to go," she said. The look of panic he gave her made her blood turn cold. She pointed to the clock on the microwave. "You'll miss your flight."

"Oh." He relaxed and she did too. It was only then she realized what she'd said.

"Sam, it's okay."

"It's definitely not okay. Look at your hand and your arm." He ran his hand over his chin in distress as she glanced down at her ripped up hand and the blooming bruises on her arm. "I did that."

"You weren't trying to hurt me. I know that."

"But I did hurt you." This was said as the undeniable fact it was. Riley's heart hurt for him.

He let out a breath and looked over at the clock again.

"Go on your trip. We'll talk when you get back. Luca is going to be fine," she said to reassure him.

He nodded and bent down in front of her so he could be eye-to-eye with Luca.

"I'm sorry I scared you. I didn't mean to yell." He paused and looked up at her, his normally happy eyes were filled with misery. "I don't know how to explain this to him so he knows I didn't mean it."

She didn't know either.

"Luca, Sam needs to get on an airplane. Let's give him a hug good-bye." With Luca in her arms she reached up and wrapped her arms around Sam. To her relief, Luca did the same thing.

Sam squeezed them close for an instant and then quickly released them and went to the door where his bag was waiting.

"I'll see you later," he said without looking back, and she thought she heard tears in his voice.

"Oh, hell," he muttered to himself as he drove to the airport.

He was almost in a full scale panic by the time he boarded the plane to head out for his next job near Houston. How had he let this happen? Sure he knew he was getting closer to them than was safe, even serious as his sister had pointed out, but up until now he thought he was still in control.

He was sure he could walk away at any minute. Now he wasn't so sure.

"Are you nervous about flying?" the older woman next to him asked.

"No. I'm nervous about something else."

"Something else" being how comfortable he was in this relationship with a single mother and a little boy. There was no more denying what it was. And how much it would hurt when she asked him to leave.

But again that was his choice. No one had forced him into this. He knew all along it could end. But it had been so easy to think he could handle things and be part of their lives. Even the party; it was a simple invite. Cake.

Ever since the incident with Jessica he'd always played it safe. Kept his distance so no one would find out how messed up he was.

But he'd let his guard down and Riley and Luca had worked themselves into his life. He had no exit strategy.

He was in too deep. It was time for an evasive maneuver before it was too late. He didn't want them to have to deal with his problems. The only way to save them from the demons that haunted him was to get out.

With that decided, he settled into his seat on the plane and relaxed.

He was going to focus on this job and let the rest work itself out.

It was a good plan, but two days later he found himself reading a text from Riley and smiling. Dammit. He wasn't good for someone like her, and she sure as hell wasn't good for someone like him.

Someone who couldn't get attached.

His phone beeped with another text. This one was a picture of Luca wearing a pair of sneakers Sam had left at her place. He looked like he had clown feet. Surely something he'd learned out of his cute kid playbook. They had already forgiven him for his episode. But he hadn't.

Sam put his phone away and didn't answer. He needed to do the right thing.

For the entire trip, his nerves were frazzled from worry. He hardly slept, and when he did his dreams were filled with all the normal ghosts.

He even found himself face-down in the Texas dust at the sound of a nail gun the next morning at the jobsite. After dusting himself off and making sure no one had noticed, he made his decision.

There was no way of getting out now without causing everyone pain. But that didn't mean it didn't have to be done. It was time.

He stayed on the job longer than was necessary, wanting to give himself more time to get his head on straight. He couldn't do this anymore. His friends had been right all along. He was going to bail or worse, and Riley and Luca would end up hurt.

And so would he.

When Riley stepped in her sister's kitchen to help with the party, Roz froze with a pile of tractor plates in her hand.

"What happened to your arm?" she pointed at the yellowing bruises. Five distinct marks left by Sam's long fingers.

"It's not what you think. Sam got surprised by Luca's toy, and he grabbed my arm to pull me to safety." She held up her bandaged hand. "Safety was actually a pile of broken glass."

Roslyn frowned.

"He didn't mean it. It was a reaction. He can't help it," she explained, wondering if the woman across the street who lived with the abusive boyfriend said the same kinds of things.

"Where is Sam?" Roslyn asked.

Luca was at his grandmother's. She was going to bring him over later so everyone could yell "surprise." Cooper and Roslyn had rented a bouncy castle which was already filled with the Montgomery children.

"I'm not sure if he's coming," Riley answered. She hadn't heard a peep out of Sam since he left. She knew he was probably still upset about the incident. She'd tried her best to convince him that everything was fine, but she couldn't stop him if he continued to punish himself.

"What do you mean he's not coming? Is he still out of town?"

"I don't think so. I don't really know. I thought he was supposed to be back on Wednesday, but it's Saturday and I haven't heard from him."

"Did you call him?"

"Yeah." Once, but it still counted. She wasn't going to keep calling him like some kind of crazy person, begging him to come to her child's birthday party. If he didn't want to be here, then screw him.

"What did he say?" Roz asked, not knowing when to stop pushing.

"He didn't say anything. I got his voicemail. I left a message and he didn't call back. I think you can figure out the rest from that information."

"I'm sorry." Again, Roz glanced down at her battered arm.

"Don't worry about it. It happens. We had a good run. I knew he wasn't stick-around material."

"I don't know why you can't meet a nice guy. Why do you always end up getting screwed over?" Roz asked as Nichole walked up.

"Oh, no. Sam?"

"Not coming," Roz told her.

"I'm sorry, sweetie. Do we hate him?" Nichole asked, ready to come to Riley's defense like the good friend she was. "What the hell happened to your arm?" She slipped into doctor mode, examining the bruises and then checking the cuts under the bandage.

"We don't hate Sam. It was an accident. He didn't do anything wrong."

"He's really not coming today?" Nic asked.

"I'm not sure," Riley replied.

"He could have at least called." Roslyn frowned.

"Okay. That would have been nice," Riley agreed as Lexi came in.

"What happened to your arm?" Lexi pointed while Riley wished they all would have been in the kitchen at the same time. Once again she explained the issue. Everyone seemed appeased with her answer—which was good since it was the truth.

"Ian has your website ready to go," Lex said as she crunched on a carrot.

"Did you finally set up a website for your jewelry?" Roz asked excitedly.

"Yes."

"It's about time. I've been telling you to do that for years!"

It was true. Roz had encouraged her to start her own business last year. But necessity had been a better motivator than her big sister.

"Oh, that reminds me, I have an order from one of the nurses," Nic said as she dug around in her bag. "Give this girl a call. She's getting married next month and she wants her bridesmaids to have the same kind of necklaces."

"Thank you." She had great friends. And her sister had already bought six bracelets.

"No problem."

Riley's phone vibrated as she tucked the paper in her bag, happy for the business. "Anita is bringing Luca over now. We have about ten minutes."

"I'll tell Cooper to bring Maddy out."

Everything was pretty much done. They blew up a few more balloons and gathered everyone together so they could sing when he walked through the gate.

When it opened Riley gasped.

Luca came through the gate on the top of Sam's shoulders.

"Happy Birthday, Luca and Maddy!" everyone cheered, making him giggle. Maddy turned into her father's neck and refused to look. The small crowd sang to them as Sam flipped Luca over his head and set him safely on his feet. Luca's eyes were on the bouncy castle, and he tore off in that direction before the last chorus was sung.

To her shock, Sam walked straight to her, bent down and kissed her. "I missed you," he said as he pulled her away from everyone else.

"I—I didn't know if you were coming."

"I wasn't planning on it. I freaked out, Ri. It was bad." He rubbed his palm over his hair. "I'm sorry."

"It's okay. I know you didn't sign up for this. You asked me out for dinner and a night of fun, and now here you are at my kid's birthday party."

"I'm not good at this. I have a lot of issues from the war. As you've seen. But the thing is, I don't want to be anywhere else."

"Because there's cake?" she joked because things felt too serious. She was in danger of saying something she shouldn't. Something she couldn't.

He pulled her against him and kissed her hair.

"I love you, Sam." Yep. That was exactly what she didn't want to say. "Don't freak out."

He didn't say anything back, but she felt his arms tighten and pull her closer before he relaxed. It wasn't an admission by any normal standards, but Riley knew his body. She knew what he wasn't saying. He felt something too. It wasn't her imagination desperate to believe a man cared for her. She knew he did.

"Come on. Let's go watch Luc bounce around," he said as he released her. "He won't stop if he has to pee, and I doubt you got flood insurance for the bounce castle."

He linked his fingers through hers and they walked over to watch Luca giggle every time he fell down.

Instead of going to the outskirts of the party to hang out with the other males, Sam stayed by her side. Twice she saw him glance down at her arm and frown, pain still there in his eyes. He helped light the candles and held the door so she could carry the cake out to the table where everyone cheered.

To the casual observer they must have looked like an ordinary family. Well, except for the obvious physical differences.

"Did you make a wish when you helped Luca blow out the candles?" Sam asked her.

"I did. I wished his father would sign off his rights so he never has to know him, or how horrible a father he is."

"He didn't send a present?" Sam asked.

"No."

After cake they helped Luca open his gifts. Not that he needed much help anymore. Somewhere between two and three he'd become a pro at ridding toys of their elaborate packaging. He even helped Maddy open her presents too.

Luca seemed happy with the movies she'd bought him. Movies neither of them had seen yet. It was as much a gift for her as it was for him.

As she gathered up the discarded wrapping paper she noticed Sam sneak out of the yard.

A few minutes later he came back pushing a small blue bicycle, complete with training wheels and a bow.

"A bike!" Luca pointed.

"Happy Birthday," Sam said while Luca all but pushed him out of the way to get on. "Hold on. You need to get suited up before you ride." He pulled the helmet from the crook of his elbow and held it out, spinning it around so it was the right way. "You need to wear the helmet and pads every time you get on the bike, got it?"

Luca nodded, the helmet making the gesture wobbly.

With the pads Velcroed in place Sam assisted him onto the seat and helped him down the driveway.

"I do it," Luca told him, not wanting any help. Sam backed off, but went down to the end of the driveway to block his path out into traffic.

"He's a natural," Anita said. Whether she meant Sam or Luca, Riley wasn't sure.

"He's pretty great."

"Has Evan called?" Anita asked. Riley could hear the worry in the woman's voice. Riley understood her need to believe her son hadn't forgotten Luca's birthday. She wanted to think Evan was a stand-up guy who would at least call.

"No. Not yet. If he doesn't call, I'll call him after the party so Luca can tell him about it."

Anita nodded. "You're a good girl. I raised him better than this. I don't know where I went wrong."

"I know it wasn't you. Do you think I'd let my son stay with you if I thought you were to blame for Evan?" Riley smiled so she would know it was a joke.

"I thought it was because I was free."

"No. I wouldn't sell my son's soul to the devil for free childcare."

Anita patted Riley's shoulder and went to go take pictures of her grandson on his new bike.

Sam had his phone out as Riley walked up.

"Are you going to give me grief for spoiling him with a big present?" he asked.

"No."

Sam snapped a selfie of them while he kissed her cheek.

"Good. Then maybe I'll let you ride it when he's done."

"It looks a little small for me. Maybe I'd like to ride something . . . bigger."

"Are you propositioning me for sex at your kid's birthday party?"

"Yep."

"Doesn't sugar keep kids awake?"

"Hmm. Yeah. I guess I wasn't thinking about how it would affect me."

"You're such a good mom." He kissed her again. "He has to sleep sometime." They laughed together as Luca yelled for them to watch him.

When they got home, Sam helped carry all of Luca's loot into the apartment. He fussed about leaving his bike on the porch, but eventually came inside to play with something else.

With a deep breath Riley pulled out her phone and dialed.

"Yeah?" Evan answered, sounding annoyed.

"Hey, it's me. I'm here with the birthday boy."

"Oh. Crap," he said. "I got him something. I'm not sure where I put it during the move."

More excuses. She frowned at the phone and once again worried for her son. She'd wanted him to have the father she never had. Someone to love him and teach him how to be a man. Instead he had Evan.

She took a breath and braced herself for seeing a lifetime worth of disappointment on her son's face.

As it turned out, Luca was too busy playing with Sam to even come to the phone. With a quick, "Hi Daddy, I hafta piss," he was running down the hall and Riley was able to end the call.

Maybe it wouldn't be so bad after all.

Once Luca was in bed she went to her room, eager to be with Sam.

"We need to talk."

"Sam—" She could tell by his face he was planning to apologize yet again for what happened.

"No, I don't want you letting me off the hook. You told me how you feel about me today. If we have any chance at making this work, I need to explain."

"Okay."

He took a deep breath and squared his shoulders before he began.

"When I got back from the service I met a girl. I was still dealing with a lot of grief and she made me feel better. I knew I didn't deserve to feel better, but I wanted it. I wanted her and I wanted to have a family."

Riley twitched at this information. He was hers. She didn't like thinking of him with someone else.

"We moved in together and I thought things were going to be great. But then one night I woke up from a nightmare with my hands around her neck."

She gasped.

"She kicked me, the pain woke me up. As soon as I realized what was happening, I let go. When she caught her breath she started yelling. I couldn't blame her. No one deserves that." He shook his head.

"It wasn't your fault," she said.

"One of the neighbors must have heard the screaming and called the police. They took one look at the handprint around her neck and suggested she file a PFA."

"Surely she knew a protection from abuse order wasn't going to stop a nightmare," Riley said.

Sam sighed.

"I'm not sure if she was really that scared of me, or if it wasn't working for her and this was a tidy way to get rid of me. But she did it." He bit his lip and looked up at her. "I thought she would drop it, but she didn't. Fortunately the judge was a vet. He ordered me to three months of court-appointed therapy."

Riley let out a breath.

"It sounds like I got off easy. But it was three months of being told I was always going to be like this, and having a family might be out of my grasp."

"That's not true."

"I wanted to stay clear of you and Luca. I never meant to drag you into my shit. But I couldn't help it. And after what happened I wanted to let you go so you wouldn't have to deal with it anymore. But then I showed up today with a fucking bike, like the selfish bastard I am."

"It's not selfish to want good things in your life."

"At the cost of hurting other people?" He raised his brow.

"You said once that you sleep so much better with me."

He nodded. "Feeling you next to me reminds me that I'm not alone. I know I'm safe."

"Then come to bed and let me hold you tight."

Sam was awakened the next week by the crack of thunder. Flashes of lightning filled the bedroom and he blinked, trying to remember where he was. He was in Riley's bed. When his hand didn't encounter a warm body, he remembered she was working at the hotel.

Once he was awake, he heard another sound in the darkness. On the next flash, the room lit up enough that he saw Luca coming into the room. He was dragging a blanket and his rabbit.

"You scared, buddy?" Sam said while patting the mattress. Riley usually went into his bedroom to sleep with him, so he wouldn't get used to sleeping in her bed. But Sam didn't fit in the little bed.

Instead of crawling in bed with Sam Luca bent down beside it. According to the blank alarm clock it was sometime in the middle of the night and the power was out. Which meant Luca's nightlights weren't fighting off evil.

"Come here," Luca said from under the bed.

"Okay." He let out a breath and got down on the floor next to Luca. "Is this better?"

Luca nodded. "My fort."

"Oh. It's nice. But I don't think I'm going to fit."

"Yuh huh." Luca scooched over making room for him. Sam couldn't very well refuse an invite to a fort.

He got situated, moving the bunny away from his face. He was just dozing off again, when his phone vibrated.

"Yeah?" he said after reaching up to the nightstand to retrieve it.

"How's it going?" Riley asked.

"I'm under the bed with one leg inside a tiny Buzz Lightyear sleeping bag."

"I forgot to warn you about the storm fort," she said. He was sure she was laughing.

"Your power is out."

"Oh hell. How long?"

"I have no idea."

"Don't open the refrigerator or the freezer. It will stay colder in there if the doors aren't opened." *Well, duh.* He didn't say that. "My shift is almost over. There was something on TV about some flooding on this side of town. I'm getting ready to head out."

"Be careful. Don't go through standing water."

"Well, duh." She said it out loud.

"I'll see you when you get here. Just so you know, there's no more room in the fort, so you'll have to chance it on the bed."

"Poor me."

Thirty minutes later she still wasn't home, and he was getting worried. Before he got the chance to call back she called him.

"Are you okay?" he asked right away.

"No," she said, but he could tell she wasn't harmed as much as inconvenienced. "There's a tree down on Sycamore, and flooding on Elm. I can't seem to get through to the other side of town. Every way I try, it's blocked."

As much as he wanted her home, having her safe was most important.

"Can you get as far as Randall Avenue on Elm?"

"Yeah, but that's as far as I can go."

"I live on Randall. Just go to my house for the night."

"How am I going to get in?"

"There's a panel on the garage door. The code is four, four, four, four."

"Four fours? Really?"

"Shh. It's a secret. Call me once you get in."

"All right. Is Luca okay?"

"Sleeping."

"Thanks." They hung up and he continued to worry until she called back fifteen minutes later. Something shifted in his heart at the sound of her voice. The way he relaxed when he knew she was safe. It wasn't something to fear, it was actually quite nice.

The stairs from the garage led up into his immaculate kitchen. Didn't Sam know he was a bachelor? He was supposed to have empty beer cans and pizza boxes everywhere. Not a spotless kitchen that made her feel inadequate because she had dishes in the sink.

She shook the rain off at the rug, not wanting to drip on his clean floors.

Clean floors? Seriously?

She kicked off her shoes and pulled out her phone to call him back while she looked around.

"Is there power there?" he asked.

"Yes."

"You can turn the air conditioning on if it's hot. The thermostat is at the top of the stairs." The apartment was a little muggy and the air smelled stale from being closed up, but clean.

"I'll be fine." She walked down the hall. The bathroom was to the right and then the bedroom. "Holy cow!"

"What?"

"Your bed is huge! Why don't we sleep over here?"

"Because there is only one room and there wouldn't be anywhere for Luca to sleep." She smiled at his answer. The way he accepted Luca as part of the deal, without complaint, warmed her heart.

"Aww. Are these your parents?" she asked as she picked up a photo next to his bed. The other picture was of two children. Most likely Sam with his older sister.

"If it's next to the bed, yes."

"They look happy."

"They were, I guess. I don't know." Right, his father died when he was a child.

"Hmm. Someone was kind of pudgy when he was a kid."

"I was husky, not pudgy. I was between growth spurts," he defended.

"Okay, okay. Don't get a complex. You turned out fine." More than fine. He was sexy and muscular with nothing that resembled pudge. "I'm going to sleep in your bed nude."

"I don't need to hear the details. Just make yourself comfortable."

"Actually, can I borrow this Braves T-shirt?" she asked.

"Damn."

"What?"

"Well, I don't know which is worse. Picturing you in my bed nude or in my Braves T-shirt."

"Hmm. Maybe next time McKenna comes to babysit, we'll come over here and find out." She waited for a smart response, but there was nothing. Maybe he fell asleep? "Sam?" she whispered so not to disturb him.

"I'm here." There was some tone to his voice she didn't recognize. It gave her a chill.

"What's wrong?"

"Nothing." Again, she could tell something wasn't quite right.

"Just tell me. If you want me to sleep on the sofa, I can."

"No." She could hear a breath. "This probably isn't the right way to do this. Over the phone with you across town, but I just need to say it."

"Say what?" Her heart was in her throat. Surely he wouldn't break up with her in the middle of the night during a storm.

"I love you, Ri."

She covered her mouth and felt it pull up into a smile.

"Ri?"

"Yeah. I heard you. Are you okay? I know that wasn't the plan."

She could hear a soft laugh from his end.

"I don't see any way of getting out of it if I'm not okay with it," he admitted.

"Best just to go with it then, huh?"

"I guess so."

"It's not so bad. I've been in love with you for a little while now, and I'm still here to tell about it," she teased him.

"But you don't have—I'm just sorry I'm not—better." The words sounded as if they were ripped from his soul. He honestly thought he was too damaged to be part of a loving relationship. And why wouldn't he? The last girl hadn't cared enough to stick it out. Sure it wasn't easy being woken up by night terrors or pulled to the ground at loud noises. But Sam was worth all of that. She wasn't delusional. She understood what she was signing up for. But she was willing to stick it out for the person he was when he was awake. And he loved her.

"Sam, you're an amazing man. We'll work out the rest. It's going to be okay," she assured him the best she could from miles away.

"I guess what I'm saying is . . ." He paused and she waited. "You can use my toothbrush if you want."

Chapter 10

They only had time for a quick kiss when Riley got home the next morning. Sam was relieved they didn't have to go through the details of his revelation from the wee hours of the morning. It wasn't that he didn't mean it. He'd been honest about his feelings. He knew he loved her. He just wasn't sure what to say next. He'd never gone this far before and he didn't want to mess it up. He'd spent years worrying about how he would handle another person being this important and integral to his life. But now that it was here, he felt content.

She was perfect.

Instead of wanting to run the other way, he found himself not wanting to leave town for his trip the next day. As long as he didn't scare her away, he might actually have a chance to be happy. Something deep inside of him twitched at that thought. A part of him didn't think he deserved to be happy. He knew he needed to let it go, but it was hard when he remembered his men. The ones who didn't make it home to their loved ones.

"You're sitting in my office," Dalton said as he rubbed his temples with his fingertips. "Please don't have bad news, Sam. I can't take it. Audrey just told me she's pregnant and I'm going to have to find a new assistant. My sister knows what I need done before I do. How am I supposed to replace her with a stranger?"

"Oh." Sam winced, not wanting to kick him when he was already being abandoned.

"You're bailing on me too?" Dalton's eyes widened in horror.

"I don't *want* to bail, it's just that I'm . . ." He wasn't sure if he wanted to go into all the gory details with Dalton. Guys didn't talk about love and feelings. "I'm seeing Riley, as you know, and it's getting serious."

"Serious? How serious?" Dalton looked as if this was the most absurd thing he'd ever heard. Maybe it was.

"Serious, serious. Like I want to stay in town instead of going away all the time. I'm even thinking about maybe moving in." He shrugged. "Or more."

"More?" A smile was hinting at the corner of his lips. "I never had The Talk with you before, but after moving in with someone the only way there is more is if you get"—he glanced over his shoulder, playing it up before he whispered the forbidden word—"married."

"Would that be so bad? Other people do it."

"Holy shit!" All joking around was over now. "You're serious!"

"I just said I was serious like twelve times in a row. You aren't too bright. You'd better get two assistants. One to do the work and the other to wipe away your drool."

"This is unexpected. I always thought I had my shit together better than you and would end up with someone way before you."

"Thanks for that," Sam said.

"Do you blame me?"

"No." Sam couldn't argue. He thought Dalton would have been with someone before now too. Maybe that girl from high school he whined about after three drinks.

"Marriage," Dalton said it now as if he was impressed with Sam.

"I don't want to put you in a bind, but I wanted to let you know that I would be looking for local work. So while you're putting in an ad for an assistant, you might want to start looking for a foreman. I'll make sure the person is settled before I leave."

"Well, hold on a minute." Dalton scratched his head for a moment while he thought. "I had wanted to talk to you about something."

"Oh?"

"Yeah, you know Timmy McGuire."

"Sure. Is he hiring?" Timmy owned McGuire Builders. They were a fairly large construction company in Roanoke, with a good reputation.

"No. He's retiring. He wanted to know if I'd be interested in buying him out slowly."

"And what did you say?" Sam asked.

"I was still in the thinking it over stage. Mainly because I didn't have anyone to stay in town to oversee things, but it looks like now I might." Dalton raised his brows in question.

"I'd be interested if you're offering." This would be the perfect opportunity for Sam. He'd still be doing the thing he loved, but in the same town with Riley and Luca. He'd already started daydreaming about taking Luca to Little League games when Dalton interrupted his thoughts.

"Would you maybe be interested in buying in with me? We could get it from Timmy quicker."

"Like partners?" Sam asked.

"Yeah. It wouldn't have to be fifty-fifty. I don't know what your financial situation is, but we can work out something that says it's partly yours. If you want that."

Sam swallowed. He'd never wanted people to count on him for anything. He hadn't thought he was cut out for a long-term relationship with a woman, and he hadn't wanted ties to the community or to invest himself in a career. These things were to be avoided at all cost. It meant he was at risk of letting someone down. How was it that these things were now his goals?

"I would be interested. I have some money put aside to invest," Sam said.

"Take a few days. Think it over." Dalton stood and walked to the wall where all the drawings were kept. "Maybe this should be the first house we build if we decide to go for it." He unrolled a drawing and held it out.

Sam only needed to look at it for a fraction of a second before he recognized it. The house was his design. He'd taken things he'd loved from other homes as he tore them down or built them up. He'd given Dalton a rough drawing and here was Dalton surprising him with an actual blueprint. A few supporting walls had been moved but other than that it was Sam's dream home. Thoughts of Riley and Luca living in it with him flooded his mind and the jolt almost brought tears to his eyes.

He could have it all.

Everything he thought he could never have.

He could have Riley.

* * *

"Everything is messed up," Riley announced as she set Luca down and watched him run off into the playroom with the other kids. She plopped down at the kitchen table next to Roslyn, Lexi, and Nichole. They sometimes had girls' night at Ralphy's Bar, but anymore, they generally had afternoon playdates at Lexi's house.

Lemonade replaced margaritas, and bad words were either whispered or spelled. The important thing was they were together. They were able to support each other and share the burden which was life.

"What's messed up?" Roz asked. "Sam?"

"Yeah. We're in a relationship."

"How do you know?" Nic asked.

"He told me he loved me." The memory of his words still made her heart speed up. She had been caught completely off guard.

Every mouth dropped open. They looked back and forth at each other, expecting someone else to come up with the right thing to say. No one did.

"See?" Riley held out her hands and let them fall to her lap. The lemonade wasn't going to cut it, but she needed to drive home and then go to work in the evening so she'd have to make do.

"He didn't seem the type," Lex noted.

"What's the problem?" Roz gave her the look like she was being ridiculous. Maybe she was.

"What if he wants to get married? I can't get married again. I can't risk it." She remembered how it felt. Being married was wonderful. It was the point in her life when she felt content. Like life was safe. She wouldn't need to worry about things because she had a partner who would always be there for her.

That was crap.

Roslyn put her arm around her sister. "Do you think Sam is like Evan? In any way?"

Riley took a second to give the question thorough consideration before she answered. "No."

"Then why would you think he would handle things the same way?" Roslyn asked.

"I don't. I'm just afraid he'll come up with his own way to ruin my life." It was a valid concern despite the fact Roz rolled her eyes.

"So what are your options? If you're not willing to move forward you either have to stay in one place or get off the ride," Lex said and pulled her lips to the side.

"You know, the fact that two of you have all this mental training is unnerving." Riley sighed. "I don't stand a chance. Sam will be home tomorrow. I need to have a plan with how to deal with this, or a place to hide."

They all laughed until someone started crying from the playroom. Riley knew it wasn't Luca so she stayed, fiddling with her glass. Since Nichole didn't have kids, she stayed too.

"If you love him, you need to be strong enough to take a chance on him," Nichole said while the other mothers were taking care of the altercation. Nichole was married to Tucker Matthews. He was a rock star, but he was also a recovering alcoholic and addict. Nichole knew what she was talking about when it came to strength and trust. And Sam didn't have those kinds of issues.

Sure, he often woke up in the middle of the night covered in sweat and gasping for breath, and he over-reacted to loud noises, but they were small things in comparison to dependency or infidelity. Sam was great with Luca, and he loved her.

She knew she loved him back, but that was only because her inferior walls of protection had been easily compromised by his willingness to care about her and her son. She was such a pushover when it came to his hazel eyes and ability to make a killer toasted cheese sandwich.

But was it enough?

When the visit was over, Riley loaded up a sleepy Luca in her car and started for home.

"Sam?" Luca said while pointing to a truck on their street.

"No. That's not Sam's truck. Sam's working."

Luca let out a sigh which sounded remotely like annoyance or disappointment. "Tomorrow, he will come," Luca said, sounding as sure about that as anything.

Sam's heart gave a pleasant skip when he pulled in at Riley's house and saw her and Luca out on the porch.

He could already hear Luca yelling his name as he opened the door. A big smile took over his face. He was home.

"Do you hear something?" Sam called to Riley as he opened the back gate. She stood up with that amazing grin on her face. She was wearing a sundress. No doubt she wore it for comfort, but it made her look sweet and sexy. Especially with the way the sun outlined the image of her body through the fabric.

Luca was now jumping at Sam's legs, desperate for attention.

"I don't hear anything," Riley played along.

"Me! You heared me!" Luca said. Sam looked down, pretending to notice him for the first time.

"Luca!" Sam grabbed him up.

"Oh, no! He's hungry," Luca squealed while Sam made the customary chewing sounds at Luca's neck. It was their greeting.

To Riley he simply leaned down and kissed her lips. Mmm. Gloss. He winked at her, accepting her silent invitation for later. Lip gloss equaled sex.

Sam carried Luca inside upside down and giggling while he wrapped his arm around Riley. This was how he wanted things to be. He hadn't talked to Riley about their future, but they would be having a conversation soon. And he was ready.

"Penguins," Luca said, holding up the movie.

"No. Not tonight. Sam is tired, and it's almost time for bed," Riley said.

It was only ten after eight, but Sam smiled knowing why she was getting Luca ready for bed early. She'd missed him. He'd missed her too. And not just the sex.

He'd told her he loved her, and tonight he would get to show her how much.

Luca pouted and held up the movie again, trying his best.

"Sorry, buddy. But I'm off tomorrow, so you and I can watch penguins tomorrow while Mommy's at work. How's that? Deal?" Sam held out his hand and Luca shook it.

"Bath time," Riley chimed. Sam jokingly pulled his shirt up. "Not you. I'll give you a bath later." She licked her lips and his penis leaped into action, obviously not hearing the part about later.

Fortunately Luca cooperated and was in bed in no time. Sam took over storytelling, making Luca laugh when he did the squeaky voices of the mice.

"Goodnight," Sam said when he was finished.

"Night. Love you," Luca said.

"Love you, too." Sam kissed his head and turned to see Riley by the door wiping at her eye. "Really?" He teased her for getting emotional.

She smacked his arm. "Don't try to ruin it. It was sweet."

"Did you get weepy when I told you what I told you the other night?"

"No. Mostly I got scared," she admitted.

"Oh, good. That was what I was aiming for when I shared my feelings. Fear."

"Maybe worried is a better word than scared," she allowed.

"Whatever. It's not like I just go around saying it without meaning it. I mean it. So stop worrying. I think it's time for my bath."

"How about a shower, and then we can go to bed quicker?"

"I like the way you think," he said as he led her into the bathroom and pulled up the sundress.

When he was thoroughly cleaned and they were moving toward the bedroom, he paused. "I want to talk to you about something."

"Now?" She gestured down to her naked body. "Now is not time for talking. Now is time for making Riley feel less like a mommy and more like a sex goddess."

"Yes. We'll get to sex goddess in a second, but I need to do this now."

"Okay." She bit her bottom lip, and not in the good way.

"Don't do that. It's not bad. At least I don't think it is," Sam said.

"Go ahead." She folded her arms under her naked breasts which pushed them up into his vision.

He checked out for a second and shook his head to get back on topic. "I talked to Dalton about staying in town more often. We're considering going into business together. Buying out a local builder. I might still have to go out of town occasionally, but not as much as before."

"That sounds great." Clearly, she wasn't seeing how this affected her. She was just assuming it was good news for him. He was hoping it would be good news for her too.

"I've been thinking about how much time I spend here. Would you be opposed to me moving in? I could get rid of my apartment, and then we could go halves on expenses here."

"You want to move in?" she said, her brows pulled together. That was not a happy look. It was not a "yes" kind of look.

"I pretty much live here already when I'm in town. Is it really a big deal?"

"Yes. Moving in together would be a big deal. It's a commitment."

"So is telling someone you love them. I know what it is. It's a step toward other places I want to go with you."

"I—I don't know. It's kind of fast."

"Think it over and let me know. I'm not going to start packing tomorrow or anything." He shrugged, hoping the gesture alleviated the tension that had taken over her body.

She was right to be leery of him. While he knew he was in love with her and he loved Luca as if he was his own flesh, Sam was aware of what he was. A wild card. Rather than push her into a corner, he decided to back off for now.

He stepped closer and let his fingertips trail down the bare skin of her arm.

"Come here, sex goddess," he whispered. As he bent to kiss her he felt the stiffness in her muscles dissipate until she melted from his touch.

Things were different between them. Sure it was still hot, and he couldn't get enough even when he was exhausted from the second time. But there was a comfort and a familiarity that he'd never felt with a woman before. Even Jessica.

He felt safe.

At least until he fell asleep.

He was on that blasted hillside again. He should have known it was a dream by now, but it felt so real. Not to mention he was asleep and not thinking clearly . . .

The same insurgents were moving closer, taking cover behind rocks when he and his men fired at them.

He still referred to them as his men, even though there were only two of them with him. He hoped the three men in the other vehicle made it out okay. The chopper had been called in. They only needed to hold the hostiles off for about twenty minutes until EVAC arrived.

As he surveyed the movements below him, he knew the chance of making it that long was slim. There were too many.

Simmons and Desmond were behind him, and he barely

registered their discussion. They didn't want to be taken prisoner. Hell, he didn't want that either.

Before he got the chance to come up with another plan, shots came from his left. They hadn't seen anyone coming from the left.

Another pop, and he felt fire flash through his left arm as he fell to the ground. Pebbles and sand dug into his palms as he struggled to get up again.

He heard the sound of quick footsteps and hoped it was help.

It wasn't. He was being pulled by his left arm. They were trying to take him away. No doubt they were going to torture him for information. He couldn't let them take him off that hill. He wouldn't have a chance.

With all the strength he could muster he shoved the man away from him, causing him to stumble back.

Sam waited for the expected sound of the gun hitting him in the skull as he always did in the past, but instead he heard the loud wailing cry of a little boy . . .

Luca.

Chapter 11

Riley was shocked out of her restful sleep by the sound of Luca screaming his head off. She knew all the different nuances of his cries. From a whimper of discomfort to this: all-out pain.

Without thinking she flipped on the light by her head and was out from under the covers in a flash to get to her child.

She had made it to the doorway before she realized he wasn't in his room. The sound was coming from her room, and she looked down to see Luca on the floor next to the wall on Sam's side of the bed.

He was hysterical and blood was running from his mouth.

"Oh, God!" She gathered him up as Sam sat there staring. For a long second it didn't look like he was with them. Then he blinked and covered his mouth in shock.

"Luca? Oh, shit, Luca! I'm so sorry," he said, his face pale.

"What happened?" she asked as she picked Luca up and carried him out to the kitchen.

"I was having a nightmare and I think—I think I might have *hit* him." The pain in his voice was unmistakable. She knew it was an accident, Sam would never willingly hurt Luca, but he had, and her maternal instincts had her moving Luca away protectively.

Luca's lip was swelling and bleeding and Riley noticed a large bump on the back of his head.

"I think I need to take him to the ER."

"I'll get dressed." Sam ran back to the hall in his boxers.

"I don't think you should come—"

"I'm coming," he said. She could have argued, but she didn't want to take the time. Luca had moved into the ugly sobs stage and wouldn't let go of her.

Sam was only gone for a minute and when he returned, he was

fully dressed. Even shoes. "Here, let me take him while you put on some clothes. I'll put him in the car." Riley didn't get the chance to answer when Luca screamed again and pulled away from Sam. "Just grab my sweatpants. I'll pull them on in the car."

She secured a sobbing Luca in his car seat and slid in next to him, so he wouldn't get more upset. His little hands were clenched in her hair so she couldn't leave him.

Sam drove them to the hospital while Riley pulled on her pants and tried to soothe her son with singing. It wasn't working. Not even when Sam tried to help. Luca just kept crying and her heart broke.

The ER wasn't horribly crowded at three in the morning. A young, female doctor took them right back while asking questions. "What happened?"

"We're not exactly sure," Riley said. "Sam was having a bad dream and we think he might have pushed or hit him. I found him on the floor. He has a lump on the back of his head."

The doctor flashed a small light in Luca's eyes and frowned. There was nothing worse in the world than seeing the doctor frown at the response time of her son's pupils.

"Is he okay?" she asked.

"He has a concussion. I'd like to get an x-ray to make sure nothing is broken in his face as well as check his neck."

"I'm so sorry," Sam said. Riley could tell the words were ripped from his chest. She knew he hadn't done it on purpose, but at the moment she only saw the man who hurt her kid. She wasn't capable of telling him it was fine.

Riley stayed with Luca as they prepped him for the X-ray. They'd told her there was nothing they could do for his lip. The cut was inside so they couldn't stitch it. She put on the heavy apron and sat next to him while he got his x-ray.

"Luca, let's be very still for a second, okay baby? Can you pretend you're a rock?" He whimpered in response. "Come on. Be a rock with me. Ready? Go."

She felt his hand tense in hers and the hum of the machine above her.

"You were a very good rock." The woman came in and positioned him for the next film. He fussed a little, but had settled down. "Are you ready to be a rock again?" she asked.

He nodded once. He did great, but as soon as they were done he was hanging on her neck again.

"Please have a seat here, and we'll take a look." The woman gestured to a smaller waiting area in the hall. Sam was sitting there. His head hung in his hands miserably. He looked up when Luca said his name.

She watched as he swallowed and stood. He was a wreck.

"Hey, big guy. How are you feeling?" Sam reached for his hand, but Luca pulled away and curled up under her chin. Sam's eyes glistened and he pressed his lips together. "I'm sorry, Luca. I didn't mean to."

She felt horrible for both of them.

They all sat silently in the waiting area. She had been instructed to keep Luca awake, but he wasn't sleeping. He just rested his head against her chest and stared at the wall. Sam was holding her hand, rubbing it intensely. She wanted to pull away, but she knew it would only hurt him worse, so she adjusted it slightly instead.

At the sound of footsteps, everyone looked up.

The woman in front of them wasn't a doctor. Or at least she wasn't wearing a white coat. She was wearing black slacks and a pink T-shirt.

"Are you Riley Fisher?" the woman asked as she stepped closer.

"Yes."

"I'm Danielle Rogers, from Child Services."

Riley's hand almost jerked back to her side, but she was able to steady herself long enough to shake the woman's outstretched hand.

Sam swallowed as he shook her hand as well.

"And you are . . . ?" the woman asked.

"Sam Brooks," he answered.

"Can I get an ID? Are you the boyfriend? Fiancé? What's the relationship here?" Danielle sounded all business as she wrote in her tablet.

Sam blinked and looked at Riley for the answer.

"Uh, boyfriend," she said.

The woman nodded before turning toward Sam. She handed back his license after writing the number down.

"Would you mind giving us a few moments alone? I believe there's a waiting room down on the first floor. I'll come get you when we're finished."

Sam stood and walked away like a robot.

When he was gone, Danielle started asking more intense questions. Everything from how long she and Sam had been together, to where Luca's biological father was.

Another fear gripped Riley's stomach at the questions about Evan. Could this incident hurt her if Evan followed through on his threats to try for custody? It surely wasn't going to help. She suddenly felt trapped. This had been an innocent mistake. Sam hadn't meant to hurt Luca, but she knew how it looked. She was shacked up with an ex-marine who suffered from night terrors and PTSD. She knew he didn't sleep soundly. She should have seen the potential risk. Sam had a PFA on file from his ex-girlfriend. This woman would know that when she ran his license. He would seem dangerous.

No, he *was* dangerous.

When Danielle was done drilling Riley with questions, she leaned down to Luca with a smile.

"What happened to your lip, Luca?" she asked.

"Sam push me," he said sadly, and Riley knew it was as bad as it looked. She'd brought a man into her son's life who had caused him pain. Whether it was intentional or not. She had always promised herself Luca would come first. She'd failed him.

It felt like forever before the woman showed up in the waiting room. Sam's mind had been going a mile a minute, trying to come up with some way to excuse his behavior.

Nothing came to him. He'd hurt an innocent little boy, pushed him. Split his lip and thrown him into the wall so hard he'd given him a concussion. Whatever this woman thought of him, Sam felt ten times worse.

She sat beside him and smiled as if she wasn't there to rip his heart out.

"I finished talking with Luca and Riley, now I'd like to hear what you say."

Sam blinked. "Whatever they say happened is what happened. They wouldn't make something up, and neither would I."

"I'd still like to hear it in your words."

Sam nodded. "I had a nightmare. I guess Luca came in and tugged at my arm. I defended myself in my dream, but in reality I hurt Luca. I'm not sure if it was just a push or if I hit him. I wasn't awake. I just know he's hurt, and it's my fault."

"Have you ever had this happen before?" she asked.

"Hurting a kid? No."

"But the night terrors are common?"

He wanted to say no. Common made it sound like it happened all the time. But they did happen more often than frequently or rarely. He nodded. They were common. Why didn't he realize he was a danger? He'd already hurt someone while he was sleeping. Why did he think he could do this?

"I had an incident a few years ago. I woke up from a dream and I—" It sounded awful.

He didn't need to finish. The woman tapped her phone and read it to him. Sometimes technology was a bitch.

"The report says you strangled your girlfriend while you were having a nightmare. She filed a protection from abuse."

Sam nodded again.

"Have you ever lived with any other children?"

"My niece. When I first got back I stayed with my sister and her daughter until I found a job and got a place of my own."

"And you never had a similar incident?"

"She never came in my room. She was eleven at the time."

"Have you seen anyone—a therapist—about your PTSD?" God, he hated those four letters. It was so much easier to think they were just nightmares. Maybe if he'd taken it more seriously, Luca wouldn't have a concussion right now.

"Yes." He nodded. "When I was released from Landstuhl, and I was ordered to three months of therapy after the other incident."

"You were treated for your injuries in Germany, but did they suggest you get a psych eval when you got back to the States?"

"Suggested? Probably. It wasn't mandatory. I just wanted to get home. I was in physical therapy for months. By then I thought I was doing better. The dreams weren't as bad. I thought I was going to be okay. After I hurt Jess I went to my meetings. The therapist signed off."

"But you've been diagnosed with PTSD," she said, and he couldn't help but hear the mild accusation in her voice. He nodded. "So you are aware you still have a problem, but you refuse to get treatment."

When she put it like that, it sounded like negligence on his part. Was it?

"I would have seen a therapist after what happened with Jessica even if I hadn't been forced by the court. I didn't continue to go after he signed off because he made it sound like there was nothing that could be done. He didn't seem all that concerned. He said it was something I would learn to live with. Here I am, trying my best to

live with it. And like I said, I thought I was getting better. I felt better."
If there was a way he could have a normal life he would have done
whatever it took to make it happen. Didn't she get that?

"I understand, but unfortunately it doesn't matter how you feel
when a small child is put in danger."

"What are you saying? I can't be around Luca until I see another
therapist?" He just wanted her to spit it out.

"I'm recommending that, yes."

"What did Riley say?" he asked, but she didn't answer his question.

"I suggest you get help, Mr. Brooks. Not just to appease my office, but for your own well-being. I'm sure it's not fun to talk about,
but generally we feel better when we let the demons out so we can
deal with them."

When she was gone, Sam stood and paced in the room until Riley
and Luca came down.

"Is he going to be okay?" Sam asked.

"Yes. We can take him home. I'm supposed to monitor him for the
next twenty-four hours. His neck is fine."

"Good."

Sam leaned down to Luca and held out his hands, expecting another rebuff, but Luca unwound his arms from his mother's neck and
leaned out for Sam to take him.

He kissed the kid's forehead and closed his eyes.

"I am so sorry, Luca. I didn't mean to hurt you, okay? I had a bad
dream. Do you understand?"

Luca nodded, looking very sleepy. Sam wasn't sure if he was able
to comprehend how horrible Sam felt.

They got him home and in bed. Riley said she would have to wake
him up every hour to check on him, and Sam offered to take the first
shift. It was the least he could do.

She frowned and bit her bottom lip. Seeing the look in her eyes
made his heart shudder. He knew what was coming. He couldn't
blame her. She was doing the right thing. Sam was a potential danger,
and a mother's job—above all else—was to protect her child from
danger. He swallowed as he waited for her to end it. End him. "Sam."
It should have made him feel better that it wasn't easy for her. She
couldn't just cut him out without a care. But nothing could make him
feel better at the moment. "I think we need to spend time apart."

"For how long?" he asked, knowing there wasn't going to be a magic answer.

"For as long as it takes for us to make sure something like this never happens again."

"So I won't sleep over. I can leave after he goes to bed," Sam suggested an alternative.

She let out a pained sigh, and he knew he'd lost.

"It's more than that," she said. "What if Evan tries to use you as a way of getting custody of Luca? What if he hires someone to say you're unstable and that Luca is being raised in unsafe living conditions? You have a history of this. I can't take that risk, I'm sorry."

Sam honestly hadn't thought of that, but she was right. He was more of a risk to them than he ever knew. He nodded and walked slowly to the door. "Let me know if you need anything, okay? I still want to help," he said.

"We're not your responsibility. I can take care of myself and Luca. You need to take care of yourself."

With a nod he stepped out of the house. He knew she could take care of herself. She didn't need him. That didn't mean he didn't want to help.

"I'm sorry it has to be this way. I really am," she whispered as tears filled her pretty eyes.

"I'm sorry too." He kissed her on the forehead and strode off toward his truck.

By the time he got home, he had convinced himself that this was all for the best.

After all, it was only a matter of time before he messed it up. He would have been the bad guy at some point. So it happened now. The decision was out of his hands. This was for the best.

If only he believed it was true.

Riley had just cried herself to sleep when the alarm went off for her to go wake up Luca again. It was almost seven and she would need to get up soon anyway.

She'd called Anita to tell her what happened. They weren't sure if Luca was going to be okay to stay with her. When he was sick or hurt he only ever wanted Riley. But they decided to try so she could go to work.

Their little trip to the ER wasn't going to be cheap, and things were already tight. In addition to emptying her savings to pay for the deductible for her car, Evan hadn't sent her a dime in the last month. She sighed when she remembered she wasn't in a good position to make him pay. If she pressed him, she could end up having to defend herself in court. And after the events of the night before, she didn't know which side the court would come down on.

"Sam? Penguins?" Luca said as soon as he came out of his bedroom. He went straight to the shelf and pulled the movie out. Despite his very adventurous night, he hadn't forgotten Sam's promise to watch the movie with him.

"Actually, Sam had to go. So you're going to Grammy's today. But you can take the movie along and watch it with her."

That earned a frown and slumped shoulders. The pout was emphasized by the fat lip, and her chest throbbed with pain.

Luca went to Anita easily after a long hug.

"Momma loves you. I'll see you tonight."

"Sam?" he asked and her heart nearly broke in two. She'd stupidly assumed it would be easy to get over Sam. But her son had cared about him too.

"Sam is away," she told him again as she always did when Sam was on a trip. It appeased him enough for her to get out of the house and in her car before she broke down.

How was she just going to cut Sam out of their lives? It had only been a couple of months, but somehow he'd managed to break down all her walls and become an important part of her and Luca's lives. She wiped at the tears as she pulled into her parking spot at work.

She was Luca's mother. A mother's sole purpose in life was to protect her child from harm. Sam—despite the fact that he didn't do it intentionally—had harmed her son, and she needed to protect Luca. No matter how much it might also hurt both of them.

"You look like hell," Pauline noticed right away. Riley had run some concealer under her eyes, but apparently there was no cosmetic tough enough for the challenge.

"I was up most of the night after a trip to the ER. Luca has a concussion and I had to keep waking him."

"Do you need to go home?" Pauline was always very accommodating when Riley needed to rearrange her schedule. This was why Riley tried not to take advantage.

"No. I'll be fine. I just need another cup of coffee." And Sam.

Pauline frowned. Riley probably didn't seem convincing, but she put a smile on her face and carried on. She couldn't miss work. She had a little boy to support and she was on her own.

This thought reminded her of the plans she and Sam had made the night before. How he was going to move in and share the burden with her. For a few hours she had some peace, knowing she wasn't alone.

But then, like always, her world was turned upside down and the weight of it was back on her shoulders.

Sam sat at his small kitchen table looking at his hands. They were large and calloused from work. But they seemed harmless enough while just resting on the table.

He knew those hands were capable of so much. They could fire a weapon, or tickle a little boy until he laughed so hard he had to run to the bathroom. The night before his hands had stroked Riley's bare skin as he made love to her, and then a few hours later they had slammed Luca into the wall, ending the stolen bit of happiness Sam never deserved in the first place. His fingers clenched into fists and he brought them down on the surface of the table, making it shake from the force.

He wasn't angry with Riley for cutting him out of her life. She did what any good mother would do. She'd removed a danger from her home. The efficiency with which she made this removal still stung. So did the emptiness. He glanced at the clock, knowing Riley would be at work. When she'd asked him to leave, he thought it was for the best. But already he knew he needed them.

He spent the morning making a list of therapists in the area, and reading articles about PTSD on the Internet. Regardless of how much he didn't want to talk about his issues, he knew he would do anything to get Riley and Luca back. As he looked over the list, gathering the courage to make the call, he remembered what he had planned for today, before everything went to hell. He was going to stay with Luca while Riley worked. He'd promised Luca they would watch the penguin movie. Now his day stretched out in front of him. Just bleak nothingness.

He only lasted an hour before he was in his truck. He knocked on the door, not sure if he was doing the right thing. If he thought for one second he was a danger to Luca, he wouldn't have come. He would keep his distance, and be on alert for anything that could trigger a wild reaction. One of the articles he'd read said he couldn't close himself off from the world. Finding a way to control his reactions and facing the problem was a step in the right direction. The night before Luca was scared of him. Sam couldn't get the image out of his mind. Luca recoiling from his touch.

Mrs. Fisher opened the door before Sam had the chance to reconsider and run away.

"You look just as bad as the other two," she said with a frown. Sam's muscles tensed, ready to lock himself down if necessary.

"It's okay if you don't want to let me see him. I just wanted to check in on how he was doing. Is he okay?" Sam asked.

To his surprise, the woman opened the door and let him in.

Luca jumped up from in front of the television and ran to him the way he always did. Only this time his lip was twice the normal size, with an ugly red scab forming.

"I'm so sorry, Luca," Sam said as he leaned down to scoop him up and hold him to his chest, abandoning his plan to keep his distance. Tears pricked at his eyes. "Are you okay? How's your head?"

"We just gave him some medicine, because he said it hurt. But he's going to be okay," Mrs. Fisher said.

"Penguins!" Luca pointed to the television. "Come." Luca was already sliding down. He took Sam's hand and tugged him toward the living room. Just like that, Sam was forgiven for his horrific act and was being invited to watch a movie.

He'd heard how kids were resilient. He remembered seeing McKenna snap back from things quicker than an adult could when she was little. But he had never been the cause of her pain. He shouldn't be forgiven this easily.

"I don't think I should." Sam looked up at Luca's grandmother.

"He told me you were going to watch it with him, but you had to leave. He seemed pretty upset about it. Maybe enough men in his life have broken promises and you should just sit down and keep this one," she suggested with a firm pat on his shoulder.

She was forgiving him too.

"Thank you," he said, giving her a hug.

She returned the embrace. "I don't know how you boys do it. My Roger kept so much ugly stuff locked up in his head. It only ever came out when he was sleeping. I think talking helps; if you ever can, you should."

Sam nodded and allowed Luca to pull him to the sofa. "I'm going to do that, ma'am. I promise."

Sam sat down and Luca crawled up into his lap without an inkling of fear. He rested his head on Sam's chest, giggling at the funny parts. The movie went by in a blur. Sam dreaded the happy ending because he knew it meant his time was up.

"I have to go now," Sam said, working to keep his voice steady.

"No," Luca whined. "Penguins again."

"I can't. I need to go." Sam got down on Luca's level so he could look him right in the eye. "I'm not going to be around very much, but I want you to know I love you, okay? Don't forget."

Luca nodded and wrapped his arms around Sam's neck.

"Love you." He gave Sam a smile which was contorted from the injured lip. "Bye-bye, Sam."

"Bye, buddy."

Mrs. Fisher patted his shoulder as he passed by her. He didn't stop to say anything other than offer another, "Thank you."

When he got in his truck he was more determined than ever to get his family back. He knew now that he considered Riley and Luca his family, and he couldn't imagine the rest of his life without them.

Talking about it helps, Mrs. Fisher had said. It was time.

He held his phone to his ear as it rang.

"Hey. How's it going?" Ian answered.

"You once mentioned seeing a therapist. You said she helped you get your head on straight," Sam said, not caring if he sounded desperate or frantic. He was both those things.

"Yeah."

"Do you think she could help me? My head is on straight, but it's full of all kinds of shit that keeps messing me up."

"Her name is Dr. Younger. Hold on while I get you the number."

A few minutes later, Sam had an appointment for a miracle.

Chapter 12

"Sam came to see Luca today," Anita said when Riley got in the door.

"What?" She'd obviously heard the woman, she just couldn't believe Sam would sneak behind her back to disobey her wishes.

"I wasn't sure how you wanted me to handle it. But he'd promised to watch a movie with Luca before everything went wrong and he wanted to make good on it as well as wanting to check on him. I didn't think you would mind. It's nice that he's not the kind of guy who could just walk away without a care."

"Was Luca okay?" Riley asked, because that was the most important thing.

"He was very excited to see Sam, and then he cried by the door when Sam had to leave. Just like every other time Sam has to leave."

"Do you think he'll come back?" Riley wasn't sure if she wanted that or not. If Sam came to Anita's, Evan wouldn't be able to use him against her.

She hated that Evan was dictating who was allowed in her life with his threats. But unfortunately she wasn't in a position to stand up to him.

"I'm not sure. He seemed pretty upset when he said goodbye. I think he'll respect your wishes and stay away." Riley nodded. "Are you sure that's what you want?"

"It isn't what I want. But . . ."

"Evan." She sighed. "Maybe I could talk to him."

"Maybe you could get him to sign away his custody." She hadn't meant to say that out loud. She knew Anita wouldn't want her son to give up his rights as Luca's father. Not that he was any kind of father.

"I did ask him," Anita said quietly, shocking Riley.

"*Really?*"

"I asked him to step away if he wasn't going to step up." She crossed herself and looked up at the sky.

"Wow. Thank you." Riley was deeply touched.

"Don't thank me. It didn't do any good. He just yelled and hung up. I haven't talked to him since. I don't know whatever happened to the sweet boy I raised."

"I married him and then one night he went to work and never came home." Riley remembered the almost instant change in Evan's personality.

Anita gave her a hug. "You know if it ever came down to it in court, I would take your side. That would have to count for something," she said.

Riley appreciated the sentiment, but she'd never be able to ask Anita to stand up against her own son. No matter how horrible he was now. "Thank you. The problem is I don't want it to go to court. They would force me to allow visitation, and I can't let Luca go across the country for weeks at a time. It's just better if we don't make waves. I can take care of Luca on my own. I'll be okay."

Anita smiled, but Riley could see what hid behind it. Doubt.

Riley was feeling the same way. Her savings account was nearly dry. She was getting a few orders for her jewelry, but so far she wasn't making a lot of money. She just needed to push on. Things would work out.

She dropped Luca off at home and got ready for her extra shift at the hotel. McKenna showed up right on time in her new-used car.

"So two more weeks until you're off to school, right?" Riley said.

"Actually it's only one more week." McKenna frowned as she looked into the living room where Luca was sitting on the sofa. "I'm only going to be able to watch him until Wednesday. I need to pack, and my mom wants to spend a day doing girl things before I leave."

"Of course! I'm sorry I got my weeks mixed up. I appreciate how much you've watched him. He has a great time with you. I'm sorry I couldn't pay you."

She gestured out at the car. "I got what I wanted out of the deal."

"I know, but I'm pretty sure he would have given you the car anyway."

"I'm pretty sure he would have too. But then he would have thought he had a right to boss me around. Now I can say it's mine."

"Smart girl." Riley laughed. "Luca, I need to go." He came over and she bent down to give him a kiss. "I love you."

"Love you, Momma." Those words would get her through her shift at the hotel.

She had this.

Sam sat down in the waiting room beside a large plant that was encroaching in his space. The place was small, with only four chairs. If he didn't sit next to the plant, he would have to sit next to the other lady without a buffer chair in between them. He'd have to deal with the plant.

He picked up a magazine and moved a leaf out of his face so he could read. Most of the times he'd had an appointment with a doctor, he sat in the waiting room for long periods of time. He never understood why he was supposed to arrive fifteen minutes before the appointment just so he could wait for thirty minutes past his appointment time.

Of course that wouldn't be the case with this appointment. Not when he wanted to put it off as long as possible. No. He couldn't catch a break.

The doctor opened the door and said good-bye to her teenage patient before turning her eyes on him.

"Sam?" Dr. Younger startled him even though he expected he was next.

"Yes."

"You can come on back." *Shit.*

He stood, knocking a leaf off the aggressive vegetation.

Her office wasn't what he expected. The furniture wasn't dark leather, and there wasn't even a couch. Everything was some shade of green. Moss, forest, hunter, he was sure it was supposed to be calming, but he felt like he was in the jungle.

Sam wondered how many Vietnam soldiers she saw for PTSD, and thought her color choice probably set them back on their recovery.

"Have a seat," she said. Sam sat in the first green chair inside the door, ready to escape if needed. He worried she might know why he chose that spot. Did that make him seem unstable? Hell, his mind was flying a million miles an hour and he broke out in a sweat.

The doctor sat down across from him and crossed her legs. She was wearing black slacks and flats. She was attractive enough, but the fact she could see into his thoughts made her too intimidating to consider. Besides, there was only one girl he wanted. And even though he'd rather jump out of the window than talk about his problems, he was going to stay and try to get better. For her. He needed to do this so he could be with Riley and Luca. And he needed to do it for himself too.

"So what's going on with you?" she asked as she flipped over a piece of yellow notebook paper.

He took a deep breath, ready to do his best. The only way to have Riley and Luca in his life was to get through this hell. He could do it. "Since I've been home, I've been jumpy around loud noises. I also have nightmares." He'd already filled out a novel-sized questionnaire so he knew she understood where he had been before he came home.

"Jumpy?" she asked, calling him on the understatement.

"Right. I react before I can think. Sometimes protectively, some-times . . . the opposite. My girlfriend has a three-year-old, Luca. He was playing with a toy gun and I yelled and broke it. I hurt his mother when I pulled her to the floor. It happens so fast."

"And what about the dreams?"

"Mostly it's the same thing every time. I had an issue a few years ago, but I was doing better until Luca tugged on my arm while I was in the middle of a terror. I woke up swinging, and he got hurt."

Sam swallowed down the lump that truth still brought to his throat.

"I hurt him." He rubbed his forehead. "His mother doesn't trust me to be safe around her boy, and I don't blame her. I don't trust my-self either. I would never hurt him intentionally, never. But I'm not myself when I'm having bad dreams or something startles me."

She nodded.

"Can you fix me?" he added.

She smiled. "I can give you the tools to help you fix yourself, but there are no guarantees. You might always have issues." Sam frowned. He had heard this same line from the last therapist. "It doesn't mean you can't have the life you want." That was exactly what it meant. "We can come up with ways for you, your girlfriend, and her son to cope with your sleeping issues. It would be the same as if you snored and kept them awake."

"Snoring doesn't land a little boy in the hospital with a busted lip and a concussion." Sam shook his head. "It could have been so much worse. What if I had snapped his neck?" Sam had tried very hard not to think about this possibility, but it was important this doctor knew what she was dealing with.

"Could you do that?" she asked.

"I've been trained how to do that sort of thing." And more. He could tell from her pale face she understood. He didn't need to go into the details.

She nodded and reached over to the edge of her desk to pick up a prescription pad.

"How's your blood pressure?"

"Fine," he answered as she began writing. "Look, I'd really rather not have to take some drug that makes me tired or loopy. Can't you show me how to meditate or something?"

"I'm not prescribing you an antidepressant. We've had some success with a blood pressure medicine that can help you sleep better. I'd like to start you on a very low dose and see if you notice a difference. If you feel dizzy stop taking it right away."

"Okay."

"We're also going to work at this from the outside, and yes, even meditation."

She laced her fingers together and rested them on her legs. It was a casual gesture, but Sam knew what came next. The hard part. Talking.

He had to tell her about the dream.

She asked very detailed questions. Things he had never noticed before, like how young the boy was that shot him. How many insurgents were coming up the hill? Had it ever changed? Did he feel responsible for his men?

That question took him by surprise. He knew he did feel responsible. They had been placed in his command. He was responsible for carrying out the mission and keeping them safe. But until she asked the question straight out, he didn't realize how much he felt responsible for their deaths.

The force of it hit him so hard, tears sprung to his eyes. He held them back, but barely.

"I'm sure you were briefed once you healed from your injuries?" she asked.

"Yes."

"And was it determined you had done anything wrong?"

"No. I followed protocol," Sam repeated the words he had been told. Empty words that couldn't bring back those men.

"But you have doubts?" she asked.

"Of course. Doesn't everyone wonder if there was something else they could have done to stop something bad?"

"Yes. That's completely normal. What have you come up with?" she pressed.

He shrugged. "I don't know."

"Okay. Let's look at it methodically, shall we?" She stood and handed him a large drawing tablet from her desk. "Let's draw it out. Show me where you were. Where your men were, and which direction the insurgents came from. I'm sure you remember every detail. Let's take a look."

He stared at the blank paper for a moment before he drew out the scene with a pencil.

When he was finished she asked him to walk her through different scenarios. Ways he could have avoided being closed in. Each time he came up with something, she had a countermove that cut him off again and again.

"There were just too many. Do you see?" she finally said after his last action failed. "You had two guys with you. There were eleven of them. You needed to get to the hill. There was no way to get to the hill without being surrounded. No matter how you played it. No matter what order you gave. It was impossible. You did your best. Now you have to find your peace with it. Because no matter what you could have done, it wouldn't have changed the outcome."

Sam nodded in defeat, though he was still looking at the paper trying to figure out another way. It had always been his fault. For the last six years, he carried the weight of that, despite the Purple Heart he kept in his sock drawer.

But looking down at the paper with all the futile scribbles, he realized it was a hopeless situation.

When he left the office twenty minutes later he felt lighter.

He'd always believed he'd failed because he didn't try hard enough. Now he knew the truth.

Sometimes people fail, no matter how hard they try.

* * *

Riley wiped her tears away before Luca noticed she was crying. He kept asking for Sam, and every time a truck drove down the alley behind their apartment, Luca would run to the window to see if he was there.

The lump and the fat lip were gone, but even after two weeks Sam was not as easily forgotten.

"Sam?" Luca asked as he sat at the table to eat his breakfast.

"Not today, sweetie."

"Workin'." That was what she used to say when Sam wasn't there. When he would be traveling and Luca would ask. She wouldn't lie to her son, but if that was what he assumed she would let him. At least for a little while longer.

"Come on. We have to go. We don't want to be late to Grammy's," she said when he was still chasing the last of his Fruit Hoops around his bowl.

"I don't want to go to Grammy's," he said, perfectly clear.

"Why not?"

"I want to stay here." She sighed. It did seem like the only time they spent at home was to sleep the few nights a week she didn't work at the hotel. Now that McKenna was back in school, it meant Luca was at Anita's all the time.

"In two more nights I will be off work and you and I can watch movies and make mini pizzas. How does that sound?" It would be Anita's bingo night and Riley didn't want her to miss it. Anita was giving so much, Riley wanted her to at least be able to go to bingo. Especially since the week before she'd won a hundred dollar gift card to a children's clothing store.

Riley had been able to get Luca clothes for fall. He was getting so big so fast.

"Can Sam come?" Luca asked.

"I'm not sure, baby. Come on. Let's go."

With a sigh, Luca got up and went to get dressed. He was a good boy, never throwing a fit, even when she felt like she wanted to.

She had become a master at catching a few moments of sleep at the desk between guests coming and going. Her shift was usually quiet. Tonight though, a group of cheerleaders had come to town for a competition. The hotel was full of squealing, giggling teenage girls who had limited supervision. She was getting calls all night. Two of them had locked themselves out of their rooms. One had been locked out on the balcony. There were complaints about not having enough towels and hot water. Not to mention the steady stream of boys sneaking into the hotel and back out.

She was exhausted by the time her shift was over. She stopped by Anita's to give Luca a kiss and then she was back out to shower and change before her shift at the jewelry store.

"You don't look so good," Pauline noted as Riley walked in.

"You say that almost every day. Maybe you should just tell me the days I look good. It might be more efficient."

"Maybe. I'll start another pot of coffee."

"Thank you. I should have brought a funnel so you can pour it in if I fall over."

"I'll find a way." Pauline laughed as she went to the back of the store.

Riley wanted to break down in tears. This was no life. Not for her or Luca.

She missed Sam like crazy. She missed his strong arms around her at night. She missed his kisses and his smile. She missed the comfort and stability he brought to her life.

"Excuse me?" the woman in front of her brought her back to reality.

"Yes. Sorry. I'll send it off for repair, and I'll give you a call when it's ready to be picked up." Riley snapped her smile in place.

"Do you want to take down my phone number so you can call me?" the woman asked with a brow raised.

"Right. Yes. I was just going to ask."

Riley wrote down the number and watched the woman leave. She needed to hold it together. Two jobs was a lot, plus her new jewelry business. But it meant she didn't have to worry so much about paying her bills and supporting her son.

She was doing it. So far.

Chapter 13

"Have you noticed a difference in your sleep?" Dr. Younger asked Sam as soon as he sat down in her office.

"Actually, yes. I only woke up a few times that I noticed." Not only was he feeling better rested, he sure didn't miss the dreams.

"Any dizziness?"

"No."

"I'm going to up the dose. See if we can't get it to be less than a few times."

They talked about some other things. Riley, for one.

"I feel like a jerk having Mrs. Fisher lie to her. But it's the only way I can help. Last week I had Mrs. Fisher tell her she won a gift card at bingo. This week I broke into her house to get the extra set of car keys, and I filled up her car while she was at work. She probably thinks she's going crazy. Her car keeps magically going back to full when it gets to a quarter of a tank."

"Do you feel responsible?" she asked.

Sam gave that a moment to consider before he answered.

"No. I want to help her because I know she's struggling and it's not right."

"But you think it's your fault."

"I'm sure she's not pushing for child support because of the incident with Luca. That's my fault. Although she wasn't pushing before either. Her ex might want to enforce visitation and he just moved to Arizona."

"What have your other relationships been like?" Dr. Younger asked.

"Other? I told you what happened with Jessica. I choked her, she panicked and kicked me out. There weren't any others after that."

"What about before you went in the service?"

Sam looked up at the ceiling while he thought it over.

"I had a few serious girlfriends in high school. As serious as you could get in high school. We talked about forever and stuff like that. Forever seems great when you're seventeen. Not so much later when you understand what it really means."

"So you've not had a serious relationship for a few years." It was a statement, not a question.

"No. Not until Riley."

"And you fought that every step of the way."

"Right."

"Why is that?" she asked.

"I don't know. You're the one with the fancy paper on the wall. You tell me." He smiled, hoping the dimples would save him. She seemed immune.

"Fine." She shrugged. "You're suffering from survivor's guilt. Both of the men you lost on that hill had wives and children. You don't think you deserve to have a family because they can't."

He knew she was right, but he shifted uneasily in his chair. She could see into the nooks and crannies of his head. Spooky.

"I'm going to suggest something you're not going to want to do," she told him.

"I don't really want to do any of this, but go ahead."

"You need to visit the families."

"I already did. As soon as I was released from the hospital I went. It's what we do when we lose people under us, we visit their families. Talk them up, tell them how great they were. I was lucky, because it was true of both of my guys."

"But you were there when their grief was fresh. I want you to follow up. See where they are now. It's been six years. They're not going to be the same people you met before."

"I don't think they'll appreciate me opening up old wounds."

"Trust me, you won't be opening up anything. Their wounds are just as exposed as yours are. It's not like they've forgotten. Do this." She wiggled her fingers at him, knowing how he teased her about being a witch. "Soon."

Sam had flown many times. Both in the marines and recently with his job with Dalton. Never had his stomach been such a mess as this flight to Colorado where Richard Desmond's family lived.

He had been married to his high-school sweetheart. They had three kids, the youngest, Little Richie, was three when Desmond died on that hill in Afghanistan.

It wasn't a surprise visit; he'd contacted RayAnn and asked to come. She smiled when she answered the door.

"Hi, Sam. How are you?"

"Fine," he answered, sounding casual.

"Really?" She led him to the kitchen, pulled out a beer and held it up.

"No." He sat at the island and nodded that yes, he wanted a beer.

"I figured you wanted to visit because you were either dealing with something, or because someone made you."

"Both, I guess." There was a picture of Desmond and the kids hanging on the refrigerator, along with other snapshots. RayAnn with another man. The kids, older, were lined up at the wedding.

"The kids will be home from school soon. I also asked Andy to stop by. He wanted to meet you."

"How are you doing?" Sam asked. After all, that was why he was there. To make sure she was okay.

"I'm good. It's different. Andy is so different from Richie. I never thought I would have fallen for someone like him. But I guess I changed too. Who knows, maybe Richie and I wouldn't have worked out." She took a sip of her iced tea. "Life is strange."

"I know. I was seeing a girl with a little boy. I never thought I wanted that responsibility. I didn't think I was cut out for it. But now we're apart, and all I want is to have them back so I can take care of them."

"And let them take care of you." He shrugged at that. "So stubborn." She rolled her eyes, making him laugh.

A man walked through the door then, offering a smile.

"You must be Sam. I'm Andy, Ray's husband. It's nice to meet you."

"Nice to meet you too," Sam said as he took him in. To say he was the exact opposite of Richie was an understatement. This man was short, thin and slightly balding. He had the word accountant written all over him. From his glasses, to his tie, to his polished loafers.

It didn't take long for Sam to see they were happy together. By the time the kids came in, Sam was sold on Andy Reynolds. Little Richie, now just Rich, was nine and already the spitting image of his father. The older girls were twelve and fourteen, and looked like trouble. But Andy interacted with them as if they were his own children.

"Was it hard?" Sam asked Andy when they were alone after dinner. "Getting involved with someone with all these kids?"

Andy smiled. "No. The kids were the least of my worries. I had more trouble getting RayAnn to take another chance. Kids love someone without fear. It's adults that can't seem to get out of their own way."

Sam laughed at that. "I'm in my own way a lot," he admitted.

"Ray said she hasn't seen you since right after Richie died. I bet you thought she was still going to be that grieving widow with the three little kids."

"Yes. That's how I've pictured them all these years."

"She's happy. The kids are happy. I don't pretend that they wouldn't be just as happy if Richie was here and I wasn't, but I do my best. We all go visit Richie's grave. At first it was just a stone with words, but because of them, I know the man he was. I feel guilty and grateful all at the same time. I hope he would be okay with me loving his family."

"I'm sure he would be okay with it." Who wouldn't want that for the family they left behind?

Sam left Colorado with a little less of the weight he carried around.

That night he woke up in the hotel room from a dream, but it wasn't a nightmare. He wasn't pinned down on a craggy hill in Afghanistan, he had been in Riley's bed. She was warm and naked as she slid her leg over him, her thigh teasing his growing erection as she giggled.

With a playful growl he rolled over on top of her. Blonde hair spilled across the pillows and she looked up at him with big, brown eyes. He felt like he could see everything in her eyes. All her worries, and pain and happiness. But most of all he saw love. She loved him and God, if he didn't love her so much his chest hurt.

He leaned down to seal their bond with a kiss and she was gone.

Gasping for air, he glanced down at his constricting boxers and frowned. It wasn't just the sexual frustration, he wanted to hold her and feel the way he felt before. He wanted to be loved.

"And you don't know what could be causing something like that?" Riley asked Cooper as he looked under the hood of her car.

"I'm sorry, I'm a lawyer not a mechanic. I have no idea why your car isn't using more gas. It didn't have this issue when we drove it. It seems like a good problem to have though." He shrugged.

"Until it blows up or something." Riley sighed.

"Maybe you're so tired you don't remember filling it up," Roz reasoned while watching Luca and Maddy playing in the backyard.

"Even if I forgot—which, okay, is possible—my bank account would remind me. I haven't gotten gas in almost a month. How can that be?"

"Maybe you paid in cash."

"I wouldn't have." She didn't think so anyway.

"It seems more likely that you *have* and then forgot, rather than that some *Fuel Fairy* is coming and filling your car with gas while you're sleeping."

"It doesn't happen while I'm sleeping, it happens while I'm at work." Riley bit her lip as she thought about the option of a Fuel Fairy. "Hold on a second."

Riley ran in her house and went to the drawer where she kept her extra keys. They weren't there.

So she had a Fuel Fairy after all.

"That—that—" She couldn't think of an acceptable term for the man who had taken the keys to her car to put gas in it without telling her. "*Sam.*"

She stormed back out to the yard as Cooper was shutting the hood.

"Can you watch Luca for an hour? I have to go take care of something," Riley asked.

"Sure. Can you pick him up at our house?"

"Yes. I'll see you there." Riley gave Luca a kiss and then headed off. First stop, Anita.

"I'm surprised to see you. It's your first afternoon off in weeks," Anita said as Riley walked in the house.

"I'm going to ask you a question and I want you to tell me the truth."

"Okay."

"The gift card you won at bingo?" Riley raised her eyebrows and Anita let out a sigh. "Was that from Sam?"

"Yes."

"What about the free groceries you got for being the one thousandth customer last week?"

"Sam."

"Did you know he's been filling up my car with gas while I'm at work?"

"I didn't, but he was trying to figure out a plan."

"Why would you help him do this?"

"Because he loves you and Luca, and he wants to help. He understands why he can't be part of your life, but he's trying. Maybe you could give a little."

"I can handle it on my own. I don't need his help." Riley refrained from stomping her foot.

"Riley," Anita said sternly. "You're not *handling* anything. You're a wreck. You don't sleep. You hardly eat. How long do you think you can keep this up? Sam wants to help. Sometimes it's a gift to the other person to allow them to give you a gift. Doesn't Sam deserve that?"

Riley understood what Anita was saying, but she didn't want to hear it. She didn't want to rely on Sam. She had to do it on her own. Because in the end she was the only person she could count on.

She left her mother-in-law's and went straight to Sam's apartment.

His eyes were huge as he opened the door. He wasn't wearing a shirt and for a second she thought she'd interrupted something.

"If you're with someone I can come back—"

"I'm not with anyone. Come in."

She stepped inside and held out her hand palm up. "Keys."

"Excuse me?" Was he really trying this tactic? She was a mother, for crying out loud.

"I know you have the extra set of keys to my car. I know you've been filling it up with gas while I'm at work. I want them back and I need you to stop."

"I just wanted to—"

"Help me. I get it. But I'm not your charity case."

His hazel eyes narrowed. "Do you honestly think that's why I'm doing this?" The muscles in his chest flexed. She only noticed because they were at eye level.

Sam had never been angry with her before. Despite his size, she wasn't frightened of him.

"Riley, I'm in love with you. If you think I'm going to sit over here across town and do nothing while you struggle to take care of the little boy, who I also love, you're crazy!"

"It's not right. It's my responsibility," she defended.

"I know." He calmed down, rubbing his hand over his face. "Nothing is right. If I wasn't so fucked up, I could be safe for you and Luca. We could be together like we should be." He looked so heartbroken she wanted to give up the fight.

It would have been so easy to wrap her arms around his waist and let his warmth take away all of her problems. "I don't blame you, Sam. It's just I can't risk it. What if Evan decides to push for custody? I have an incident on file with child services, while he is moving into a house with a stable partner and another child. I'm worried about my odds. I can't compete with a sometimes live-in boyfriend who suffers from PTSD and has a history of throwing my kid against a wall and giving him a concussion."

"I understand. Believe me, I know exactly why you don't want me around. I'm working on it, okay. I really am. But until I know I can be safe, please let me help. Please?"

"I don't like lying," she pointed out while pointing at him.

"I know. I don't like hardheaded women who can't accept a helping hand." He crossed his arms across his chest.

"No more sneaking around, or making other people lie for you."

"Agreed. Can I buy a few groceries? I seem to remember you liking the size of my peanut butter."

She couldn't help it, she smiled. She needed to be strong. She needed to keep distance between her and Sam. She knew if she saw him, she would want him. And wanting Sam right now wasn't a good thing. "I could probably use some peanut butter from time to time. But no more grand theft auto."

He nodded quickly. "Okay." Then he frowned. "You should probably know the gift card was from me too."

"Yeah. I figured it out." She rolled her eyes.

"I knew he would need clothes soon. He's growing so damn fast."

She didn't know how it was possible that Sam noticed important things like how fast Luca was growing, while Evan still hadn't sent Luca's birthday present.

"He is. I appreciate it. Thank you." She probably should have thanked him first instead of yelling. She didn't like feeling like a failure. "I'll work on being less hardheaded."

Sam sniffed. "I have a better shot of getting over my PTSD than you do getting over that." It was meant as a joke, but Riley frowned.

"I do hope you get through your issues, Sam. Not just so you will look good on paper, but for you. It can't be good walking around with all of that bad stuff inside of you."

"It's not. But I'm making progress," he said. She had noticed something lighter in his eyes. He didn't seem to be as haunted as he had been.

"Take care of yourself," she said as she moved for the door.

"You too. You look kind of worn out." She couldn't argue or even act offended. She knew she looked like hell. Worn out was a compliment. Her hair was a mess, and she had dark circles under her bloodshot eyes from lack of sleep.

"Yeah. I think I'm coming down with a cold or something." It wasn't an excuse, she didn't feel well. Just what she needed. She'd felt achy all day, and her nose was stuffy. Now her chest felt weird. "I'd better get going."

Sam leaned down and kissed her cheek.

"I hope you'll give me another chance someday." Great. Now her chest felt weird in a different way.

"I have three lots here for you to look at," Dalton said when Sam went in to work the next week.

After his visit from Riley he'd gone to Texas to visit with Mrs. Jackie Simmons. Like RayAnn, she had moved on. Not with a guy, but with her own business. She sold gift baskets, and was doing pretty well for herself and her daughter.

Jackie got a little teary when she saw him, but she pulled it together and assured Sam that they were fine, and they definitely didn't blame him for what happened.

With that second hurdle over, Sam was waiting for the magic to happen. Unfortunately, there was no such thing as magic when it came to healing from PTSD.

The medication seemed to be helping. He'd only had one nightmare in the last week, and that wasn't even about the blasted hill. It was about kittens. He surely wasn't going to tell anyone about the kitten dream.

He picked up the file Dalton had tossed on his desk.

"I heard back from Cooper. He looked over the agreement with McGuire. He says it looks straightforward. I have the accountant working the numbers now. In the meantime, I want to get ready to move once we decide. I don't want a lag time after we take over. We have guys who will want to keep working."

Sam flipped through the properties where they would potentially build the home he had designed. One in particular stood out. Four acres on a partially wooded lot in the foothills of the Blue Ridge Mountains. He shook the thought away before he could even start seeing himself there with Riley and Luca.

"Actually, I'm not sure I'm going to be buying a house. Riley and I kind of broke up."

"Seriously? I thought you were good to go." Dalton looked personally offended.

"I was. I am. It's just with my issues, I'm more of a liability."

"Issues?" Dalton tilted his head to the side.

"I have trouble sleeping." *Freaking kittens of all things!*

"Uh-huh." It was obvious Dalton could tell Sam wasn't telling him everything, but he didn't push for details, which made Sam grateful.

Fortunately they were interrupted by a tap at the door.

"Officer Porter, what brings you by?" Dalton asked Malcolm as he sat down. Malcolm Porter kept an eye on the warehouse and the business while Dalton and Sam were out of town. It was always nice to have a cop for a friend.

"I just got off duty. Anyone want to go get a drink?"

"Can't. And not just because it's only nine-thirty in the morning," Dalton answered for them.

"Come on. You guys work for yourselves. You can leave if you want to."

"We're getting ready to take on another business. And apparently my partner has issues, and broke up with his girl."

"Sorry, man," Malcolm said sincerely. "Well, if I can't corrupt you, I guess I'll go home and get some sleep. It was a toss-up anyway." With that he tipped his hat and left Sam alone with a miffed Dalton.

"I already have a few applications for people to take over your stuff on the road. Are you still planning to give that up?" Dalton asked.

"Yeah. I mean even if I can't be with Riley, I'm going to want to settle down someday, right? I might as well lay the groundwork."

"What do you think of the lots? If you're laying groundwork . . ."

Sam looked at the photos again. "Let me go out and take a look."

This turned out to be a bad idea.

He stopped at the one he liked best, and got out of the truck. He could see the way the house would be tucked in a clearing down a long driveway. It would be secluded. He liked that idea. The driveway would be great for the kids to ride their bikes. There was a tree at the edge of the yard that would be perfect for a clubhouse. There was a small creek. Surely Luca would have hours of fun getting muddy in that creek.

He and Riley could watch from the deck.

This was exactly what he hadn't wanted to happen. But no matter how hard he tried, he couldn't stop thinking about a future with Riley and Luca.

Another week had gone by and Riley was no closer to getting over Sam. He'd dropped off groceries while she was at work, using the key from the porch to bring them inside and put them away.

"I thought I said I was okay with *peanut butter*," she muttered to herself as she looked in the cupboards. They were full. Cereal. Snacks. There was fruit on the counter, and ice cream in the freezer.

Damn it, why did he have to make this so hard? She missed him and loved him, but what would happen if he caused her to lose Luca? She would never be able to forgive him for that, even though she knew it wasn't his fault.

On top of her broken heart and her foul mood, she was officially sick. She'd held it at bay, but unfortunately she was no match for the microscopic germs that had taken over her body. It was apparent by now the congestion in her sinuses and chest were not going to go away.

She popped a Dayquil and washed it down with a cup of coffee.

"Finish up and get dressed so we can get going," she told Luca. "You're going to go play with Maddy while I go to work." Even though she had just gotten off work an hour ago.

"Sam?" he asked as he did every day.

"Hey, look! Do you want some fruit snacks?" He was distracted enough to forget his question for the time being.

Three days later, the cold from hell had somehow gotten even worse. Pauline cringed every time Riley coughed and swayed. She was feeling a little off kilter, but she was sure it was just because she hadn't been sleeping well. A stuffy nose and an empty bed kept her tossing all night when she finally got the opportunity to go to bed. On top of that she now felt chilled and although she hadn't taken her temperature to know for sure, she no doubt had a fever.

"I think you should stay home tomorrow if this isn't better. Maybe you should go to the doctor again."

The truth was, Riley hadn't gone to the doctor at all. She let Pauline assume she had gone and didn't correct her.

What she had done was call Nic at the clinic and asked her to call in an antibiotic. When Nichole said she would actually need to see her first, Riley put it off. Riley didn't have time to spend sitting in the waiting room at the clinic. She had two jobs and a toddler.

She also had more groceries in her house when she got home.

"Damn it, Sam," she grumbled as she put them away. She hated that he kept bringing her groceries. After all, she wasn't helpless. She could feed and clothe her child. But knowing Sam did these things because he wanted to and it made him feel needed made her feel guilty for not allowing his help.

She sent him a text.

Stop bringing me food, I mean it! And thank you.

She added that last part right before she hit send, not wanting to seem ungrateful. If ever there was a mixed message it was that one.

In an effort to stop his coming in her house like some kind of peanut butter fairy-godfather, she went out to the porch and found her spare key under the pot where she kept it. She had to put her hand out on the wall to steady herself, having stood up too quickly. Squeezing the key in her palm for a second she deliberated, and then she walked back in the house and tossed the key on the counter next to the growing pile of bills.

The next morning, she moaned when Luca crawled in bed next to her. His skin felt ice cold against hers as she shivered.

"Momma, up?" he asked. He was probably hungry, and she needed to get up to go to work, but she didn't know how it was going to be possible in her condition.

She quickly calculated how much money she would lose if she didn't go in. Pauline would understand, but she couldn't afford to lose the day. Especially if it seemed inevitable that she was going to need to go to the doctor's. For real.

With all the strength she could muster she pulled back the covers and sat up on the edge of the bed. Luca had already run off, expecting her to be right behind him. Unfortunately, she was having difficulty. The room was slanted and her burning skin was covered in goosebumps.

As she made her way to the kitchen, it became very apparent this was worse than she thought. She obviously had a fever, probably a high one from the way her head was throbbing. She was also off balance. There was no way she was going to be able to drive.

Hell, she'd be lucky if she could make Luca's cereal.

She got a bowl down and filled it with Fruit Hoops, then focused on getting the milk out of the refrigerator and pouring it over the colorful circles in the bowl. In a fog she closed the refrigerator and carried the bowl to the table where Luca was sitting patiently.

She was royally screwed. It was time to do the mature thing and ask for help. Actually the time for the mature thing had been two days ago when she couldn't seem to lie down without coughing, but she was ready now.

Her cellphone was on the counter next to the refrigerator. She just needed to make it that far. She leaned on the counter and picked up the phone. She would call Anita and she would come over to help.

It was a simple goal—just a few swipes of her finger—but she didn't make it that far.

Chapter 14

With a deep breath, Sam walked into the jewelry store expecting to see the frown line on Riley's forehead. He'd had a breakthrough at therapy the day before, and he decided he was ready to get his life back.

The first step started with Riley and Luca. He hadn't had a dream in the last week, kittens, insurgents, or otherwise, and Dr. Younger had made some suggestions to help keep Luca safe until he was old enough to understand not to touch Sam while he's asleep.

He glanced around the small shop and was surprised when only Pauline greeted him.

"Hi Sam. What can I do for you?" she asked.

"I stopped in to see Riley." It was nine-thirty. She should have started her shift a half hour ago. "I brought muffins."

"You're so sweet, but she's not here. You must not have spoken to her or you would know how awful sick she is. Poor thing. I told her to stay home."

"I'll go check in with her," he said, leaving the muffins with the woman who was eyeing up the bag. "Thanks."

He was disappointed that Riley wasn't there. He had psyched himself up to state his case, and the delay was making him nervous all over again.

He tapped his fingers against the steering wheel as he drove down her street and parked in the alley behind her apartment. As he got out of the truck he thought maybe he should have stopped to get her tissues or cough medicine. Some gesture to show he cared. But the screams coming from the house made every thought fall right out of his head.

"Luca?" he called as he stepped up on the porch. He knocked on the door, but didn't wait for anyone to answer before he went to the window to peer inside.

Luca was screaming as if he was being tortured, and every instinct Sam had told him to get inside that house. The air conditioner blocked his view on the bottom half of the window so he leaned up to look in through the top part.

Blood.

Luca was sitting on the floor in the kitchen next to the counter with blood all over him. Where was Riley? Why wasn't she helping him?

Sam went to the pots at the side of the porch and picked up the one where she kept the spare key. Nothing. He picked up two more and then pushed them all over trying to find the key. It wasn't there.

"What the hell?"

Luca let out another long wail and Sam couldn't think. All he could do was act. Without consciously planning it, he grabbed hold of the air conditioner and ripped it out of the window, letting it crash to the floor, bits of plastic and splintered wood scattered at his feet.

A second later he was climbing through the window to help the little boy.

"Luca? What's wrong?" he asked, but then he saw her.

Riley was lying on the floor in a large puddle of blood. Her skin was pale, her blonde hair stained red. Small bloody footprints marked the floor where Luca had ran down the hall. Hops, his white bunny sat next to Riley, soaked with blood.

Sam pulled his phone and dialed 9-1-1 at the same time he checked Luca over. None of the blood appeared to be his own. Sam told the woman on the phone to send an ambulance and repeated Riley's address twice before he hung up.

He paused a second and ran his hand over his hair before he gathered enough courage to reach down to check for a pulse.

His mind raced. *Please don't let her be dead. Please don't let her be dead. Please,* he repeated over and over as his hands shook and Luca continued to cry next to him.

Then he felt it. A faint thump against his fingertips, nearly made him weep with relief. She was alive, but for how long? She was bleeding from a head wound. There was so much blood.

For a moment, Sam's mind transported him to another place where there was too much blood. He remembered seeing his own blood dripping from his fingertips into the sandy soil beneath him.

"Momma!" Luca said while tugging at Sam's T-shirt. The little boy left bloody stains on the white cotton and Sam forced the panic down so he could deal with what was happening now. He didn't have a bullet wound on a hill half a world away. He was in Riley's kitchen and she needed him.

"Luc, stay back. Your mommy is going to be fine." Sam stood and went to the drawer with the dishtowels. He grabbed a bunch and brought them over.

Turning Riley just enough to be able to put a folded towel on her head he applied pressure to the wound.

"Come on, baby. Please be okay." He couldn't help but notice how hot her skin was. She was burning up. Pauline had said she'd been sick. Why hadn't she called for help? Luca was still crying, but that wasn't the sound Sam had honed in on.

Sirens.

He could hear them coming closer as he remembered the door was still locked. When the sirens got near he let go of Riley's wound long enough to open the door and run out to flag them down, then ran back to her.

He kneeled there in the kitchen with a screaming boy clinging to his arm as medical personnel flooded the room, yelling terse commands. The smell of blood filled the air.

He needed to run. To get away as quickly as possible before he snapped. But before he had the chance, he felt a tug at his knee and heard Luca say, "S-S-Sam."

Sam's feet were grounded to the floor. He couldn't go. It wasn't an option.

He picked up the trembling boy and held him tight, his little arms wrapped around Sam's neck in a way that said he wouldn't let go. Ever.

People shouted vitals and commands to one another as one of them asked Sam questions he couldn't answer.

"She was home sick. Her boss said she had a bad cold. Her skin feels hot."

"She may have passed out and hit her head on the way down.

She's lost a lot of blood, but her injury isn't life threatening. Is the boy okay?" the man asked.

Luca was still clinging to Sam for all he was worth.

"He's just scared."

As they loaded Riley on the gurney, Sam noticed how small she looked. She wasn't a big person but she seemed too tiny for someone so fierce and capable. Sam walked alongside her as they wheeled her outside and loaded her in the back of an ambulance.

He wasn't asked to ride along and he knew he couldn't. As much as he wanted to be with Riley, he needed to help Luca first. Riley would want that.

"We can't take him with us," the man pointed at Luca. "We'll take care of her. By the time you get to the hospital they might have some information on her condition."

Sam nodded woodenly and looked down at Luca.

"Momma," Luca whispered when they closed the doors on the ambulance.

"She's going with the doctors so they can make her better. We're going to clean up and then we'll go see her, okay?" Sam wiped at Luca's red, puffy eyes as he nodded. Sam gave him a kiss on his forehead next to a bloody smear.

"Uh-oh," Luca said, clutching his wet pants.

"It's okay, buddy. It's okay."

He turned to go back in the house and was faced with a police officer.

"Do you live here?" he asked.

"Uh. No."

"Is the boy yours?" Sam instinctively pulled Luca closer, as if the officer was going to rip him from his arms. What could he do if that happened? He had no rights. Only an incredible desire to take care of Luca.

"No," he answered honestly, because he was certain lying to a cop wasn't going to help his situation.

"I can vouch for him," someone said from behind Sam. He turned to see Malcolm Porter walking closer.

Sam nearly fell down with relief. "Thank you."

"So what happened?" Malcolm asked while pointing at the porch.

"When I got here, Luc was screaming and Riley was lying on the floor. So I"—he gestured toward the window—"I ripped out the air conditioner so I could get inside."

"Why didn't you use a key?"

"I don't know where it is." He didn't go into the details about not having one of his own. The truth was, he didn't know where it was.

Malcolm wrote something down in his notebook as Luca squirmed.

"Can we go in so I can get him cleaned up?" he asked. Luca was wet and smeared with blood.

"Sure."

Sam carried Luca down the hall and started water for his bath.

"You want Colonel Scrubs?" Luca shook his head, his fingers were still tightly wound in Sam's shirt.

He gave Luca a bath, which was difficult since the kid wouldn't let go of Sam for a second. Sam answered Malcolm's questions as best he could.

"It doesn't look good, you breaking in with a woman bleeding on the floor. It's a good thing I know you, or you would probably be in the back of a car until the girl woke up and could answer some questions."

"Then I'm really glad you showed up."

"If you had broken in and hurt the girl, her little boy probably would be afraid of you instead of clinging to you like a barnacle."

As soon as Luca was out of the tub he was latched on to Sam's neck again.

"That's as good of an answer as any," Malcolm said, closing his tablet.

"Is it okay to clean up the mess in the kitchen?" Now that it wasn't going to be a crime scene with yellow tape and him hauled off to jail. He hadn't even considered the way it looked. All he cared about was getting to them.

"Sure. Let me know if you need anything." Malcolm waved and left.

Once Luca was dressed, Sam set him on the counter while he cleaned up the floor. He didn't want Riley to come home to that.

God, he hoped she would come home. He glanced worriedly at Luca.

Sam wanted to go to the hospital to find out how Riley was doing, but he was also putting it off. He hated hospitals. He'd had to stay in one for a while after he was shot. He hated the way they smelled and the sounds.

"Momma hurt," Luca said, pointing to the bloody towels as Sam tossed them in the trash.

"She's okay. We're going to go see her." When everything was cleaned up, he put Luca on the floor and looked down at his own stained shirt. He had left clothes here. Hopefully Riley hadn't tossed them. He went to her room with his little shadow hot on his trail.

Sure enough, on the shelf in Riley's closet he found a black T-shirt and changed it out. "You ready?" he asked Luca as the boy watched him from the doorway. He wouldn't let Sam out of his sight.

"Hops?"

"Hops is in the sink soaking. He's dirty. He can't go with us."

"Hops?" he repeated as if Sam hadn't offered a perfectly good excuse.

"No Hops. Let's take someone else. How about the duck?" What the hell was the duck's name? "Um. Mr. Quacks!"

After they retrieved the duck, Sam searched for Riley's cellphone. It wasn't plugged in on the counter by the refrigerator where she usually kept it.

He had Cooper's number, who could tell Roslyn, but he knew they were out of town on vacation. He didn't have Mrs. Fisher's number. He checked Riley's purse and the bedroom. Nothing.

"Do you know Grammy Fisher's phone number?" he asked Luca who stared back at him like he was insane. "Do you know Grammy Fisher's real name? What's her first name?"

Sam had only ever called her Mrs. Fisher and he was certain that wasn't going to help him locate her number in the directory, not that he could find one. "Okay. Never mind."

Since it was almost noon, he decided he'd better feed Luca before they left. He made him a sandwich and tried to be patient as he nibbled at it. Sam tossed some crackers into a Ziploc bag for later and then went to the door.

"Let's go check on Mommy."

"Momma hurt," he said again.

"But the doctors are fixing her up, so don't worry." Sam was worried enough for both of them.

He loaded Luca and Mr. Quacks into Riley's borrowed car, not wanting to mess around with the car seat. He'd taken her keys from her purse along with her wallet in case she needed something from it.

As expected, he was assaulted by the antiseptic smell as he entered the hospital. Luca was once again stuck to his neck like a baby monkey, and he leaned closer so he could smell the kid's shampoo instead of the sterile smell that surrounded him and made his body tense.

It worked.

"Riley Fisher, please."

The person behind the information desk smiled as she looked at her monitor.

"Are you family?" she asked.

"Yes," Sam said. At least one of them was.

"Third floor. It looks like she's been admitted for the night."

"Thank you," Sam said, not liking the idea of her being admitted. Although if they'd noted on her chart it was only for the night, maybe it wasn't that bad.

At the third floor nurses' station he was given the details. "Room three twelve. She has pneumonia, an upper respiratory infection, and an inner ear infection. She most likely got dizzy and fell. She has six stitches in her head and needed a unit of blood. She's sedated and will probably be out for the night." The nurse gestured toward the correct hall and with another "thanks," Sam and Luca went to see her.

"Momma sleeping," Luca whispered and put his index finger in front of his lips.

"Yes. She is. She's very tired." Sam sat in the chair and situated the duck so it wasn't in his face.

"Boo boo," he said, pointing to the gauze on her forehead.

"Yes. She has a boo boo."

"I kiss it." Luca did his squirm maneuver to get down, but Sam held on firmly and carried him over to his mother where he dangled the boy close enough he could kiss her forehead without touching anything important.

They sat in her room all afternoon as doctors and nurses came in to check on her. She was given a breathing treatment. When Luca became upset at seeing his mother with the mask over her face, Sam took him for a walk.

They came back and at some point both he and Luca fell asleep. They'd had a rough morning, and they were both exhausted.

They were awakened by a different nurse who looked irritated. "Visiting hours are over. You'll need to come back tomorrow."

Maybe it was being woken up, maybe it was the kink in his neck from sitting in a crappy chair. Maybe it was the fact the woman woke up Luca who was now crying. Or maybe it was just the fact that she looked like a snooty bitch who liked to wield her power over the commoners, but Sam glared at the woman before telling her where she could put her visiting hours.

"And I'll tell you something else! I've served three tours in Afghanistan, and this little guy was found sitting in a pool of his mother's blood crying his heart out when I got to him. If you don't think we've earned the right to stay in this crappy chair for the night, you can go fuck yourself."

"Fuck!" Luca chimed in.

"No, Luc. That's a bad word, don't say that."

"Fuck!" he repeated.

"Oh, shit," Sam said in defeat.

The nurse rolled her eyes and left the room. He'd won the battle, kind of.

"Chit," Luca said.

"Shh. Go back to sleep." To Sam's surprise, he listened.

Sam didn't fall back to sleep right away. He stretched out his legs, making sure not to disturb Luca.

Then he sat watching Riley's chest rise up and down the way it was supposed to.

She could have died today. She could die on her way to work in an automobile accident the way Georgie's husband had. He would have been devastated with loss. He should have been ready to run from the hospital to avoid the potential pain, but instead he squeezed Luca a little closer and rubbed the back of Riley's hand.

He loved her.

There was no turning back now.

Chapter 15

When Riley woke up it was dark and she felt as if something heavy was sitting on her chest. She looked around the room and her gaze fell on the two men sitting in the chair next to her bed.

One of them wasn't exactly a man yet. Though some days he seemed to think he was. Luca looked comfy where he lay against Sam's big chest. Sam on the other hand looked uncomfortable in the silly chair.

A nurse walked in with a bag of clear fluid. "How are you feeling? Any pain?" the woman asked. The sound of her voice caused Sam and Luca to wake up.

Luca pointed at the woman. "Fux jurself," he said with a frown.

Riley looked over at Sam who was wincing.

"Seriously?" Riley said, her voice sounded like a frog that had been run over by a truck.

"Ma'am, I'm very sorry about that," Sam said to the nurse. "Luca, tell the nice nurse you're sorry. She's helping your mommy."

"I'm sorry, ma'am." Luca looked at Sam for approval.

"They were both so worried about you, they forgot their manners," the nurse explained with a smile. "The doctor will be in to check on you and go over the plan."

"Can I go home?" Riley couldn't help but ask.

"Maybe in the morning." The nurse wrote something on the whiteboard and left. It wasn't as if Riley could argue. She sounded like death, and felt pretty close.

"How are you feeling?" Sam asked as Luca shimmied down and tried to get up on her bed. Sam leaned over and gave him a little lift and Luca crawled from her feet up her body until he was by her face.

"Boo boo," he announced while pointing at her head.

"You must have been so scared. I'm sorry, baby." Tears came to her eyes as she thought about what trauma she'd subjected her child to. Would he grow up to be a serial killer? There weren't any more available outlets in his room for additional night lights.

"He was upset when I found you, but he seems fine now," Sam told her. "He fell asleep with no problems."

"You found me?"

"Yeah. I stopped by to talk to you. I'll apologize now for your air conditioner." She didn't care about the air conditioner. Someone had given it to her, and she barely used it in an effort to keep her electric costs down. "The key was missing and I had to get inside."

More tears ran down her cheek.

"I was trying to stop you from helping me," she admitted.

He shook his head. "Key or no key, I'm still going to help you, Ri." He stood and came to sit on the edge of her bed. "You can't get rid of me that easily. I came to tell you I'm making progress in therapy. I'm taking a medication that's helping with the nightmares. I'm trying to get better, so I can be good enough."

She started full out crying which prompted a horrible coughing fit. Sam picked Luca up as a nurse came in, followed by the doctor. They put a clear mask over her mouth and told her to take deep breaths. The task seemed impossible as more coughing racked her body. Every breath felt like fire in her lungs. Eventually the fit subsided.

"Ms. Fisher, you have pneumonia and an inner ear infection. We're going to need to keep you here for a few days," the doctor said.

Panic set in as she immediately shook her head and pointed to Luca.

"I'll take care of him," Sam said. "He'll be fine, I promise."

She wasn't able to speak, but she didn't need to. Sam seemed able to understand her thoughts.

"Don't worry about work and bills right now." His deep voice soothed her a little bit. "You need to rest and get better. We'll figure things out later. I'm going to take him home now that he's seen you awake. We'll be back tomorrow."

She mouthed the words "thank you" from behind the mask as whatever they'd injected into her IV started pulling her under.

Sam was there. Her hero.

* * *

It was two days before Riley was released from the hospital. She couldn't wait to get out.

Sam and Luca had come to visit her as much as possible. Luca had fussed and whined when it was time to go, but he listened to Sam.

"Thank you for cleaning up," she said as she looked at the spot on the floor where she had fallen. Unfortunately she'd been dizzy when she fell and hadn't blacked out completely until she was on the floor with blood everywhere.

She remembered hearing Luca call her name, and not much after that. She kissed Luca's hair at the memory and set him down so he could go get all the pictures he'd drawn while she was away.

Sam pulled out a chair and pointed.

"I'll make you some tea. The doctor said it will help."

"I don't have any tea."

"I got some yesterday." He opened her cupboard and pulled down a variety box of tea. "What kind do you like? Earl Grey? Breakfast Blend? Mint? Lemon?"

"Earl Grey is fine. Thank you."

She started to get up to help, but he pointed at the chair again.

"Unless you're going to agree to wear a hard hat, I'd appreciate if you would sit until my hands are free to catch you. Just in case."

She smiled at him.

"I love you, Sam."

He paused in what he was doing for a moment and then nodded before going on. "I love you too. We need to come up with a better plan. Kicking me out of your lives isn't working for me," he said.

"Okay." It wasn't working for her and Luca either. He brought her the tea and sat down next to her.

"My therapist suggested we sit down with the agent at child services, and make sure my being with you doesn't impact your custody arrangement. A lot of people have PTSD, and they have kids and lives. My life is at a standstill right now, and I'm miserable. Can we work this out?" he asked point blank before he added, "Please."

She looked into his hazel eyes and knew what he meant. Her life felt like it was at a standstill, or worse a tidal wave. She was miserable, and not just from the pneumonia.

"Yes," she answered simply. "Before I got so sick, I had been reading up on PTSD while at the hotel. I read a few articles on how to deal with this. I don't want to lock Luca out in case he needs us, but we could put bells on the door so it wakes us when he comes in."

Sam swallowed loudly and looked up at the ceiling as if praying. "Thank you," he said as Luca ran in with colorful papers trailing behind him.

Sam had his life back.

The contracts were all signed, and he and Dalton were set to take over McGuire Builders the next week. Sam would have a steady job in town doing what he loved. And when his day was over he was able to come home to Riley and Luca. The people he loved.

As Riley suggested, they installed bells on the door knob of Riley's room that would ring when Luca came in the bedroom. Dr. Younger had agreed with Riley. She didn't like the idea of locking the door—at least for sleep—as it might stress Luca if he couldn't get to Riley when he needed to.

They also had a talk with him about staying on Riley's side of the bed if he needed to come in. Luca seemed more than willing to avoid getting thrown against the wall again. He occasionally brought up the incident, and every time Sam felt like crap. It wasn't that Luca was scared of Sam or angry. It was just what it was. Something horrible that had happened.

Sam carried Luca into the offices at Child Services and instinctively pulled him a little closer, as if a horde of workers would come steal him away. It would take a horde to get Luca away from Sam. He would protect the boy with his life.

"Ms. Fisher? You can come on back."

It was a different woman than the one who had been at the hospital. Sam took Riley's hand as they walked back the hall together. She squeezed it tightly. Tighter than he would have expected for someone so small. She was fierce, and not to be underestimated. He'd learned that by now.

"Have a seat. I'm guessing you are Sam, and this is Luca, right?"

Luca nodded and Sam said, "Yes, ma'am." Which made Luca repeat him.

The woman smiled. "I'm Evelyn Winters. I took over your case. It's not every day that someone wants to make an appointment to come talk to us." She seemed surprised.

Riley looked at Sam. They hadn't discussed who would be doing the talking, but it appeared it was going to be him.

"Uh. Yes. Well." He swallowed and rubbed his hand on his pants. "We had an incident, and I accidentally hurt Luca when I was having a nightmare."

"Yes. That's in the file. You suffer from PTSD."

"Yes. But I've been seeing a therapist, and I'm on medication to help with that. I still have an occasional nightmare, but we've taken measures to make sure Luca stays clear of any possibility of getting caught up in one." He held Luca closer. Luca's fingers were clenching his T-shirt, as if he was expecting the horde too.

"It says here it was suggested that Sam be removed from the household until he was deemed safe." She flipped over a paper.

"Yes. Here is a letter from my therapist. She's willing to talk to you personally if you want." Sam thought he might suffocate while the woman scanned the document he handed her.

Finally she looked up and took off her reading glasses. "I don't think that will be necessary. She's pretty clear in this letter that you're no danger to Luca."

Sam wasn't sure if he agreed with the letter. There was really no way to guarantee that. But as Dr. Younger had said, other people live with this every day and they have kids. They find a way to work around it and keep everyone safe.

"Our main concern is how this might affect a custody hearing if Riley's ex-husband tried to push for full custody. I don't want this to be used against her."

The woman flipped to the front of the file and scanned another paper.

"Evan Fisher?"

"Yes," Riley said, after clearing her throat. She was sounding more like herself and less like a duck.

"He lives in Arizona?" the woman asked, her brow pinched while she slipped the glasses on again.

"Yes."

"He's court ordered to pay support through garnishments, and I don't see any record of anything for two months."

"That's right," Riley said.

"He's not working?" Ms. Winters asked.

"I don't believe so," Riley answered. "Is there any way to force him to give up his rights to Luca? If he's not paying support, can I have his rights revoked?"

"You could try, but it probably wouldn't work. If he's not willing to sign off, you'd be hard pressed to get anything better than a ninety-ten split on custody. As for the support, you would need to file a complaint with domestic relations and they could go after him for it."

"But you're sure he can't use this issue with Sam to try to take Luca from me?"

"Again, he could try, but he wouldn't have any more luck with that than you would with getting his rights revoked. It would just be a lot of name calling and finger pointing and in the end the judge would most likely keep things the way they are now."

Riley seemed to relax next to Sam. He wanted to relax too, but there was something still bothering him about the idea that Evan could just come by one day and take Luca back to Arizona for a week or more. Luca belonged with him and Riley, not with strangers. Evan was a stranger, despite his DNA.

Riley smiled as they left the office holding hands. "I feel better. How about you?" she asked.

"Yeah," he said. He did feel better.

"What?" She could read him well.

"I don't like that he still has a claim on Luca. Evan's a wild card. It makes me nervous," he shared. "I feel . . . helpless."

"Welcome to my world," she said. "Who wants ice cream?"

"Me!" Luca said with big eyes.

They went for ice cream like any other family. Then they went home and got Luca ready for bed before they climbed in bed together and relieved the stress that had been bottling up since making the appointment.

Riley had a strength about her that made her seem invincible. But when she softened in his arms and cried out his name in passion, he could see the soft sweet parts that made her everything he would ever want.

The next night after work, Sam stopped by to pick up Luca at Grammy Fisher's house.

Riley was working a later shift at the jewelry store. She'd agreed to cut back her shifts at the hotel. Sam was ready to broach the topic of moving in again, but thought he'd give it a couple more days.

"Hello, Mrs. Fisher. How's our boy today?" Sam asked as he stepped into the woman's living room.

She gave him a smile as Luca came running, arms up.

"Oh, my goodness. You've gotten heavier since I held you this morning. Did you eat Hops or something?" Sam joked.

Luca giggled and shook his head.

"Luca, why don't you show him the picture you drew today," Anita—he'd asked her first name—suggested.

"Oh, no," Sam said as he let Luca slide down to his feet. "How bad is it?" He winced remembering the drawing of them in bed together.

"I don't think it's bad at all, really. We'll see what you think."

Luca shoved a paper at him. It was a mess of colors and scribbles.

"What is this?" Sam asked.

"My mommy and daddy and me," he said, pointing at what was most likely the body of his daddy.

"Oh. It's very good." Sam nodded.

"And what is this?" Mrs. Fisher prompted her grandson while pointing to the mass of color in the middle of the blob.

"Tattoo," Luca explained.

"What is the tattoo of, Luca?" she continued. Sam got the impression she was going somewhere with this, but Sam didn't know what tattoos Evan had.

Luca didn't answer, instead he pointed at Sam's chest where his tattoo was.

"Dis," he said.

"Does Evan have a tattoo like mine?" Evan wasn't in the marines so Sam doubted it would be the eagle, globe, and anchor he had on his chest.

"Evan doesn't have any tattoos."

Sam looked at the drawing again in confusion.

"Who is this?" he asked the little boy as he pointed to the blob he'd just said was his daddy.

"You," Luca said.

"And who am I?"

"Daddy." Oh. Shit.

He looked up at Mrs. Fisher who was smiling down at him. Why was she smiling?

"I didn't tell him to call me that," Sam told her.

"I know. Christian was over this afternoon. He drew a picture of his mom and dad, and Luca drew you and Riley. Apparently he thinks of you in that way."

"Oh jeez."

"You act more like his father than my son ever has," she said as she patted Sam's shoulder.

"Still, don't you think it's disrespectful?" Not that he felt Evan deserved any respect. After all, what kind of respectable man leaves his family and won't help provide for them? But still this was Anita's son. He didn't want her to be upset.

"More disrespectful than a man cheating on his wife and then moving away so he doesn't have to support his child?" So she did get it. "No. My son should just waive his rights if this is how he's going to act. That way Riley wouldn't need to worry so much."

"Riley has been saying she wants him to sign off. Do you think she really means it or is she just angry?"

"She definitely means it."

"Is there any chance you might be able to—?"

"I've already tried and he refused. I don't know where I went wrong with Evan. If his father were here . . ." She made that look like it would have been a horror. "Honestly, I'm embarrassed to call him my son. I'd rather adopt you the same way Luca has."

Sam swallowed, understanding the honor this was. He'd never considered himself good enough to be anyone's father. While he wasn't going to correct Luca on calling him Daddy, he wasn't going to encourage it either.

He didn't know what Riley would think about this. If she got spooked and worried Luca was getting too close to him, she might try to run Sam off again.

"Let's not mention this to Riley, okay?" he suggested. Mrs. Fisher nodded with a grin.

He loaded Luca in his truck and got in the driver's seat. It took him a few minutes to start the truck and leave. He was having trouble breathing.

Luca had called him his daddy. This was a very big deal. He was both thrilled and scared to death. He was tired of being in between. He needed to commit or bail, and he needed to decide before it was too late for all of them.

*　*　*

Sam was acting weird. She wasn't sure what was going on. She only knew that every time she asked him if he was okay, his lips said yes, while his eyes said no.

"I have a meeting tonight, so I need to get going," he explained after dinner.

"Okay. Will you be coming back?" she asked.

"I don't think so. I need to stop by my place and I'll be heading out the next morning."

"I thought you didn't need to go away anymore." He had told her he was taking over for a local builder so he could be home more.

"I have something I need to take care of first."

"Oh. All right. Well, have a nice trip," she said. She was sure he hadn't mentioned having a trip scheduled. She kept track of his schedule on the calendar so she could show Luca when he asked. She even showed him what state Sam was in on his map puzzle when Luca wanted to know where Sam was.

Something twisted in her stomach.

Had Luca called Sam *Daddy* to his face? She knew he had been referring to Sam as Daddy lately and she'd tried her best to explain that Sam wasn't his father, and that his daddy had moved away. But Luca was three. Explaining biology and geography to a three-year-old was like herding cats.

"I'll check in with you later, okay?" Sam gave her a kiss, and then gave Luca a hug and a high five before he left. There was something about his kiss that made her nervous. Mostly it was because *he* was nervous. She could feel the tension in his lips when they touched.

"Sure." She knew what this was. The beginning of the end. He was running.

She fought the urge to cry as she watched his truck pull away. She knew this could happen. She had tried her best to keep her heart protected so it wouldn't hurt so much, but damn if he hadn't found a way in anyway.

It wasn't a surprise when Sam didn't call her the next day, or the next. She helped a couple pick out wedding bands and bit her lip to keep from breaking down. This was not the Riley she knew herself to be. She was stronger than this.

The last time she had been left alone with a baby. She took care of herself then, she could take care of herself now. She didn't need Sam.

If only that were true.

* * *

Sam was way out of his element. After speaking with Cooper and getting the proper paperwork, he now found himself standing at Evan's door hoping to God he was doing the right thing. Riley had said many times how she wished she could be free of Evan. He was taking her at her word.

Arizona was fucking hot. People always said it was a dry heat, but heat is heat.

It was worse because Sam was nervous. He needed to make sure he applied the appropriate amount of pressure without losing his cool. Losing his cool seemed inevitable when it was a hundred and two degrees in the shade.

Malcolm had warned him about keeping his temper in check before he left. And if he failed, Mal said to have the Arizona police call him.

"Hello?" a woman who could only be described as Riley's exact opposite greeted him as she opened the door. She was tall and large boned with black hair.

"Um, yes. I would like to speak to Evan if he's available." Sam was surprised by how pleasant his voice sounded.

"Of course he's available. Where would he be? Work?" She snorted at this and backed up to let Sam inside. "Someone's here to see you."

Evan was sitting on the sofa playing a video game and wearing a headset. He paused the game, but left the headset on. As if Sam needed another thing to push him over the edge, the guy was the poster-child for losers. The only thing that would make it official was if he lived in his mother's basement.

Sam smiled at the thought. No way would Anita Fisher allow her son to live in her basement. But Sam might have a shot.

"What the hell are you doing here?" Evan asked, standing up and moving toward the door. As if Sam had flown the whole way to Arizona to beat him up. "Is this about the support?" Evan asked as his glance flickered toward Celia. "I'm doing the best I can. I can't pay any more than I am."

Sam gave him a doubtful look and also glanced at Celia who had her arms crossed impassively.

"You can't pay more than you are?" he repeated in disbelief. "You haven't paid anything in months."

Evan immediately got defensive. "That's not true. I just sent her money last week." Again he glanced toward Celia and Sam was starting to put it together.

"How did you send this money last week? A check, money order?"

"Cash."

"You sent three hundred dollars in the mail?" Celia stepped in. "Are you crazy?"

Sam didn't think Evan was crazy as much as lying, but he bided his time.

"Is she saying she didn't get it?" Sam had to hand it to him, Evan was a pretty good actor. The guy was doing a fair impression of concern.

"What about the other payments?" Celia asked.

"Others?" Sam said, raising his brows.

"Yes. Evan sends her a hundred dollars a week. Except he missed the last three weeks so he paid them all at one time."

Sam swallowed and looked at Evan, giving him the opportunity to fix this on his own. He wasn't surprised when Evan sat there staring at his feet waiting for the final blow.

Sam shrugged and turned to Celia. "Riley hasn't received a payment since before you left Roanoke. He came to her home telling her she was going to have to be patient because he wasn't going to be able to pay anything for a few months."

"But that doesn't make any sense. He's sent—" She seemed to hear what she was saying and stopped talking. "What have you been doing with the money, Evan?" She came to stand in front of him, and she looked more than impassive. She looked downright hostile.

"I'll figure out what happened and take care of it. This is between me and my ex," Evan tried, but Celia wasn't having it.

"Except it was my money."

"We're married, Celia. Your money is my money."

"We'll see about—"

"Excuse me," Sam interrupted. He had a return flight to catch. "I'm not here about the money."

"You just came here to stir up trouble," Evan assumed.

"I came to talk to you about signing over your rights."

At this announcement, Celia sat down looking confused. Evan said nothing, so Sam took a deep breath and went on. "You have a nice home here, and a great family." Sam glanced around at the neat house. Celia relaxed at the compliment. "But you left people back in Roanoke that were your family too."

Evan had the decency to look away in shame.

"All I want is to pick up the pieces of that family so Riley and Luca and I can move on and make our own. But that's difficult if you still have this hold over them. Especially when you're still threatening to take custody."

He saw Celia's back stiffen. She was a mother. Despite how she might feel about Riley, she could put herself in her position. She glared at Evan and he cringed.

"It's not true. I never threatened to take custody."

"Why would this guy fly all the way out here to make this up? Why?" Celia's voice raised a full register.

Sam pulled out the forms Cooper had given him. "I have the papers right here. All we need to do is go to a notary and you can sign them and I'll go. You won't have to worry about child support again. Evan, it's time to do the right thing by your son. You need to be a man."

Chapter 16

When Riley went to Anita's house to pick up Luca on Friday, she was surprised to learn he'd already been picked up.

"Sam came by around one. Is there a problem?" Anita asked.

"No. I must have forgotten he was picking him up. It's fine. Thanks."

She hadn't forgotten anything. Sam hadn't called or so much as sent a text in days. She had this weekend off, and they were going to make plans, but that was before he'd vanished.

"You're off this weekend, right?" Anita asked as she picked up an envelope. Then Riley noticed a familiar duffel bag sitting on the floor. It was hers.

"Sam asked me to give you this when you got here." Anita held out the envelope and then bent to pick up the bag.

"What's going on?" Riley wasn't big on surprises. Especially not when she wasn't sure if they were good or bad.

"I can't say," her mother-in-law answered in a way that made her think she *could* say but she just chose not to.

Riley opened the note and stared down at Sam's writing.

Come up to the cabin. We'll see you soon. Be careful.

The cabin?

She did have the entire weekend off. She hadn't thought to ask Lexi to borrow the cabin, but now she was excited about the idea— despite Sam's disappearing act for the last few days.

An hour later, she pulled in next to Sam's truck in front of the Montgomery cabin. She was excited to see Sam, but nervous too. Why would he bring her the whole way up to the cabin if he was just going to break things off? Giving up on figuring it out, she grabbed the duffel bag that contained her clothes and toiletries, and went inside.

Riley walked in the door to the smell of flowers and wood. There was a bouquet of roses on the table next to the sofa. So Sam was going for romantic. She could hear Luca laughing from the kitchen. She wasn't sure how they were going to have a romantic night with a toddler, but they'd figure it out.

Just then, said toddler came running out of the kitchen toward her.

"Momma!" he said. She picked him up with a shock, especially when Sam stepped into the living room too.

"What's going on?" she said. "Why are you dressed up? Is he wearing a tie?" She looked down at her son. Sure enough it was a tie. A clip-on, but a tie. He also had a little suit that almost matched the one Sam was wearing.

She looked down at her button down shirt and khakis.

"Yeah. We have a little something planned out, and then we thought we'd go out for dinner."

"But I look like this," she pointed out.

"You look beautiful. You always do." Sam winked at her. "Give us a second." He motioned to Luca who wiggled down from her arms and went to Sam. "Go ahead." He handed Luca a business-size envelope and turned him toward her.

Luca brought it over and handed it to her.

"Here, Momma. From Daddy." He pointed at Sam and she worried for a second that Sam might run out of the room hearing the mistake. She'd tried to explain to Luca that Sam wasn't his daddy. Obviously he hadn't listened.

With shaky hands she opened the envelope and pulled out the thick sheaf of tri-folded paper. The crest at the top indicated it was a court document of some sort. Seeing that made her nerves kick up a notch as she scanned the pages. She paused when she noticed Evan's signature at the bottom and then backtracked.

"He's signed away complete custody?" Riley wanted to hope. She wasn't a lawyer, and this form was riddled with lawyeresque words. But it appeared Evan was signing over his rights.

"Yes. I had Cooper draw them up. Anita gave me his address and I went out to meet with him. After we discussed things we went to a notary office. He's no longer Luca's father as far as the court is concerned. You don't have to worry about him ever showing up and taking him anywhere. I knew you were concerned about that, and it wasn't like he was paying support anyway."

"Oh, my God, Sam! Thank you so much!" Happy tears came to her eyes as she read over the document more closely. Part of her wondered what Sam had said or done to get Evan to sign these papers, God knew she'd tried and so had Anita. But she decided she didn't care. The important thing was Evan had signed them. He couldn't take Luca. Not for a day or a week or a month. Never.

She was so busy dealing with her wet eyes, she hardly noticed Sam prompting Luca with another envelope until he placed it on her knee and said, "Daddy" again. Like the first time he pointed at Sam, and Sam just smiled nervously.

"What's this?" she asked as she opened the flap on the second envelope. She didn't know how things could get better. She was already thinking about the celebration dinner.

This document was also from the courthouse, though it didn't have any seals or signatures other than one. Samuel Alvarez Brooks. Like the first time, she backed up when she saw Luca's name.

It was a petition for adoption.

"You want to adopt Luca?" she said, her words barely made a sound.

"I do." He stepped closer and sat next to her. His eyes serious. "I know there's no guarantee with my PTSD, but I'm still seeing my therapist, and I'm working out my issues. I'm trying. The meds are helping with the nightmares. I promise to take care of him and provide for him and love him, Ri. Just as if he was mine, because in my heart, he is."

More tears filled her eyes and rolled down her cheeks. She glanced at Luca who was standing by Sam's knee fiddling with his tie.

"If you don't think I'm good enough, I would understand. I know I have a problem with my vocabulary, but I'm working on that too. If you don't want to do it officially, I'll still make sure he has everything he needs."

"Daddy," Luca said and pointed at Sam while he wrestled with his tie. Sam helped Luca fix the tie and patted his shoulder.

"Luca said yes when I asked him, by the way, but he's three. He doesn't know what's good for him." Sam winked at her and she knew her answer.

She didn't even need a lot of time to think about it. It was as natural as hearing Luca call Sam *Daddy*.

"I think he does know what's good for him. You've already proven to be a better father than his biological one. If you're sure, Sam. I would never push this on you."

"I know you wouldn't. That's why—" He leaned down and whispered something in Luca's ear. Luca nodded and reached in his pocket. He stepped closer to her and pulled out a diamond ring, holding it up proudly.

"Pretty for Momma," Luca said. She looked at the ring and then her gaze moved up to Sam as he knelt next to Luca. Was this really happening?

"I want it all, Ri. Call me selfish, but if I'm going to have a kid, I want a wife too. The whole package. A family."

"You don't need to do this," Riley said. The last thing she wanted was for him to feel some sense of obligation.

"I do need this. I need you and Luca in my life forever. Please say yes, so we can all go out to eat as a family."

He picked up Luca who was still holding out the ring saying, "Pretty."

"Do you want Mommy and Daddy to get married, Luca?" Sam asked before he whispered something in his ear.

Luca giggled and then yelled, "Yes!"

"Is he always going to take your side?" Riley asked.

"Of course. We men need to stick together."

"You're sure about this?" she asked, giving him one last chance to change his mind, since she'd already made up hers.

"I'm sure."

Riley took the ring from her son and slipped it on her finger. "Then yes."

Sam wrapped his free arm around her waist and pulled her close. "Thank you. You won't regret this. I promise."

She already knew she wouldn't.

Epilogue

L eaves crunched under tires as he noticed Riley pulling in at the jobsite where Sam was working. He hadn't told her much about this project, mainly because he wasn't sure how she'd feel about it.

His wife got out of the car and the late autumn sun glinted in her golden hair. He could already hear Luca in the back seat calling his name. *Daddy*. He never thought hearing that word would feel so good.

As soon as his feet hit the dirt Luca was tearing off toward him. Sam crouched down and waited for impact.

The boy had a paper fluttering in his hand. No doubt another piece of artwork. Luca was four now, and his artwork had improved from colored blobs and squares to actual trees and people with giant bodies and little heads.

"Hello there, Mr. Brooks," Sam said with a wink at Riley. The adoption had gone through easily, and now Luca had Sam's last name. Luca was his son.

"Daddy, I drawed this for you."

"You did? That's awesome. We can hang it inside." He looked over at Riley and leaned down to give her a kiss. The wind was biting and she pulled her jacket tighter around her.

"We brought you lunch," she said.

"I'm glad you're here. I could use your help picking some things for inside."

"This is beautiful," she said as she took in the structure behind him. The outside was mostly finished. The cedar siding was set off by the river rock accents. It was a handsome-looking house. But to him, she was the only thing he found truly beautiful.

They'd only been married a month, but every day with her and

Luca was even better than the day before. He felt so lucky to have them. And sure, Sam had to listen to the guys tease him about how right they were every time they got together for drinks, but it was a small price to pay.

They'd had a simple ceremony. Just a few friends and family. Mrs. Fisher sat next to Sam's sister and cried as if she was his own mother. Riley had her sister as her matron of honor, and Sam chose Luca to be his best man. It wasn't every day the best man sat on the groom's shoulders for the duration of the wedding ceremony. But Luca produced the ring when asked, and he made the cutest damn speech.

Sam began working on this house the week after she'd agreed to marry him, knowing it would take a while to finish it. He swallowed as he led them inside.

"Oh, my God," Riley said as she stepped through the front door and looked around. He hadn't bothered with a foyer in the design. Instead the door led right into the great room. Open timbers and skylights were the only details in the whole open space for the moment.

"So I have some samples over here of flooring, and cabinet finishes. Countertops and backsplashes. Also, what color do you think the walls should be?" he asked as she gazed at the large fireplace that took up most of the side wall.

"Shouldn't you ask the person who's going to live here?"

"Well . . ." He swallowed. "Actually, I hope I am." Every muscle in his body was tense as he watched the news sink in. He'd taken a chance by doing this without having her involved from the start.

This was his dream house. He'd worked on the plans for years. He'd saved up restored pieces he thought would be perfect from jobs here and there. But that had been before he knew Riley. Before he planned to live in this house with her and Luca. He'd made some changes since then to accommodate children. They'd talked about having another baby. At least one more. She went off her birth control two weeks before the wedding so they were going to see what happened.

Her eyes were huge as she turned to look at him. "You hope you are what?" she asked, clearly confused.

"I hope I'm talking to the person who's going to live here. I designed this house. For us. Dalton's having it built and if you like it, I'm going to buy it from him. If you don't, then he'll sell it to someone else."

"He's not going to sell our house to someone else!" she said adamantly. He smiled as he picked her up and spun her around.

"I was hoping you'd say that."

"This is amazing, Sam. You designed it?"

"Yep. Come on. Let me show you the rest of it." He stopped to kiss her. "God, you make me so happy."

Riley watched Sam as he showed her the rest of the gorgeous house he'd designed. He seemed nervous at first, but she quickly put his mind at ease. It was perfect. She loved seeing the pride on his face when she pointed out something she particularly liked.

Luca was in his normal spot on Sam's shoulders and he giggled every time Sam pretended to run into a beam or a wall.

When they got to the master bedroom that looked out over the yard she decided now was the time to let him in on her secret. She was just as nervous as he had been, hopefully it would work out the same way.

"It's perfect, Sam. I can't wait to make it our home." He kissed her while Luca looked out the windows.

"I'm so glad you like it. I wanted it to be a surprise, but then I realized I was going to need your input on the details. This could have blown up in my face."

"You did good." She swallowed and pulled away. "Luca, why don't you show Daddy your picture."

Sam knelt down while Luca held up his drawing proudly.

"So what's this?" Sam asked while his brows creased. Luca's art still wasn't very identifiable, since all the people were the same size, but all Sam needed to do was ask and Luca could fill him in.

"Dat's you and Mommy and me and baby sitter," Luca said while pointing at the four blobs on the page.

"This is McKenna?" Sam asked, having misunderstood because Luca didn't say it clearly. McKenna had watched Luca over the summer when she was home from college, giving Anita the summer off to take a trip.

"No. *Baby sitter,*" he repeated getting a little indignant.

"Yeah. McKenna is your baby sitter."

"No." Luca shook his head and walked over to Riley, pointing at her stomach. "Baby sitter. In Momma's belly."

Sam looked confused.

"I believe he's trying to say *sister* instead of sitter. Not that we know it's a girl yet, but I guess he's decided—"

She didn't get the chance to finish. Sam was holding her and kissing her again.

"Are you fu—Are you kidding me? You're pregnant? We're having a baby?"

"Baby sitter!" Luca said excitedly.

"Yep. I just found out for sure this morning. Luca came with me while Nichole ran the test."

"You're going to be a big brother." Sam picked up Luca and gave him a high five. Luca nodded. "I guess I'd better get this house finished."

"Guess you'd better." Riley laughed as Sam kissed her neck and Luca giggled in her ear. She had everything she could ever want. And she wasn't afraid.

ABOUT THE AUTHOR

Allison B. Hanson lives near Hershey, Pennsylvania. Her novels include women's fiction, paranormal, sci-fi, fantasy and mystery suspense. She enjoys candy immensely, as well as long motorcycle rides and reading. Visit her at allisonbhanson.com.

Don't miss the other

Blue Ridge Romances

WHEN LEAST EXPECTED

And

NICK OF TIME

Available now

From Lyrical Shine

WHEN LEAST EXPECTED

First in a new series!

Sometimes happily ever after
takes a major swerve…

ALLISON B.
HANSON

A Blue Ridge Romance

WHEN LEAST EXPECTED

Whispering breezes, clear mountain lakes—and her ex.

Alexis Montgomery thought her marriage was fine. Sure, they were going through hard times, struggling to get pregnant—but she and Ian had chemistry, friendship, and love. Or so she thought, until she found the separation agreement waiting for her on the countertop.

Ian Montgomery feels like life is spinning out of his control. He's got a new girlfriend, even if he can't remember why he's supposed to want one. His family clearly likes his ex-wife more than they like him. And then he inherits the romantic family cabin in the rolling Blue Ridge Mountains, where he and Alexis honeymooned. Or rather, they both inherit it. Together.

A weekend alone with fresh air and fresh wounds seems like the worst thing that could happen to an ex-couple trying to keep it civil. But life is full of surprises—and Ian and Alexis are in for a big one . . .

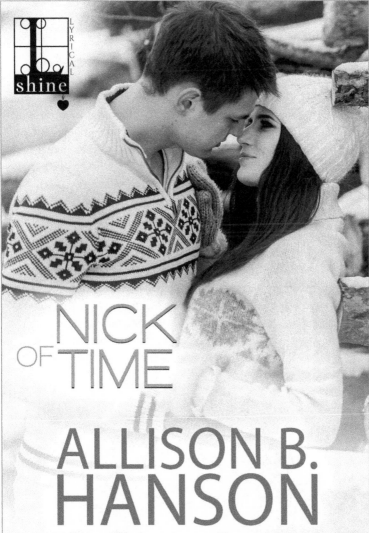

NICK
OF TIME

ALLISON B.
HANSON

A Blue Ridge Romance

NICK OF TIME

*A romantic cabin in the mountains. And a man who knows
how to get lost . . .*

With a brand-new M.D. behind her name and a wonderful man by
her side, Nichole Atherton thought she had her happily-ever-after all
sorted out. Then her fiancé told her he was gay. Nic can fake a smile
better than anyone, but she's hanging by a thread. She just has to
make it through her best friend's wedding . . . and an encounter with
his nightmare little brother, Tucker Matthews.

Weddings make Tucker antsy—he's got a bad track record with
"forever." The family screw-up became a screw-up famous rock star,
and bottomed out fast. Now he's putting his life back together, and
the last person he wants to see is perfect Nichole. No matter how
hot the fantasies he had about her growing up, Nichole is out of
his league and he knows it. It's just too bad they have so much
chemistry. Because there's no way the two of them could ever
make it last . . .

9 781616 509651

HOW NOT TO SAIL

(SCREWING UP IS PART OF CRUISING.
LET ME SHOW YOU HOW!)

BRADFORD ROGERS

worldsongs